A Search for Justice

Also by Monty R. Garner

Buckshot

Canyon: Life Is a Gamble

Card Jordan Series

Card, Kill Them All

Card, Man of Justice

Card, Taking Care of Business

Card, Day of Reckoning

Card, Duty Calls

Card, Unleashed

Card, A Test of Faith

Card, Revenge is Mine

Sawyer McCade Westerns

Life After War

Take No Prisoners

A Rancher's Revenge

A Search for Justice

Brody Connor
Book 2

Monty R. Garner

A Search for Justice
Paperback Edition
Copyright © 2026 by Monty R. Garner

Wolfpack Publishing
1707 E. Diana Street
Tampa, FL 33610

www.wolfpackpublishing.com

All rights reserved. No part of this book may be reproduced in any form or by any electronic or mechanical means, including information storage and retrieval systems, without express written permission from the publisher, except for the use of brief quotations in reviews. Any use of this publication to train generative artificial intelligence (AI) technologies is expressly prohibited.

This book is a work of fiction. References to historical events, real people, or real places are used fictitiously. Any similarity to real persons, living or dead, is purely coincidental and not intended by the author.

All brand names and product names used in this book are trademarks, registered trademarks, or trade names of their respective holders. Wolfpack Publishing is not associated with any product or vendor in this book.

Paperback ISBN 979-8-89567-263-1
Ebook ISBN 979-8-89567-262-4

A Search for Justice

Chapter One

The Missouri Mule stood with his head in the feed bucket while Dr. Brody Connor checked over the packsaddle and its cargo, covered with a tarpaulin. The strong pack animal had the young doctor's medical books, medication, tools of the trade, and food for the long journey they were about to embark on.

The young doctor graduated at the top of his class from the Kansas City Doctor School on May 13, 1876. He turned down prestigious jobs from hospitals in some of the larger cities, all because he wanted to go west and help folks in need.

Brody spent time in Indian territory two years ago, when he thought the law was after him for killing his stepfather, Ludwig Muller, but it was ruled an accident after he went on the run. Those months in Indian territory put a burning desire inside the young man to pursue his dream of becoming a modern doctor.

Dr. Milrose of Wichita, Kansas, gave the boy a job helping in his office after school and on weekends. His name back then was Thaddeus, but after running away when Ludwig was killed, he changed his name to Brody Connor. The boy's pa was named Connor, and he wanted it to be his name. During his time going to classes in Kansas, Thaddeus had a patient who was a judge, and he had his name changed officially to Brody Connor.

Brody bought the mule and a cow pony off some men who brought a small herd of cattle up from Texas. The herd had to be quarantined because of tick fever on the border of Indian territory and Kansas. During the quarantine time, the men used up most of their profits on buying extra grub. When the herd was finally released to enter Kansas, the men needed to sell some mules and horses to have enough money to make it back home.

Brody heard through the gossip line that if a man was in need of a horse, mules, and saddles, he should head to the cattle shipping pens. A deal was made for a horse and cowboy saddle for one hundred dollars. The mule and packsaddle cost him sixty-five dollars. The man who sold him the animals guaranteed that both were four years old and solid as they come.

Brody worked hard filling in at the newly built hospital after hours in Kansas City every chance he had. The money was good, and he was able to save a good amount, knowing where he would go when he finished school.

It just so happened that he also knew a beautiful young lady on a ranch in Central Texas. They wrote to each other a few times, but he hadn't heard from her in almost six months.

Last night when he went to tell Dr. Milrose goodbye, the doctor offered him a partnership in his practice if he would stay in Wichita. Brody hugged his friend and mentor before turning him down. The older physician smiled. "Brody, you're a fine doctor, and I know you'll blaze a path a mile wide across the prairie to find that young lady we operated on before you went off to school."

Brody only smiled and walked out to pursue his own destiny. He walked to his mama's house that night, and the following morning she fed her only son a good breakfast before he took off.

Brody mounted up on his horse which he named Scalpel. He renamed the mule also, and he would be called Forceps. The mule followed along well since being led from Texas to Kansas.

At first, the young man thought about heading due south through Indian territory until he arrived in Central Texas, but he had never ridden that way and decided to go where he had been before.

Another reason for going the way he knew was that he wanted to stop by and see his good friend William Longtooth. William taught Brody how to fight, how to shoot, and how to survive in the wild on his own. William was also a healer who taught the young doctor about natural plants, roots, and herbs used for different functions in healing.

Brody was almost to the Arkansas River, where it made a curve back to the east. He was passing by Lester's Gun and Leather Store when out came two men shooting guns back into the store.

Brody stopped his horse and transferred the bridle reins from his right hand to his left hand. The young man had time to remove the safety strap off his gun when one of the men turned and rushed off the porch.

One of the men pointed his gun at Brody and fired, but the bullet went wide. Brody drew his gun, and his first shot hit its mark, and the man was jerked backward and fell to the ground.

The second man fired a shot, and it was so close that Brody felt the air part as it passed by. The man's gun fell on an empty chamber, and when he decided to run, it was too late. Mr. Lester came through the door with a double-barreled shotgun and fired both barrels. The power of firing both barrels drove the old shop owner back through the door. The force of the buckshot flung the robber a good six feet from where he was standing.

"Mr. Lester, don't shoot anymore, they are both down."

Brody knew the man hit by the buckshot was dead, but he didn't know about the one he shot. He dismounted and went to the man who was still alive. After a quick examination, the bullet had hit him in the upper abdomen on the right side, and the slug went clean through.

Mr. Lester came out loading two more shotgun shells in the double-barrel.

"Move aside so I can put him out of his misery."

Brody raised up and put his hand on his gun handle. "No, sir. This man may be a criminal, but I'm a doctor, and I won't let you shoot him."

"I said move out of the way."

Brody pulled his gun at amazing speed. "Mr. Lester, are you willing to die over some no-good outlaw?"

"Who are you?"

"I'm Brody Connor. My mama is Ellen Muller."

"Are you the one who killed Ludwig and his no-good brother?"

"Yes, sir, that was me, and I won't hesitate to kill you if you try to shoot a helpless man. I suggest you send someone after the law."

Mr. Lester broke open the barrels and removed the

shells. "I'll send my daughter after the law, but I ain't helping you care for that outlaw."

Brody took out his folding knife and cut off two large pieces of the hurt man's shirt. He made a ball and shoved the material in the hole where the bullet entered the man. With all his might, he was able to roll the man over and plug the exit wound.

The man was unconscious, and that was fine by the doctor. Mr. Lester came back out.

"Would it be okay with you if I retrieved what they stole from me?"

Brody watched as the store owner took a roll of bills from the dead man. He came to the injured man and started going through his pockets, and pulled out fifteen dollars.

"Mr. Lester, I don't think that money belongs to you. I'm thinking you should give it to the undertaker as his payment for burying that man you killed, don't you?"

He threw the money on the ground and went inside.

The city marshal and one deputy came running to the scene, while a second deputy came in a wagon. Brody told the marshal what he saw and how the men tried to shoot him. The conversation was interrupted when the marshal called out to his deputy, "Put shackles on the injured man's wrist and irons on his legs. Get him loaded in the wagon and take him to Dr. Milrose."

When the marshal was finished giving orders, Brody asked, "Would it be all right if I went on my way? I have a far piece to go today."

"Yeah, you can go."

Brody walked to his horse but took the time to reload his gun before he mounted up.

Chapter Two

WHAT A COINCIDENCE IT WAS TO BE LEAVING town and almost get shot by two men trying to rob a gun shop. It seemed that there was never a dull moment in Wichita, especially down by the river. As he crossed the Arkansas River, leaving Wichita and heading south, the young man thought back to the situation that had just happened.

The first thing he had to change was using his left hand to guide the horse. When he saw what was happening, he transferred the reins to his left hand so he could get to his gun with his right. Also, he had the shoulder holster rig on, and it didn't have a safety strap on the gun. He could have pulled it if his right hand was clear.

Thinking back to his training on fighting and gunplay, a smile formed with the thought of going to see his old Indian friend, William. The old man had taught him many things, and he had better start using those skills again to survive out on the trail.

It would be a stretch to make it to Wellington today with the pack mule. It was still in the cool of morning, and time to increase the speed of his horse and mule. Forceps didn't like loping, but the big, long-eared mule didn't have a say in the matter. The man who sold Brody the animals had told the truth about them being solid on the trail.

Riding along the Chisholm Trail was much easier than going across country to Wellington. The few wheat fields that he could see were still mostly green, and the corn was coming along nicely. Farming was something that Brody never had a hankering to try.

He did try cowboying with a herd coming up the Chisholm on his way back to Wichita from Kingfisher two years ago, though. It was hard, dirty work, but he had actually enjoyed learning how to rope a calf. Although, it could be dangerous if you happen to rope the wrong cow and she decides to charge your horse.

After traveling at a good pace for five miles, Brody slowed the animals to a walk, giving them a well-deserved breather. Two or three miles to the south was a huge cloud of dust, indicating a herd was coming his way. He didn't want to be caught up in the clashing of horns, the dust cloud coming off their hooves, and the fear of an angry longhorn coming after them.

By watching the dust cloud, he figured the wind was out of the south, so he veered off to the east and would ride around the herd. When it passed, he would get back on course.

It wasn't long until he could hear the bawling of cattle, horns hitting horns, cowboys hollering, and the crack of a whip. He felt a little sorry for the drag riders, even though the wind was out of the south, they were still covered in trail dust. That was his job when he hired on. Ride drag and learn how to stay away from the mean longhorns.

It wasn't a large herd, and with him going south and the herd heading north, it wasn't long until he rejoined the main trail and started to lope the horse and mule again.

By high noon, the temperature had to be in the high nineties, and the young doctor was covered in sweat. There had to be something he could do to get cooler. Then he thought back to the city boys who attended doctor school with him. In the summer months, they would wear short-legged britches.

That gave the young man a great idea. When he gets to Wellington, he would find a seamstress and have her remove the sleeves from one of his shirts and cut off the legs of a pair of his older britches.

He may look funny riding a horse in those clothes, but it would be much cooler than a long-sleeve shirt and long-legged britches.

Riding another five miles, he slowed down again, but this time he let the animals stop for ten minutes under a shade tree. Brody removed the vest he was wearing and tied it to the packsaddle. He unbuttoned his shirt and let the wind cool off his stomach while sipping water from his canteen.

It would be nice to sit in the shade, but there was still a far piece to go before they were in Wellington. They would have to cross the South Fork Ninnescah River right before they entered the town.

Wellington was only incorporated in 1871 and a stopping place for the crews bringing cattle up the Chisholm Trail. Not only was it a good location where trail bosses could buy supplies, but it also catered to the cowboys' drinking and blowing off steam.

LATE IN THE AFTERNOON, Brody, along with his tired horse and mule, stood on the bank of the river examining the crossing where the last herd had crossed. The ground was so torn up that he figured the mud in the riverbed would be knee deep to his horse.

Mounting back up, they turned downstream and got away from all the mud. They were able to cross some two hundred yards from where the cattle had come through the water.

The little town was quiet as he came down the street leading his mule. The livery stable was going to be the first stop, so he could get his animals' grain and rest.

The hostler came out. "Howdy, you want to put them up for the night?"

Brody slid to the ground. "Yes, sir, I want them fed grain, rubbed down, and watered. I'll pick them up in the morning. How much for the night?"

"That'll be two dollars. There's a good hotel across the street and one block east if you're of a mind to sleep in a bed."

"I do want a bed. I also need a seamstress. Do you know where one is?"

The hostler thought for a second. "Oh, you mean a woman who mends clothes for people. Yeah, Lucile can do that for you over at the mercantile."

Brody handed the man two dollars and went to his mule. "Say, I have a packsaddle on here. Do you reckon that the two of us can remove it without unloading everything?"

The man pointed to the barn. "I have rope blocks hanging from the rafters that are put there for that very reason. Let's lead him inside, and I'll have the saddle off in a jiffy."

Sure enough, the man knew what he was doing and

lifted the packsaddle off without harming any of the cargo. Brody decided it would be easier to purchase a new shirt and britches than to unload the pack.

He walked across the street and found the mercantile where he inquired about Lucile. She was a jolly woman in her sixties with gray hair and missing a few teeth.

"I'm Dr. Brody Connor and I need a pair of britches and a shirt. I'd like for you to remove the sleeves off the shirt and cut the legs where they come to above my knees."

"Mister, I've been sowing for almost fifty years, and this is a first for me. Are you sure you want me to do that?"

"Yes, ma'am. I'm riding to Central Texas, and it's mighty hot on the back of a horse in this heat. I need something to help keep me cool."

"Let's go find you them britches so I can mark where you want them cut off."

She held a pair up against him and put a pin where to cut off the legs. "Give me an hour and I'll have both of them fixed."

"Thanks a lot." Brody left the store, heading to the hotel.

Chapter Three

THE TOWN SEEMS LIKE A GROWING COMMUNITY, and the people on the way to the hotel either spoke or made some sort of acknowledgment as they passed by.

The newly built hotel was a narrow, long, three story wooden structure painted white with blue trim. The clerk was mopping the floor in the lobby when Brody stepped inside.

"Good evening sir. Would you like a room?"

"Yes, and a hot bath."

The man pointed to the ledger on the counter top. "Sign in, please and I'll fetch your key. What time would you like your bath?"

"Can you have it ready in an hour. I have to pick up some clothes and would like to clean up after that."

"Certainly, sir. Is your first name, Doctor, or are you a real doctor?"

Brody smiled. "I'm a real doctor heading to Texas."

"Here's the key to room 107. It's down that hallway on the left. The bath is two rooms past on the same side. If the door is open, it'll be ready for you."

"Much obliged," said Brody and started to his room.

The room was a little small but the bed and other furnishings were nice and looked clean. With time to kill, he walked out without locking his door and went out looking for someplace to eat supper.

Not far south of his location was a café that seemed to have a good business by the amount of people going in and out. As soon as the young doctor stepped inside, he saw why so many male patrons were there. Two beautiful girls who looked to be around his age were waiting tables while flirting with the men.

One of the girls smiled at Brody and pointed to a small table with only two chairs. "Have a seat, and one of us will be right there, sugar."

Brody didn't like where she wanted to seat him. That particular location would have him out in the open, and anyone could sneak up on him. Instead of sitting at the little table, he went to one farther back where he could have his back to the wall.

His classmates at school used to tease him about being paranoid when they went someplace to eat or have beers. Brody never told them of the training he had received from his Indian friend. One of the main subjects that the old man taught him was self-preservation. Know where to sit so no one can shoot you in the back. Let your eyes adjust to a room before going in. Keep the sun to your back in a gunfight.

The waitress came over. "You moved."

"Yes, ma'am, I like my back to the wall."

"I hear that a lot around here. I'm Candy, by the way. Do you want coffee to drink?"

"No, ma'am. I'll have a tall glass of water and whatever you have cooked."

"Coming right up. By the way, what's your name?"

"I'm Dr. Brody Connor, and it's nice to make your acquaintance."

"You a real doctor?"

"I certainly am. I just graduated from the medical school in Kansas City."

"I'll go get your food, Doctor."

The food was delicious, and Candy kept busy filling cups and cleaning off tables. More people came in and the place was filling up when Brody stood up, laid money on the table, and walked out.

As he came out onto the boardwalk, he accidentally bumped into a cowboy who was walking with two other men. It was an innocent mistake, but the man didn't think so.

He put his hand on Brody's shoulder and shoved him out of the way. "You need to watch where you're going, pretty boy."

Brody had been called a lot of names, but pretty boy wasn't one of them. "Sorry, mister, I didn't mean to bump into you," said Brody.

The cowboy turned, and when he did, Brody caught a whiff of whiskey on the man's breath which could escalate the situation. Brody didn't wait around to see if the man wanted to start something and walked off into the street. He wanted to put distance between himself and the man.

The cowboy called out, "Don't you walk away from me. I think it's time I teach you a lesson on manners."

Brody was a good ten feet into the street before turning to face the man. As he pivoted on his left foot, he removed the leather string off his gun hammer.

Brody stood with his feet shoulder-width apart and the sun at his back. "Mister, you're in no shape to come at me. I suggest you let it be and go have your supper while you can still eat."

The cowboy bolted off the porch, picking up speed to bullrush the tall, slender man standing in the street. He was almost within striking distance when Brody went down on one knee and swept the rushing man's legs out from under him with his other extended leg.

The man was getting up when a hard right hit him on the temple and then a left to the chin. The man's eyes glazed over, and he slumped back to the ground unconscious.

Brody looked back toward the boardwalk to see what the man's two friends were going to do. They were standing with their mouths open in shock at seeing their friend taken down so easy.

Not trusting the men, Brody commenced to walk backward across the street, all the while watching them. When he was certain that it was over, he continued to the mercantile to get his shirt and pants.

Lucile had his shirt and pants on the end of the counter when he came in.

"Here's your things. Look them over if you want."

"No ma'am, that won't be necessary."

"I will give you my two cents' worth, though, you be careful and only wear them for short periods of time so you don't get sunburned."

"Thank you, ma'am, for the advice. I'll only put them on when the temperature is unbearable. I do appreciate you doing this and the advice."

Brody took his clothes and headed back to the hotel, where he would take his bath and then find something to do until it was time for bed.

The bathtub was in a designated room that had three tubs with curtains separating each one. He happened to be the only one in the room and was also surprised by the smell of the water. The hotel put lavender in the water, giving it a nice fragrance.

The first time Brody was in Indian territory and practicing medicine in Kingfisher, he had a saloon girl as a patient, and she taught him how to play poker. They would play for hours with her explaining to him the percentages of each hand and when to fold or hold.

That training had come in handy during his two years at medical school. It became a way for him to make money, and he was good at it. Tonight, he would go to the saloons and find a friendly game and add a few dollars to his poke.

Looking at himself in the mirror revealed a handsome young man with a clean-shaven face, short brown hair, blue eyes, and a smile that would make most young ladies blush. He stood six feet, one inch, and weighed one hundred seventy pounds. The new shirt with no sleeves revealed his muscled arms, even if they were white from not getting any sun.

That last observation of his appearance caught his attention. Lucile was correct when she said to limit the exposure to the sun so the arms and legs wouldn't sunburn.

He would wear the shirt without sleeves tonight and see if it helped with the heat, but tomorrow, he could only wear it out in the sun for a short period of time. He would have to do that each day until his arms and legs were tanned enough that they didn't burn.

Chapter Four

The Cowtown Saloon was having an off night since no cattle herds were bedded down outside the small town. Normally, when the herds came through, getting a chair at one of the tables was almost impossible.

The entire town profited from the cowboys off the range as the drovers passed through. They not only frequented saloons to wash down the trail dust, they ate meals, bought boots, clothing, and some wanted haircuts and a bath.

There were also problems with the drovers, especially when more than one herd was close to town. Opposing cowhands like to fight, and some were even killed in gunfights. The trail bosses tried to keep their men from fighting, but most of the time it happened regardless of their efforts. When one of the drovers got hurt and couldn't do his job, the others had to step up and work harder.

Wellington catered to the flux of herders that came through, and most of the townsfolk stayed away from the popular places when the drovers were in town. Tonight was one of those few occasions when it was mostly locals and a few men passing through in the Cowtown Saloon that evening.

Brody had on his new shirt with no sleeves, the shoulder holster gun, a holster and gun on his right hip, britches, and boots. He left his hat in the hotel room along with the bandana that he had washed out and left to dry.

He stood just inside the batwing doors, letting his eyes adjust to the dim lights, observing who was playing cards. Two tables were occupied with men who he suspected were from town. They were playing five-card draw and drinking beer. The second table only had three men playing, and one of them didn't fit in. He was dressed in range clothing, but what got Brody's attention was the ring on his finger and the ring in his left ear.

Brody watched as the ring man picked up the cards and started shuffling with such ease that the untrained eye wouldn't catch him placing cards. This man most likely makes his living cheating men at playing cards.

The young doctor walked up to the table where the ring man was getting ready to deal the cards. "You fellers mind if I play a few hands?"

The ring man smiled and motioned to an empty chair. "I'm fine with you playing if these gentlemen are."

The other two men nodded their heads. "Thanks, I'm just passing through for the night, and it's too early to go to bed."

The man with the cards handed the deck to the man to his right. "You want to cut?"

"No, just deal the cards."

The dealer made eye contact with Brody. "What's your name, mister?"

"I'm Dr. Connor. I recently graduated from medical school. Who might you be, sir?"

"A real doctor. I'm impressed that you would like to join in a game of chance with us here tonight. I'm Recardo Emmerson from Missouri."

The man on Brody's left stuck out his hand. "I'm Joe Jones, and me and the missus own the mercantile." After shaking Joe's hand, Brody turned to the man on his right. The man also stuck out his hand. "I'm Peter, the town carpenter."

Recardo picked up the deck. "Gentlemen, it's a dollar ante and no limit on bets."

Brody pulled out playing money and placed it on the table where everyone could see that he had plenty to bet on hands. He wanted Recardo to take notice since he suspected that the card shark would fix the deck so he could win a few early hands.

Brody was no fool for the game and had seen his share of card sharks in the back rooms of gambling halls in Kansas City.

Brody picked up a pair of kings, a ten, a jack, and a deuce. He tossed five dollars onto the table. "I bet five dollars."

The other three men also put in their money.

Normally, Brody would have discarded three cards and asked for three new cards, but today he was going to have a little fun with the card shark.

He flipped the deuce and jack onto the table. "I'll take two cards."

The rest of the men did the same, and when everyone had their cards, Brody still hadn't picked up his new cards. Instead of picking them up, he placed the pair of kings on top and threw in twenty dollars. "Gentlemen, I feel lucky tonight. I believe I can win this pot without looking at my cards." He then stared into the eyes of Recardo, who stared back.

Joe threw in his cards. "I fold."

Peter threw in the twenty. "I call."

Recardo smiled at Brody. "This game may get very interesting before the night is over. I'll call your twenty."

As soon as he put the money on the table, Brody never took his eyes off of Recardo and turned over the pair of kings. He then turned over a five of hearts and a five of clubs. "Look here, I have two pair." Brody picked up a twenty and placed it on the table away from the other money. "I bet twenty on the side that I have a full house."

Peter picked up twenty. "I'll take that bet. There ain't no way you picked up a full house."

Recardo stared into the eyes of the young man across from him. He smiled and slowly reached out with his twenty. "Doctor, you may use your bluff with your school chums, but they don't work with me."

Brody eased his right hand to the edge of the table while reaching for the last card with his left hand. When he flipped the card over, it was the five of diamonds. Peter sighed when he saw the card. Recardo never said a word and began to pick up the cards.

Brody racked in his money, folded it, and placed it in his left britches pocket. "Gentlemen, I was lucky tonight, so I think it's time for me to leave." He stood up, and that's when Recardo also stood up, and Brody saw the two guns in a fancy holster.

He was still looking into the eyes of the card shark facing him. Joe and Peter were looking from one to the other, and it was Joe who pushed back from the table.

Recardo was the first to speak. "So, you win one hand and leave?"

Brody smiled. "I'll play you one-on-one. One hand for a hundred dollars only if Peter deals the cards."

"Are you saying that my dealing is rigged?"

"No more so than mine. What's it going to be? Are we going to play one more hand or pull iron over a poker hand?"

Recardo shifted his eyes off the doctor and looked at the table. He looked back up at the young man who hadn't moved.

"I know you said your name was Dr. Connor, but what's the rest of your name?"

"It's Dr. Brody Connor from Wichita, Kansas."

Recardo took a deep breath. "Are you the same Brody Connor that killed the Muller brothers, and Rosco a couple of years ago?"

Brody eased his right hand closer to the gun on his hip. "Yeah, that was me. I didn't want to kill them, but they tried to kill me and my mama. I'm a healer, but I don't turn tail and run when trouble comes my way. I did what I had to, and they got what they deserved."

The gambler nodded his head. "I'll play you one friendly hand for a hundred dollars, and Peter can deal."

They all sat back down, the two men put their money on the table, and that's when Brody asked, "Would you rather draw for high card?"

Recardo shook his head. "You're a brave one, all right. High card is risky, but I'm in if you are."

"Fine, I'll go first."

Peter placed the cards on the table. Brody reached with his left hand, and picked up cards with only his thumb and middle finger. The cards began to fall away when he lifted them. Then he flipped a card over, and the ten of spades flipped up.

Recardo rubbed his hands together, reached down

and picked up a few cards and turned them over with the seven of hearts showing. "Well, Doctor, it is your lucky night. Here's your money."

Recardo stood up, gathered his remaining money, and took one step away from the table. Brody was still standing in the same spot, ready for what he knew was coming.

The card shark wheeled around and was bringing up both guns when the young doctor pulled his pistol and fired one shot. The searing lead hit the dealer with such impact that he went down on both knees, grasping his chest. His eyes rolled back in their sockets, and he fell over on his face, dead. Brody went to the man and felt his neck to see if there was any life. With a sad face, the doctor stood up to address the men in the room. "I didn't want this to happen. I'm a healer, not a killer, but sometimes a man's got to protect himself. Can someone go get the law?"

Everyone in the saloon gave the same information to the city marshal on how Recardo pulled first, and the doctor only shot him in self-defense.

Brody lay awake that night thinking about the lives he had helped to save and the lives he had taken. He loved helping people, but he wasn't going to be bullied or swindled if he could help it.

Chapter Five

THE SUN WAS SNEAKING UP OVER THE EASTERN horizon when Dr. Connor left the café where he had an early breakfast. The coldness of morning found him in the new shirt and cut-off britches with the intention of wearing them until he began to burn.

The attention he got when he entered the café was unreal. Most people had never seen a grown man wear cut-off britches, but it was common of little kids. Brody didn't pay any attention to the whispering and looks as he ate his meal.

His horse was saddled when he arrived at the livery stable, and the mule had on its halter. "Howdy, Doctor, iffin you'll help, we can put the packsaddle back on the mule."

"Of course, I'll help." Brody led the mule under the packsaddle while the hostler let the rope blocks lower the saddle in place.

Brody eyed the ropes over again. "That's a handy contraption you have there."

"Yep, it comes in handy. Say, I was wanting to talk to you about a little matter. My wife keeps getting headaches. Is there something we can do to stop that?"

"See if you can buy opium at the drugstore or where you buy medicine. Mix a little opium with vinegar and make a poultice, then apply it where the pain is and see if that makes it go away."

"Thanks, Doctor. I hear a person can buy it from some of those people working on the railroad."

"I don't know anything about that." Brody mounted up and took off down the dusty street, heading to Caldwell, Kansas, which was only about twenty-one miles. The decision was still in the air whether he would stop there for the night or go on farther.

It had been a little over two years since he passed by Caldwell and he didn't get a good assessment of the town back then. It was hard to see much when you rode drag behind eight hundred head of cattle.

Reminiscing over his drover days gave the young man a new look on life for becoming a doctor. The dirt caked on his face, in his ears, and matted in his hair, was something he hoped he would never have to endure again. Each night, the drag riders' clothes would have so much dirt stuck to them that a man couldn't make out the color of the material.

Brody had to push his thoughts aside when he saw a wagon parked under a shade tree up ahead. It looked like a family with children running and playing, but he couldn't see any grown-ups. This was odd for the folks to be cooling off this time of day when it wasn't even hot yet.

As he approached the wagon, one of the boys saw him coming and ran to the back of the wagon. A man in his thirties came from behind the wagon with his sweat-soaked shirt sleeves rolled up, waving his arms in need of help.

"Mister, can you help us? My wife is in a bad way, trying to have a baby."

"I certainly can. I'm a doctor." Brody dismounted and walked behind the wagon to find a half-naked woman, leaning against a tree in severe pain.

"Ma'am, I'm Dr. Brody Connor, and I'm here to help you. What's your name?"

"It's Marsha. Something is bad wrong this time."

"I need to see what's going on down there with the baby and then we'll get it out."

He looked at the man. "Do you have a quilt or anything that we can lay her on?"

"No, we didn't bring anything."

"Do you have something to heat water in?"

"No,"

"Come with me. We have to get my bags off the pack mule."

With the older boy helping, they removed all the things that the doctor needed. He put the woman on top of his tarp, got her in the position where he could perform his examination, which revealed the baby was breached.

"We have two choices. The baby is breached, and it will be really difficult out here to turn it enough so it will come out headfirst. I suggest doing a cesarean section and removing the baby surgically. I have everything I need, and she should be fine in a few days."

The woman grabbed Brody by his arm. "You get this baby out of me before it kills both of us."

The man reached down and patted his wife on the head. "Now, dear, don't be mean to the doctor."

"You get your hand off me. You're the reason I'm in this situation."

Brody pried her fingers off his arm and began to lay out rags, chloroform, Iodine, and his instruments. When everything he would need was in place, he pulled out a bar of lye soap and had the boy get his canteen.

Brody looked at the husband. "What's your name?"

"I'm Lewis Canker."

"Lewis, you're going to be my assistant. First off, you have to scrub your hands with this soap and then don't touch anything until I tell you. We're going to do this quick, and you have to follow instructions."

"I'll do my best."

Brody washed his hands, and while Lewis was washing his, Brody cleaned off the woman's belly with iodine. When Lewis was ready, Brody covered the chloroform rag to the woman's nose, and she went out like a light.

The skilled doctor worked quickly, and in a few minutes he cleared off the baby's face, gave her a pat on her little bottom, and then handed the crying baby girl to the oldest daughter, who looked to be around ten. The skill he used in stitching up the incision came from hours of surgeries at the hospital where he worked while attending school.

This had definitely not been the best of locations to deliver a child, but it wasn't his first time out on the trail. It took a little while for the chloroform to wear off, where Brody thought it was safe for the mother to hold her newborn.

The two canteens that Brody had were emptied before he was able to wash like he wanted. With the help of the oldest boy, he packed up the mule with the intentions of going on to Caldwell and sterilizing all his instruments.

Brody came around to the back of the wagon where the woman had sat up, but he could tell she was in a lot of discomfort.

"Lewis, how far away is your house?"

"It's might nigh two south and a mile west."

"Ms. Marsha, me and Lewis are going to help you stand up, and then we're putting you in the back of the wagon. I'll come follow along and make sure you and the baby are fine until we can get you home."

The poor woman took a beating in the wagon the three miles home, but it was still better than lying on the dirty ground. The only good thing about having the baby on the Chisholm Trail was the fact that no herd came by.

Marsha was able to nurse the child and clean up before she and the baby went to bed. Brody also used his time sterilizing the instruments that were used and packing them away until the next opportunity came his way.

The doctor didn't want to take off again so late in the day so he would spend the night and be on his way tomorrow if Marsha and the baby were fine. Lewis and his oldest daughter did the cooking that night, and afterward they sat outside talking.

Brody made himself a bed of hay under a shade tree that night and watched the stars, thinking about the events of late. He had killed a man over cards in Wellington but brought a life into this world today. Was that some kind of an omen of what his future would be like?

There were still so many questions about life that the young man didn't have answers for, or the experiences to know what each situation would mean to his life. One thing he learned a long time ago was the simple fact that he was good at delivering babies.

It seemed that he happened to be in the right place at the right time to use his God-given gift as a healer. William Longtooth will laugh when he tells him about delivering another baby on the trail.

Chapter Six

Brody woke up sometime after midnight when he heard the baby crying. He could tell by the loud screaming that the child was in pain. A lantern was lit in the house, and Marsha was rocking the child when the doctor came inside.

"Marsha, let me take a look at the child. That cry is more than being hungry or mad." With the baby cradled in his hand, he began to press on its stomach, which was hard as a rock.

"Has she had a bowel movement since we've been here?"

"No. Is she going to be all right?"

"Of course. She's constipated, is all. Here, hold her while I go after something."

Brody went to the pack, which he and Lewis removed after they arrived at the house. He came back in with a little bulb on the end of a syringe that he filled with some soapy water. In a few minutes, the baby got the relief she needed and fell off to sleep.

"You may have to give her a little apple or pear juice if

the constipation keeps happening. You can also rub her little belly and exercise her legs to make the poop move along."

"Thanks, Doctor. I don't know what we would have done without you."

Brody patted her on the shoulder and turned to Lewis. "I'm going back to sleep."

THAT FOLLOWING MORNING, Brody shook out his boots and sat on his bedroll for a few minutes looking out over the field of wheat to the north before pulling them on. It was going to be another hot day, and the wheat was showing it. Most of it was turned to a golden color and that meant harvest would be soon.

He would go inside and check on Marsha and the baby, with the hope that Lewis would fix him breakfast. After a good meal, it would be time to gather his things, saddle up the animals, and be on his way toward Caldwell.

One of the kids came outside. "Mr. Doctor, my daddy said to come inside, breakfast is about ready."

"Thanks, I'll be right in."

Marsha and the younger kids were seated while Lewis and the oldest girl finished cooking. The meal was simple with biscuits, gravy, and ham, but it was delicious and more than enough for everyone. Brody was sopping up the last of the gravy in his plate when he looked at Lewis. "This is some of the best biscuits that I've ever ate."

Lewis reached out and slid the pan closer to Brody. "Take another one and load it down with some of that butter. It'll melt in your mouth."

Brody didn't even think about it and did like Lewis

said. When he finished it off and drank the glass of milk he was having, he pushed back. "I best be loading up and going on down the road. I'd like to get close to Indian territory by tonight."

Lewis got up. "You kids clean up the kitchen, and I'll go help the doctor with his packsaddle. That bulky thing is more than one man can handle."

When they had the horse and mule loaded, Brody went inside the barn, put on his cut-off britches, and came back out. The kids started laughing.

"What's so funny?" he asked.

"Mr. Doctor, you have white legs," replied the giggling kid.

Brody ruffled up the kid's hair. "It's fine, they won't be white long out in the sun."

After going inside to check on Marsha one last time, he hugged the kids and shook hands with Lewis. Not looking back, Dr. Brody mounted up and headed down the road.

The late start would have him arriving in Caldwell around or shortly after high noon. That would also be a good time to change back into his long britches and shirt so he wouldn't get sunburned.

The searing sunlight blaring down on the rider with the sleeveless shirt and short britches soon showed its effect, and he had to change before he ever arrived in Caldwell.

Caldwell was the first real place where drovers could buy supplies and blow off steam after going through Indian territory. The settlement was a major Cowtown that sat just north of the border on the Kansas side and had the reputation of being a lawless, rowdy, *anything goes* community.

The saloons catered to the cowboys off the trail as

well as the outlaws that frequented the seedy establishments that employed working girls. All the activity that went on in the little border town caused it to be nicknamed Border Queen.

Lawmen didn't last long in the place, and either they were killed or the criminal element was so great that they loaded up and left.

Brody entered Caldwell around one in the afternoon with the intention of stopping for a meal and continuing on. Today happened to be an off day for the small town with no cattle drives coming through, and it showed by the activity going in and out of businesses.

What caught his eye was the white house surrounded by a pole fence and a sign with the name of Dr. Meadows written on it. Doctors in small towns like this were uncommon. In fact, most country doctors had their practices set up in larger communities and made house calls. They even made most of their medications and were limited on any formal medical training.

Many country physicians learned their limited knowledge from an apprenticeship, sort of like Brody did with Dr. Milrose. Some received their training by serving in the Army during the Civil War. Most of those doctors never had any formal training to treat illness, as they were mostly used for wounds and amputations.

Brody rode past Dr. Meadows, but something tugged at his brain, and he turned around and rode back to where he tied his horse and mule to the fence before going to the door and knocking.

"Come on in. I ain't getting up to open the door for you," came the raspy voice from inside.

Brody stepped inside to find the room cluttered with three chairs, an examining table, off to one side, where the doctor could have access to both sides of it. An upright cabinet with glass inlay in the doors where he could see medications, bandages, and common instruments. Then there was the oak desk littered with books, papers, a coffee cup, and a whiskey bottle.

Behind the desk sat an elderly man wearing round spectacles suspended low on his nose, bald-headed and sporting a mustache and goatee. He looked up from the book he was reading, pushed the glasses in place, and asked, "What's wrong with you?"

Brody didn't particularly like the old doctor's greeting, but he let it slide for now. He walked up to the front of the desk and stuck out his hand. "There's nothing wrong with me. I'm Dr. Brody Connor, and I wanted to stop in and meet you."

"What for? You planning on taking over my business?"

"No, sir. I'm on my way to Central Texas and saw your sign out front and wanted to meet you. I recently finished doctor school in Kansas City and I'm just passing through. I apologize for interrupting you. I'll be on my way."

Brody turned and started to the door. "Hold on, Doctor. Don't get your drawers in a wad. Come on back and sit down. I don't get many real visitors around here. Most of my company is about to die from getting shot, stabbed, or beat to death."

Brody turned back to the man who had stood up and put out his hand. "What did you say your name was?" asked the old doctor.

"It's Dr. Brody Connor. I'm from Wichita originally.

"I'm Dr. Randolf Meadows. I learned my trade in the Army, and when the war was over, I practiced in Springfield with three more fine physicians. My wife passed four years ago, and I wanted to get out of the city and came here. I look forward to days like today, but when the herds come in, it's *Katy, bar the door* until they pass through."

"I worked riding drag a couple of years ago, and I can tell you from experience that following behind a herd of cattle every day will give a man a bad attitude. Dr. Meadows, do you go out in the countryside and make house calls?"

"No, I did in Springfield but not out here. I'm too old to be doing that anymore."

Brody stood up and stuck out his hand again. "I best be on my way. I'm going to eat and then head on south. It was really nice meeting you, Dr. Meadows."

The old man not only shook hands with Brody but walked him to the door. "The best place to eat is that slop bucket right over there. Mattie cooks a mighty good steak with potatoes. Doctor, I must say that I've heard of you, and I wouldn't be telling anyone my name while in town. You may not know it, but you acquired a reputation with all that business in Wichita a couple of years ago. There's men here in town that would call you out if they knew who you were."

Brody was surprised by what the old doctor was telling him. "Thanks, Dr. Meadows. I'll watch what I say while in town."

Brody went out and untied his animals so he could walk to the café for a steak and potatoes. He was still processing the advice the old doctor had given him as he went to eat. Maybe he wouldn't tell anyone his first name while here, even though he was proud of the name, Dr. Brody Connor.

Chapter Seven

Brody happened to be the only person in the café at that hour of the day. The regulars had already come and gone by the time he arrived. A woman who looked to be in her fifties greeted him as he came in and sat where he could watch his horse and mule.

"Hello, I'm Mattie Lawrance. What would you like to eat? I have beef stew, or I can cook you a steak with taters."

"Nice to meet you, ma'am. I'm Dr. Connor, and I was told by Dr. Meadows that you cook a mighty good steak, so that's what I'll have with water to drink."

"I'll get started on it. Is that your mule out there?" She pointed out the window.

"Yes, ma'am."

"Keep an eye on it. The thieves will be watching to see if it's worth their time to take it or not."

"Thank you, ma'am, I'll watch it."

Dr. Meadows was spot on about the steak and potatoes, and the portions were so large that he took what he couldn't eat with him. The remarks about the thieves caused him to look up and down the street as he tightened up the girth strap and made sure the packsaddle and its cargo were secure.

Two men were standing out front of one of the saloons, looking at him, and farther down the street was another man leaning against an awning post, looking his way. It could be a coincidence for them to be watching, or was he being extra careful after the remarks by Mattie? Whatever the reason, he wasn't going to give them a chance to take his things. Two years ago, he made himself a promise that he wouldn't stand by and watch someone mistreat another person or allow someone to steal what he had worked so hard for.

Before mounting up, he removed the safety off the gun on his hip and checked to make sure the cylinder was fully loaded. He then did the same with the gun in the shoulder holster. Now it was time to see if the men were friend or foe.

Brody mounted and headed south with the lead rope in his left hand, along with the bridle reins. As he passed the first two men, he intentionally made eye contact as he came up to them. When all three men were looking at each other, Brody smiled and kind of jerked his head up to acknowledge them.

He was able to keep them in his sight until he was a few yards past. Then he began to watch the third man and that's when the feller quit leaning on the post and turned his head toward the saloon doors. He must have said something because two more men came out to watch the young man leading a pack mule by.

Brody continued to ride by and was even with the three men watching him from in front of the saloon door, and he didn't like the situation, so he did the unthinkable and reined his horse a sharp right, where he was sitting tall in the saddle, directly in front of the men.

"Is there something I can do for you fellers?"

One of the men who had just come out of the saloon took a step forward and dropped his right hand toward his gun. Brody didn't wait for the man to say anything or get into a position to draw. The healer pulled his gun with lightning speed and surprised the three men so much that they didn't have time to react.

"Whoa! Now hold on, mister. We don't want no trouble."

"Then don't be out here like you're going to try something. I don't take kindly to men watching me ride by." Brody patted the horse's ribs with his right knee so it would head on out. He kept his gun on the men until he was out of pistol range.

When he turned back and looked at the first two men, they were gone from where they were. This may not be over, and he didn't want them coming at him in the middle of the night so he started off at a faster speed.

He rode up on Fall Creek and let the horse and mule take on water before heading on out. In a little over a mile, they crossed through Bluff Creek and then were able to proceed at a faster rate. The mule surprised Brody on how easy he wanted to run. Most mules were stubborn and hard to keep moving.

Another mile or so, they were in Indian territory and traveling at a good pace across what was mostly flat to gently sloping plains or the Red Prairies. The rich soil supported a selection of tall grass and mid-tall.

This was also buffalo country, and when Brody was through the Indian Nations two years ago, he had killed a young bull to help feed some nice folks he met on the trail. He had enough knowledge of the massive beast to see where they had recently come through. Their trail was similar to the Chisholm Trail. The vegetation had been eaten or trampled down as they came through.

The farther south he rode, the hotter it got, and he knew the humidity could be terrible this time of year, especially if a storm blew in and dumped rain. The good thing about storms was, a man could see them coming from miles away. But when the sky began to turn colors, it was time to seek whatever shelter was available. The wind, rain, and even tornadoes were common.

By late afternoon, he rode up to Bullwhacker Creek, and that's where he would bed down for the night. He would go ahead and cross the stream so he would be on the south side in case of rain or if he had visitors from the north.

Not wanting to build a fire, he ate the remainder of the food he had at Coldwell before pulling enough tall grass to lay his bedroll on. Unsaddling his horse and putting hobbles on it was easy, but it took him a good amount of time to unpack the packsaddle and secure all his things where they wouldn't get wet in case of rain. He didn't know how the mule or horse would fare during the night with hobbles since this was their first night to spend out in the wild.

Brody read in one of his medical books until it got too dark to see. By his estimation, it was around nine at night and time to turn in.

SOMETIME AFTER MIDNIGHT, the mule made a noise that woke Brody up. As he was shaking out his boots, the mule started raising a ruckus, kicking and braying.

All of a sudden, a new noise sounded out like an animal in severe pain.

With his gun in his hand, the young doctor went to the mule and started petting him so he would settle down. The moon was only a quarter moon that night, and he couldn't see what had frightened the mule.

Brody lay on his bedroll for the longest time thinking about what could have frightened the mule. It could be anything out here, and tomorrow night, he would keep a fire going so there would be light.

THE SOUNDS of morning came to the young man, and when he opened his eyes, the first thing he saw was Forceps, his mule, looking down at him. The young man rose and looked around to see his horse grazing some yards away.

After shaking out his boots and rolling up his bedroll, Brody inspected the mule to make sure he wasn't injured during his bout with whatever came around last night.

Both animals were fine, and now it was time to put the packsaddle on and secure all his supplies and possessions. This was a big job, having to pack and unpack each day, maybe he overpacked for this trip.

When he was finally ready to travel again, he mounted up and had ridden less than two hundred feet when he saw the culprit from last night. A raccoon lay dead from getting kicked in the head by Forceps. So, the mule was protecting the camp after all.

With no breakfast, the young man wanted to see if he could kill a rabbit or a few squirrels and take the time to cook them along the trail. By the time the sun was overhead and nothing to eat, he made the decision to push on and stop earlier this afternoon and cook supper.

Around midafternoon, he came to the Salt Fork Arkansas River and made it across before stopping to make camp. The location of the camp had been used many times, and there was still enough wood to make a fire. With the fire going, he unloaded the pack mule again and then his horse.

Tonight was a meal of bacon and a can of beans that he heated by setting the tin close to the coals. With his bedroll moved away from the campfire, he could sleep without getting too hot and still be able to see his horse and mule.

Chapter Eight

THE FOLLOWING MORNING, BRODY WAS UP AT the break of dawn, putting the packsaddle on Forceps. Today, he was multitasking by cooking bacon while securing his supplies to the packsaddle. When the bacon was finished, he took the time to make skillet bread and eat.

One thing he did different today when he loaded his things was fix the food bag where it was easy to get to. He could possibly camp without having to unload everything tonight. Although, he was hoping that by tonight he would be getting close to his Indian friend's house.

With a full belly and his things all nice and secure, the lone rider took off with the Missouri Mule in tow. He went ahead and kept his regular clothes on with the intention of changing when it got hot in the afternoon.

The land was still mostly flat with some sloping hills, a few gullies carved into the land from excessive wind and rain. By the height and healthy nature of the grass, he surmised that someday this would be good farming land, just like the land where he came from.

Brody was at ease traveling across the prairie alone with the understanding that things could change quickly. There were lots of Indians in these parts and especially west and east.

Then there were the herds coming up from Texas. A thought entered his mind: *Why hadn't he seen a herd in the past few days?* Past experiences told him that today or the next day could be when he would come up on one. If he did, he would talk to the trail boss and see if he knew where Jennifer, the girl he operated on and who helped him rescue his mama from Rosco, lived in Central Texas. The young doctor really liked the tough, young woman, and they had even written to each other a few times, but then the letters stopped about six months ago. He remembered her pa's name was Big Joe, and they had a ranch somewhere close to Waco.

Jennifer was one of those rare people that you come across who makes a lasting impression on a man. She was beautiful, kind, loving, intelligent, but the thing that touched the young doctor's heart was her toughness, strong will, and aggressive behavior. As far as he was concerned, it was love at first sight, but he had never told her how he felt.

He had spent many nights in Kansas City wondering if he had said something in one of his letters to make her so mad at him that she didn't write him back. Or had she found someone she liked better and gotten married? Well, it didn't really matter right now since he couldn't do anything about it while riding along the Chisholm Trail.

Interruptions always have a way of putting his mind back on reality. Up ahead was something coming toward him, and not more than a mile behind the object was a cloud of dust. The object has to be the chuckwagon out in front of the herd.

That dust was not something he wanted a part of, but he could talk to the cook and see where they're coming from. Then he can ride southeast and see if he can find William Longtooth's place again.

With Brody going south and the wagon going north, it wasn't long until the two met up. "Howdy, could I ask you a few questions before I have to turn away from the herd?"

"Look, I'm tired, I'm cranky, I have a hurt man in the back, and I have to find a place to bed down for the night. I ain't got time to jaw with some kid."

"I understand. I rode with a herd a couple of years ago. The foreman's name was Delmer. I don't know if I ever heard his last name."

"Was it Delmer Hunt?"

"I don't know. Say, you said you had an injured man back there. I'm a doctor headed to Central Texas. Do you want me to take a look at him?"

"He's got a shattered leg that's in bad shape." The cook was nodding his head while talking. "I think that's a grand idea, but I can't stop the herd until we get to the river."

Brody kept riding along, beside the wagon, looking straight ahead and pondering on what to do. He went to medical school to help people and took an oath when he was declared a doctor. He had to help the man, so back-tracking was what he would do.

"The South Fork Arkansas River is not too far off. That'll be a good stop to water the stock and I can have enough daylight to examine the man. In fact, if you'll stop long enough for me to tie my horse and mule to the back of the wagon, I'll get in and see what I can do."

"Mister, you better make it snappy or them longhorns will be on us before you know it."

"Keep going, and I'll see if I can do it without you stopping."

Brody stopped his horse, and as the back of the wagon came into view, he maneuvered his horse where he could tie the mule's lead rope to the back. He then dismounted and walked fast, leading his horse so he could tie it up.

With both animals taken care of, he heaved himself into the back of the wagon to find the cowboy lying on the floor in a spot that was only large enough for him. The man's shirt was covered in sweat and his britches had one leg sliced up the side, exposing the broken leg. Someone had made a crude splint out of a couple of limbs and tied it on with twine. The exposed portions of the leg were already a different color, and it looked swollen.

"Mister, I'm Dr. Brody Connor, and I'm going to try and help you. I can tell that you're in severe pain, and I can help with that also. I'm going to move some of these supplies around so I can have room to see the extent of your injury. Before I do anything, I need to know your name."

"It's Barnabas Mingo. Doctor, I hurt so bad, and it's so hot in here that I can't hardly breathe. Can I have some water?"

"Yeah, give me a few minutes to move this stuff out of my way, and I'll find the water."

Brody went to work rearranging the back of the wagon so he had room to get to the man's leg. When he had room to ease his way to the front, he touched the cook on the back. "Barnabas needs water. Do you have a canteen up here with you?"

"Here, take this. I have another one somewhere."

Brody took the canteen to the man who drank most of it before he handed it back.

"Listen, I can't do much with the wagon moving. As soon as we stop, I can give you something for pain and then have a look at that leg. In the meantime, you'll have to fight through the pain."

"Doctor, am I going to die?"

"I sure hope not."

Brody really needed to get his medical bag off the mule, so he went to the back of the wagon and climbed over the tailgate and fell to the ground. He got up and ran to the mule, where he had to walk fast to keep up but was able to untie the tarp enough to find his medical bag.

He pitched the bag into the back of the wagon and once again climbed back in, where he could give the poor man some laudanum to ease his pain. He had much stronger opium, but he was going to save that for later in case the bones had to be set.

The jarring of the wagon didn't help the man's pain as they continued on toward the river crossing. The laudanum helped some and even helped the feller fall to sleep, but Brody could see the pain on his face.

What seemed like days were actually a few hours, and the wagon was fording the river and jolting up the far bank. Brody knew they would stop soon, and he could get busy working on Barnabas's leg. Although, he didn't know the extent of the break until he had time to remove the splint and feel the bones.

The wagon stopped, and the cook came to the back to lower the tailgate, which also served as his work table.

"I have to get a fire going and water boiling for coffee. Can you help me with the team?"

"Sure, I can help."

Brody was unhooking the team when the cook came to help. They removed the harnesses and hobbled the team for the night.

I need to get Barnabas out of the wagon and into the shade over there. Do you have a tarp and some bedding that we can lay him on?"

"There's tarps in the underbelly over there. He's on his bedroll in the wagon. That's all I have for him."

"That will do for now."

Brody got the man's bed laid out and was standing by the tree watching as the first of the cattle started through the red river water.

Chapter Nine

THE MAN RIDING POINT, WHOM BRODY FIGURED was the ramrod, crossed through the water first and then stayed by the riverbank, whooping and hollering at the cattle after they had sucked in water and went up the riverbank. He wanted the cattle to keep moving out onto the prairie so the ones behind them would have room to climb out of the riverbanks.

The cattle were pushed out by the riders as well as the men bringing up the drag. Brody waited and watched since he needed help moving Barnabas to his bed under the tree.

The cook, whom the doctor hadn't bothered to ask his name, was already busy peeling taters and onions for supper. By the look of things, it seemed they would have some sort of soup.

The ramrod started to the chuckwagon when more than half of the cattle were across the river. "Hey, Soggy. Why'd you stop here? We still have a couple of hours of daylight left?"

The cook looked up and pointed the knife he was

holding at the trail boss. "Well, now, I stopped for a couple of reasons. First, we're almost out of provisions and need fresh meat. Some of these cowhands need to kill us fresh game or butcher one of those calves from the herd. The other reason is Barnabas, he's in a bad way with that leg, but the good thing is, we have company, a man who happens to be a full-fledged doctor."

"A full-fledged doctor, you say. Is that him over there by the tree?"

Brody could hear the conversation and walked toward the two men.

"Hello, I'm Dr. Brody Connor. Yes, I'm a trained medical doctor, and I'm needing help moving Barnabas to that spot under the tree."

"How bad is his leg?"

"I'm not sure until I can get him out of the wagon and under the tree so I can examine his leg. From what I've seen so far, I'm of the impression that the bones ain't lined up straight, and that's why he's in such pain. I have medication that I can give him to ease his discomfort if I can set the bones back in place."

The foreman never took his eyes off Brody. He pointed a finger at the young doctor. "You doctored up Rufus, didn't you?"

"If you're talking about the Rufus that worked for Delmar, then yes that was me."

"Rufus is one of the outriders on this drive. I've heard a lot of good things about the gunfighting doctor. You do know that's what you're called in the cow camps, don't you?"

"No, sir, I didn't know that. By the way, what's your name?"

"I'm William Remario. You can call me Bill or Billy. I'll go get some men to help you. I'll be right back."

In a few minutes, Bill came back with two more men, and with Bill and Brody helping, they were able to get Barnabas settled down in the bedroll. The pain was still present, but he was handling it okay.

"Barnabas, I have to remove the splint and examine your leg. I'm going to give you something to make you unconscious in a little bit so you don't hurt too much."

"You do what you have to do, Doctor."

With the splint removed and the britches leg cut to mid-thigh, it was evident that the bones weren't in place, but he wouldn't know until he felt them. Brody sat back and thought about how to proceed. Almost all the cattle were across the river, and the cowboys were coming to the chuckwagon for a drink of water. That's when he came up with the crazy plan.

Brody walked to Bill. "I need help with Barnabas if you can spare a few men. The bones are not in place, so I'm going to do something and hope it works. I'll need three ropes and four men."

"We'll be right there."

The four men came to the tree where Barnabas sat, leaning against the tree trunk. "Take one rope and tie Barnabas to the tree, and make sure he can't get loose. I'm going to give him some chloroform to put him out, and then I want you to tie both ropes around the top of the boot on the broken leg. When I'm ready, I want the four of you to gradually pull on the ropes until I can get the bones lined back up. Is that clear with you all?"

Bill chimed in, "I understand what you're doing, and I'll help also."

Brody put the chloroform on a rag and placed it over Barnabas's nose and mouth until he slumped into the ropes around his arms and chest. The men tied on the other two ropes and started to pull while the doctor gave Barnabas another whiff of chloroform.

With the injured man out cold, Brody started to feel the leg and could feel the bones out of alignment. "Pull harder on the ropes."

They had the poor man stretched out when the doctor placed the side of his fist on the bone and hit his fist with his other fist and heard the bone snap back into place.

He felt some more, and when he was satisfied, he looked at Bill. "They can let him go now."

The doctor's shirt was covered in sweat as he got up. "Leave him tied up until after he wakes up. I need to find something to make him a better splint until some of the swelling goes down."

Brody went to the cook, who was cutting up chunks of meat and throwing them in a pot by the fire. "I see you found some meat?"

"Yep. A couple of the fellers killed a calf that probably wouldn't have made it to Kansas anyway. How's Barnabas?"

"He'll be fine. I need something stiff I can wrap around his leg so he don't hurt it when he gets up. Do you have any leather or thick material on the wagon?"

"I got a piece of cow hide that you can cut up if that'll work."

"That may work. Can you show me where it is?"

"It's rolled up under the seat."

Brody was able to cut the hide about two feet wide and long enough where it would wrap around his leg, and then tied it on with twine. He even went out and cut him a small tree with a fork to use as a crutch.

Barnabas woke up, and the men removed the ropes. After giving him another swallow of laudanum, he was able to sit up and visit with his friends until it was time for supper.

Brody sat down by Rufus at supper. "I see that hole where you were gored healed up."

"Yep, Delmar picked me up from Kingfisher on his way back home. You don't know how much me and those saloon girls appreciate what you did for all of us back there."

"I was glad that I could help. I've often wondered what happened to Emeral and Lilly."

Bill interrupted. "You're the man that killed Harris Chumbley, ain't you?"

"Harris almost beat Emeral to death, and when he came to finish her off, I stopped him in self-defense."

"If it hadn't been you, someone would have done it. When he hit the sauce, he got mean, and the more he drank, the meaner he was. I know that girl who you saved from him, and she's now a married woman in Fort Worth. I saw her there back in the winter, working at the railroad station with her husband. There's still a few scars on her face. You should stop by and see her when you go by."

Brody smiled at the thought of Emeral getting married and not having to work in the saloon anymore. In the short time he treated her wounds, they had become good friends.

"Doctor, I need to know if Barnabas can ride in the wagon tomorrow."

"How about this? I'll examine his leg in the morning and if it's still doing better, then I don't see why he can't. I don't want him up on it no more than absolutely necessary."

"That's fine. We can stay here a little longer in the morning until you've had time to examine him."

"Thanks, I'll hurry as quick as I can in the morning. I'll have to load up my pack mule and hit the trail as soon as possible, also."

The men sat around the camp talking, and that was the prime time for Brody to ask if anyone knew Big Joe or Jennifer Bernie from Central Texas. The men were all shaking their heads no.

Bill poured out his coffee. "Where in Central Texas are they from? That covers a large part of the state. We're all from around San Angelo, and I don't know any ranchers east of us." Brody let it drop, and the men continued to talk until the night riders had to join the herd. Brody slept in the location where he had Barnabas so he could check on him.

Chapter Ten

SOGGY WAS UP MAKING BISCUIT DOUGH AND humming a tune when Brody rolled off his bedroll and wiped the sleep from his eyes. Waking up early wasn't one of the things that he enjoyed in life. A man ought to be able to sleep until the sun was up.

After shaking out his boots and buckling on his guns, the doctor walked out behind a cedar tree to take care of some business. The cattle had spread out over the prairie, grazing on the tall grass. His horse and mule were close by, so it was also a good time to bring them in closer.

By the time he was back with the animals, Soggy was beating on the bottom of a pan with a large spoon. "Rise and shine. Breakfast is almost ready."

Soon, everyone was sitting around in a somber mood, eating the biscuits and gravy the cook had prepared. The bread was a little flat and hard for the doctor's taste but he understood since the cook was getting low on provisions.

One of the cowboys stood up. "Listen up."

Bill also stood up and looked south. "There's another herd coming this way, I can see the dust. Let's finish up and get these cattle moving before that other herd starts across the river."

Brody went to Barnabas, who was sitting up with his back to the trees, sopping up the last of the gravy from his plate. "How are you feeling?"

"I'm in a little pain, but nothing like I was. Whatever you did seems to be working."

Dr. Brody got down on his knees and felt the cowhide brace. "You'll have to tighten the twine if it starts getting loose. I want you to stay off this leg for at least four weeks, and I highly suggest you go see Dr. Milrose once you get to Wichita. He's a good physician and will go ahead and put a plaster cast on your leg."

"Thanks, Doctor. If you'll help me up, I think I can make it to the wagon on my own." With Barnabas up and using his crutch, he was able to hobble to the back of the wagon and started working his way into the bed. Brody gathered up the injured man's bedroll along with the tarp and took them to the wagon.

That herd was getting closer when he saw Bill take off across the river to see if he could slow them down until his herd could take off. Brody worked as fast as he could, packing up the pack mule and then getting his horse ready to ride.

The herd was no more than a half mile away and coming fast when the chuckwagon took off, and the herd followed. The men had to get after the cattle to make them leave the good graze and water, but there was a creek up ahead where they could stop for the night.

Brody crossed through the river and was heading southeast when he saw the cattle coming from the south start moving faster. The longhorns smelled water, and there was no way to stop them from getting to it now.

By the time the lead cattle were belly deep in the river, Bill and his men had their herd moving at a faster pace to put some distance between the herds.

Brody kept heading southeast, riding across prairie, up and down gullies and along sloping hills. His horse would scare up a deer or some other animal as they headed through. Once, when he was going through some tall grass, two pheasants flew up. With a keen eye, he watched where they went and wondered if he could get close enough to shoot one with his rifle. Something made him reach down and remove the safety off his pistol, and he no more than did it when another of the birds took flight in front of his horse. The pistol came out, and with one shot, the bird fell to the ground.

While off his horse, he went ahead and removed its innards before hanging it off his saddle. With his gun in his hand, he took off and in a few more feet, two more birds took flight, and he missed the first shot but the second one was on its mark.

Now to find a stream where there was water for his horse and mule. He would go ahead and cook the foul before it had time to spoil. Another quarter of a mile were willow trees and that meant water was near. It happened to be a spring that provided water to refill his canteen and water the animals.

Two pheasants were more than a meal, and it was hard to break camp on a full stomach. He changed his clothes before heading out this time and would wear the sleeveless shirt and cut-off britches until he felt like he was getting sunburned.

The stop was worth the time taken to eat a good meal, and tonight he could probably get by with a can of cold beans unless he happened to kill a rabbit. The country began to turn more to grazing land where the buffalo had wallowed out large depressions in the soil.

Two hours before sundown and traveling across terrain covered with scrub trees, brush, buffalo grass mixed with weeds, the smell of smoke overtook his nostrils. Someone had a fire going not far from where he sat on his horse. Did he keep going in the same direction, or did he veer off and try to avoid whomever it was?

Curiosity got the better of him, and off he went in the same direction that the breeze was bringing in the scent of smoke. Just as he topped a small hill, the object of the fire was another three hundred yards ahead. What looked like a family of Indians, were smoking meat to keep it from spoiling so fast in the heat. A deer, half processed, hung from a limb with a man holding a bloody knife, cutting off chunks of meat. A woman and two girls were cooking the venison in pans over hot coals. Two boys who looked to be in their teens also helped by packing the cook meat in leather bags.

One of the girls pointed toward Brody, and everyone began to move around and that concerned Brody some. He had spent time with Indians and had learned to understand some of their language. He had even learned to speak a little, but hadn't used it in a little over two years, and was having a hard time thinking of the words to tell them that he was a friend.

Then it hit him on what to say for peace. He held up his hand. "Nvwadohiyada."

That got their attention, and he pushed it farther. "I am anidawehi, the healer."

Brody reached back into his saddlebags and removed the pouches of herbs that William Longtooth had given him and held it up where they could see it.

Not sure what to do now, he eased on toward where they stood. "Do you speak White man's language?"

The man took his bloody finger and pointed to himself. "I speak English."

"I'm Dr. Brody Connor, a friend of the healer, William Longtooth."

"You welcome, come get food to eat."

Brody knew better than to turn down an invitation to eat with them. It would hurt their feelings, and he didn't want that. He took two pieces of the meat, sat down, and began to chew on the venison until he could swallow it.

The Indians knew what they were doing and kept working while Brody chewed on the meat. When he finished, he stood up. "Which way to the healer's house?"

The Indian pointed a little more east than the direction the healer was taking. Brody nodded his head and mounted up. He tipped his hat to the woman and kids as he rode past. They were nice people living off the land in the same tradition they had practiced for generations.

It was still too far to make it to William's house today, so he would find a place to bed down for the night. Looking up at the sky, there was still an hour of daylight left, and he would use that until he found a place to bed down, which wasn't long. Up ahead was the trading post where he and William had come and bought the Colt that was on his hip.

It didn't look like the business had any customers since no horses were tied out front. He looked at the four houses that also made up the little settlement with the trading store. Out here, it was customary to ride and not walk, but a man could never be too careful and needed to be prepared. With the safety off both guns, the lone rider leading a pack mule rode up to the front of the building, where he tied the horse and mule to the hitch rail.

Brody opened the door and stepped inside, where the only light was what came through the windows. The smell of some sort of meat cooking was the first thing that flooded his nostrils.

"Hello, anyone here?"

He was almost certain that the same man who was here two years ago came in from the back. "Evening, stranger. I have some cool beer if you need a little something to wash down the trail dust."

"That sounds good, and a plate of food too if you have some, and I'd like to know your name?"

"It's Press, Press Dixon, and those steaks are mighty good today. I've had them cooking most of the day. I'll be right back with your beer and food."

"It's nice to meet you, Press. I'm Dr. Brody Connor."

Press nodded his head and took off out the back.

Brody wandered around the store until the man came in with a plate of food and a small bucket of beer.

Brody tore into the steak, and the man was right, the buffalo steak was delicious and so tender. When he finally finished, he pushed the plate to the side. "Is there someplace that I can spread out my bedroll tonight around here?"

"I have an empty house back there that you can use for a dollar. It don't have much in it by way of furniture, but there is a bed you can spread your bedroll on."

Brody got up. "I'll take it, and I'll pay you another dollar if you help me with my packsaddle. I don't want to unload all my stuff today."

"Sure, I'll help. I think you were here with William one time about two years ago, weren't you?"

"Yeah, I bought this pistol and all the ammunition you had."

"I thought you were going to have it out with those men that were drinking that day, but you played it right, I reckon."

It was no use bringing up any more about him pulling his gun on those men, so he got up and went after the horse and mule.

Thirty minutes later, Brody was placing his bedroll on top of the bed. His things were secure in the house. The mule and horse were safe in the corral for the night.

Chapter Eleven

EVEN THOUGH THE BED WAS NO MORE THAN ropes weaved across two poles attached to a headboard and a footboard, the dirty feather mattress beneath his bedroll was all it took for the young pioneer doctor to get a good night's sleep. The sun rays shining through the dusty windowpanes is what woke him up.

After pulling on his boots, buckling on the holsters, and rolling up the bedroll, it was time to find the water well and wash off. The hand-dug well was over closer to the larger house, and on a small table beside the well housing was a bar of soap, a used towel, and a wash pan. He drew one bucket of water to fill the pan, then removed his shirt.

With his hair, face, and chest washed with soapy water, he drew another bucket and poured it over his head, then dried his face and hair with the towel before putting on his shirt. His britches and shirt were wet, but that didn't matter, as it was already hot and they would dry soon.

Press came out the back of the store. "Dr. Brody, come on in. I've got more steak with eggs cooked for four bits."

That sounded like the kind of breakfast a man didn't want to miss. Sure enough, Press's wife, who was an Indian woman, cooked buffalo steaks, eggs, and cathead biscuits covered in gravy.

Brody gave the woman a dollar for the meal, plus she gave him two biscuits with a piece of meat in each one for his noon meal. Press helped lift the packsaddle back on the mule. As Brody was securing his load, Press walked around the mule and said, "If you ever want to sale this mule, I'll give you top dollar for him. These Missouri mules are a luxury to the farmers around these parts."

"I'll keep that in mind. For now, I have to keep him. I've been well pleased with his performance so far, and I still have a long ways to go before I part with him."

Brody shook hands with Press and headed southeast. He thought he knew the way to William's house from here. It had taken him and the old Indian a half day to travel to the trading post before, but today it wouldn't take that long since his animals walked faster than the donkey William rode.

The trip to William's place revealed that more people had settled in the area since he was here last. A total of five sod houses were passed by, and the people stood outside one of the houses holding rifles. Brody didn't wave or acknowledge them as he passed by a half of a quarter away.

Up ahead was the weird formation that he remembered riding into. It looked like two hills on each side of a valley, but when you rode in, it was actually one large hill formation in the shape of a horseshoe. Cattle and horses were still inside the confines of the vast amount of land inside the horseshoe and the house that William lived in and could vaguely be seen toward the back wall. He was still too far away to see any smoke coming from the chimney, and the dogs hadn't come out to let the old Indian know he had company.

The dogs not coming out made the hair on the back of Brody's neck stick up. Something wasn't right, and he needed to be ready in case there was trouble. The leather straps were removed from his guns as he got closer to the house.

The place looked abandoned, with no smoke coming from the chimney, no animals in the corral, and no dogs yapping at his horse and mule. Brody stopped a hundred yards from the house and called out, "Hello, Healer. Hello, Healer."

There was no answer from outside and nothing moved at the house that he could see. This was very odd and uncommon for no dogs to be at the house, even if the old warrior was gone somewhere.

Still being cautious about the dogs coming out, trying to attack, he tied up his animals and proceeded to the front door, which wasn't locked. Upon entering the dark house, it was plain to see that no one had been home for a while. The hearth in the fireplace was cold to the touch. There was dust on the table where William ate his meals.

Brody stood where he was and began to search the room with his eyes. Over the fireplace where a rifle usually sits on two pegs, there was no rifle. The dishes, pots, and skillets were all clean and stacked where he kept them. The dirt floor hadn't been swept in days by the amount of dust that went airborne with each step.

Maybe his friend had been called away to administer

aid or spiritual healing on someone. But how long had he been gone?

Brody looked in the cupboards, and the bacon had already turned rancid, as well as the potatoes and onions. That meant the old man had been gone a long time for the food items to go bad.

Grabbing a large pan, he began to discard all of the food items that were no longer edible. He would take them away from the house and throw the food out.

His next move was to go out to the barn and look around, which also gave him clues that no one had been here in a long while. The garden only had potatoes and onions growing in it. By the look of the plants, no one had cut the weeds or dug any potatoes. Onions and potatoes were some of the first things planted and that was usually in February or early March.

A sickening feeling came to the pit of the young man's stomach. Something had happened to William, and there wasn't any clues here to give him the answers he wanted.

He would go ahead and unload his packed items and place them in the house. This would be his base camp until he figured out what happened to his friend. There was plenty of food between the potatoes in the garden and what he carried with him to get by for a few more days.

Tomorrow, he would ride to the family's house where he operated on the woman and see if they knew where the old healer was.

Before unloading the mule, Brody swept the dirt floor and wiped off the tables and kitchen counters. He didn't want all his things covered in dust. Next, he cleaned out the fireplace and brought in more wood so he could cook supper later.

It took a few minutes to unload and transport his supplies into the house, where he could remove the food items and have them separated from his medical supplies and clothes.

There was grain in the barn for the animals, but the water trough was dry in the corral. It took him thirty minutes to haul two gallons of water at a time to finally fill the water trough.

By the time he finally sat down under the porch to look out across the prairie, he was tired and finally drifted off to sleep.

He dreamed that he was riding across the plains when he saw bones scattered across the ground. The healer woke with a jolt, but the image of the bones stayed with him. What did the dream mean? Was it the Great Spirit giving him a vision?

Brody finally shook it off and went inside to cook his supper. He still had some of the bacon he brought from Wichita, and that plus some potatoes from the garden would be his supper. Eating alone in William's house seemed a little uncomfortable. His friend should be here, giving him pointers on healing or how to talk to the spirits.

Maybe he would get some answers tomorrow when he visited the family of the woman he operated on.

It was too hot in the house to sleep, so he dragged the feather mattress outside onto the porch where he could get a breeze. Maybe the heat, along with the anxiety of not knowing where William was, caused him to lie awake longer than usual. He finally removed his shirt and britches so the heat wouldn't be so bad.

The sky was almost black with only a few shivers of light shining through onto the parched ground. The light was shining on bones scattered on the ground. What does this mean, he asked?

No answer, only more bones and a campsite.

Brody woke up covered in sweat. He made his way to the water well, where he drew a bucket of water and dumped it on his head to clear out the dream.

Chapter Twelve

He sat in the darkness, going over the dream for the hundredth time and still didn't know what to make of it. It would be daylight soon, so he dressed and went inside to stoke up the fire enough to cook more potatoes to go with the leftover bacon from last night.

The good thing about being up so early, he would make it to the other Indian's house while it was still kind of cool, and his horse would probably like that also.

Speaking of his horse, he walked to the corral and noticed that the water trough needed topping off. Two trips to the well and the mule would have plenty to drink until he returned.

He went ahead and put the saddle on Scalpel before leading him to the front of the house. Brody hated to go off and leave his things in the dwelling unsecured, but didn't have a choice in the matter. They would probably be fine since the house didn't look like it had been used since William had left for who knows where.

With only two canteens and his guns, the doctor took on the five-mile journey to the other family's house. He made it out of the horseshoe hills and was making good time across the prairie when he noticed movement off to the east, close to some tall trees. It could be a deer, so he pulled the rifle out and started that way. The animal wasn't running off, and it was too large for a deer.

It was a donkey.

Why would a donkey be out here by itself?

Then it hit him like a ton of bricks. This was William's donkey out here by himself. Where was William? What has happened to the healer and spiritual man?

Brody rode up to the donkey, who didn't have a bridle, halter, or anything on him. Where was his gear? Someone had to remove the gear off the animal, and it could have been William if he was hurt and didn't want his donkey to die. Where had the donkey come from?

Brody thought about the situation for a few minutes, and the best thing he could do was recruit help to find William. Mounting up and heading south at a good gait for two miles took him to the house where the family lived, where he stayed after operating on the woman.

The dogs ran out barking at his horse and then the kids came out, followed by the woman. Brody rode up and put up his hand. "Osiyo."

The girl looked at her mama and spoke in her native language. Brody didn't understand since she was talking so fast, so he said, "Hisdela," which means *help me*.

The girl turned to Brody and spoke in broken English, "We help White healer. Come in house."

He dismounted, and one of the boys came and took his horse to the water trough. The woman went to a pot and dished out a bowl of stew, and poured him a mug of water from a clay pot. She set it on the table and then bent down, hugged his neck, and began to cry. Brody didn't know what to say or do, so he looked at the girl.

"Why is she crying?"

"She cry with happy to see you, Healer."

Brody smiled and patted the woman on the back. He then turned to the girl. "Where is your pa?"

She pointed out back. "Brother gone after papa."

Brody ate the stew, and when he was finished, the man of the house came in and hugged the young man also. Brody pointed to a chair and turned to the girl. "Tell Papa and Mama to sit down."

When they were seated, he said, "I came to see William. He's not home for a long time. I found his donkey on the way here." He rubbed his belly. "I feel in my belly that he's hurt or dead. I need help finding him."

The girl began to talk, and the dad was nodding his head up and down. He then said something to her, "Papa will help. We get horses and leave now."

The man, along with two of the boys and the girl, all had horses and were ready to go when Brody mounted up.

They found the donkey still grazing, and the Indian started tracking the donkey's steps. They came from the east, and Brody told the girl to spread everyone out, and that they would all head east in hopes of finding their friend.

The search party had traveled more than a mile when the Indian stopped everyone and went on alone. It took him some time and a lot of walking to find the donkey's trail. He pointed east, and they took off again. All five had about fifty yards between them as they searched the countryside for any sign of the old man.

Brody saw something to the south of them. It was more willow trees weaving in the slight breeze. Why would William be out this far from home? Was he hunting? If that was the reason, he must have known those willows were there and that meant water. If he knew there was water among the trees, so would the deer and other wild animals.

Brody called out and pointed to the willows. "Let's look over there."

Brody and his Indian friends started that way, and he had this cold feeling come over him. He remembered his dreams when he saw a humerus bone on the ground. He threw up his hand so everyone would stop. Brody pointed to the bone and then walked his horse closer to the trees. More bones were scattered on the ground where wild animals and vultures had cleaned all the meat off the skeletal.

The young healer was both saddened that William had died, but was also relieved that he had been found. But wait, were the bones really Williams?

He looked at the girl. "You and your brothers stay here and tell your papa to come with me."

The two men went the last hundred feet on foot and found the campsite where the saddle and bridle were laying. The skillet was still on long-died-out coals. The bedroll was on the ground by the saddle, and on the bedroll was most of the skeleton of William Longtooth. The healing pouch he always carried was laying on the ground beside the bones, and Brody picked it up to show it to the Indian. As he looked around the campsite, he didn't see the beads that his friend always had around his neck. They could be anywhere, the way the bones were scattered, or whoever killed the healer took them.

Yes, this was William, and he had been out in the elements for a long time. Brody kept looking and found the skull some ten feet away. The disturbing thing was the hold where someone had shot the old man in the head.

Whoever it was must have been someone that William knew, or they had waited until he went to sleep and shot him from outside the camp. Brody went back to his horse and took a pair of leather gloves from his saddlebags and picked up the skull. He placed it back with the rest of the skeleton.

The entrance hole had been fired from the south, and that was the way Brody and the Indian started walking. Sixty feet from the camp, the Indian picked up a lone .44 caliber hull. So whoever killed the old man had actually murdered him out here and left him for the wild animals.

They walked back where the others were, and Brody spoke to the girl. "We need shovels and a pick axe to dig a grave. Would you go get them?"

She spoke to her papa and then she and the other kids took off. The man looked at Brody and pointed to the few scattered bones. He went to one and picked it up and took it to the bedroll. Brody followed suit, and it wasn't long until they had recovered all the bones in the immediate area.

Shortly after when the two men were cooling off, they saw dust in the air. It was more than the children coming back with shovels. Their mama, along with a dozen other Indians, were coming to give their friend a real burial.

Brody didn't have to dig on the grave, but he did go through the medicine bag he picked up off the ground and took out a few items. When the grave was finished, the bedroll with Williams's bones on it was lowered into the earth.

Brody stood up and raised both his hands toward the heavens. "I sprinkle sage on the grave to purify the area."

He then walked around the grave, dropping small amounts on the bones.

Again, Brody then raised both his hands toward the heavens. "I sprinkle tobacco on the body of William Longtooth, a great warrior, healer, and medicine man, so he will connect with the Great Spirit." Brody again circled the grave using his finger and thumb to sprinkle the ground-up tobacco on the bones.

When he finished, the Indians in unison began to chant and sing while raising their hands up to the Great Spirit. When the song ended, the men began to fill the grave with dirt. Brody walked to his horse and was about to mount up when the girl brought her papa over. "Papa says you are a great medicine man and can stay with us."

Brody smiled at the girl and reached out to hug the man. "Tell him that I'm spending the night in Williams's house and then riding south in the morning. Williams's donkey is still at the location where we saw it, and you can go get it."

The girl relayed the message, and the man stepped forward and hugged Brody.

The young doctor rode off with a heart full of sadness but also a sense of gratitude. He was shown in his dreams where William was and that was a gift from the Great Spirit that William told him about. Maybe it was time he owned a Bible and learn more about the God of the Universe and how he works through people.

With his horse and mule fed and watered back in the corral at William's place, Dr. Brody cooked his supper and then looked through all of William's things. He took a knife that had some kind of inscription on the handle and gathered all the pouches he could find that contained herbs used for healing the body or soul.

Chapter Thirteen

THE FOLLOWING MORNING MADE THE YOUNG doctor realize that an important chapter in his life had come and gone. William Longtooth taught him many things about fighting, healing, life, and most importantly, about friendships. The warrior didn't have to take the boy in and befriend him when he was running away from what he thought was his way of life.

No! The old man saw something in the boy that was worth his time and effort to teach the scared boy how to be a man out in the wilderness. The hours and days of hand-to-hand fighting lessons, the days of target practice using his gunfighting skills, and then the art of learning to observe his surroundings. There's more to see out in front of a person than what his eyes originally see. You have to clear your mind and see not only with your eyes but with your other senses.

William taught him how to listen. Cover your eyes and listen to all the sounds around you, and you will eventually hear the different insects, a variety of birds, and animals scurrying about. Then you will hear the weather and listen to the wind and rain. Listen to the heat waves ricocheting off the ground, feel the heat and cold. Smell all the different fragrances around you.

This was William's house and a place where healing took place. A place that had seen its share of death, but it was more than all that—it was the home of a man who believed in the Great Spirit. Brody made sure the house was clean and the kitchen utensils put in place. When he walked outside and shut the door, there stood the donkey. He had followed them back to the house after all.

Brody mounted up and headed west back toward the Chisholm Trail. He would continue on toward Texas, but after what he found at Williams's, he would go to Kingfisher and see how his friends there were doing.

Instead of riding west to Hennessey's Place, he would go more southwest and see if he could cross Little Turkey Creek and the Cimarron River without going through the little town of Dover. Dover was a rough and rowdy town when the herds bedded down close by, and he almost had to shoot it out with a man the last time he was there in the café, eating a meal.

It would be hard on him and his animals in this heat to make it across the Cimarron River today. Then he remembered that he had no more meat to cook and all he could do for food now was eat out of tins. That little café in Dover was looking better by the minute.

Urging the animals to go faster would determine where they would end up at the end of the day. By going at an angle toward the Chisholm Trail, he could cut out a few miles.

By noon, he had to slow the horse and mule to a walk and once let them graze beside an almost dry creek. The stream was still moving, but had shrunk where it was only about four feet wide. It was plenty to sustain his animals, and the rest period gave him time to boil water for his canteen.

The sun had already begun to go down when he emerged onto the cattle trail and headed due south. Not sure where he was or how far the next town would be, Brody didn't push his horse or mule. They were tired, and the heat had them worn out more than he was.

Another quarter of a mile, and the sound of cattle mooing and the clash of horns hitting other horns could be heard, but there was no dust in the air. Riding on closer to the sounds and the herd had been directed off the main trail to bed down for the night on the prairie, where there was an abundance of grass.

The cattle off the trail was a blessing for Brody since he wouldn't have to move off the trail to get past the dust they produced. He kept riding and soon three riders came from where the herd was bedded down, running their horses, hell bent on getting to whichever town was to the south.

This was the same on every cattle drive, and lots of times it didn't turn out the way the drovers had planned. The men would go to the saloon, drink whiskey, start a fight over nothing that mattered, and more times than not, get into a gun battle.

A lot of the trail towns catered to the drovers with food, whiskey, and saloon girls for company. Two of the girls that Brody had helped in Kingfisher worked at the saloon when he was there. Emeral was almost beaten to death, and Lilly got pregnant, and he then helped find a good family to raise the baby. Being a saloon girl was a hard way to make a living, although there were times the girls found a good man who would marry them and take them away to a better life. That's what he was told about Emeral.

Turkey Creek was in front of the doctor, and not far to the south would be Dover. He knew where to eat and then he would be on his way. There was nothing here for him besides food to fill his belly. Tomorrow, he would be in Kingfisher, and that's where he could stock back up on provisions.

The café he had taken a meal in two years ago was still in business, and by the look of horses tied at all the hitch rails close to the saloons, it must be more than one herd close by. That could be trouble for the local law and merchants. Opposing ranch hands had a tendency to fight each other. He didn't want to be anywhere near any of that, so he would eat and leave.

The café only had a few people sitting at tables when the young man wearing a shirt with no sleeves came in and took a seat where he could watch his horse and mule. He had worn the cut-off britches earlier in the day but had changed a couple of hours earlier. The cut-off britches wouldn't be popular around cowboys, and who knows, the shirt may not, but he was willing to take that chance since it was much cooler than a regular shirt.

The waitress, who wasn't the girl that he almost got into a gunfight over, took his order for a plate of what they were serving and water to drink. It so happened that with the cattle herds near, today's menu was steak, potatoes, fried pies, and cornbread.

The food was delicious, and Brody mounted up his horse and mule, who were also watered and rested. There was still a good hour of daylight left, and if he hurried, he could sleep in the hotel at Kingfisher.

Brody was almost to the second saloon when two men walked out onto the boardwalk and stood with their thumbs on their holster belts. He saw them and then looked back for a second look. They were two of the men he had seen watching him as he rode through Caldwell, Kansas.

His first inclination was that the men had followed him so they could steal what he had on the packhorse. That wasn't going to go well for any of them if that was their intent. Out here alone and trying to survive was like treating a patient with a disease. You find out what the cause is and eliminate it as quickly as you can.

Brody turned his horse toward the two men. "I saw you fellers watching me in Caldwell, Kansas. Is there something I can do for you?"

The men took one step away from each other. "We were wondering what's so important on the back of that mule that you have to keep it covered."

Brody smiled. "Although, it's none of your business. I'm a doctor, and most of its medical books, bandages, and instruments that I don't want to get wet. The books are important for me to treat people, and I also have a change of clothes. Is there something else you want to know?"

"Yeah, what's your name?"

Brody moved his hand to his lap, where the shoulder holster gun would be easy to draw. "It's Dr. Brody Connor. What's your names?"

"Why do you want to know our names?"

"It'll be fitting for the undertaker to have a name for the wooden cross."

"You better watch what you say, boy. Your big mouth could get you into trouble."

"I reckon it could. You fellers have a good day. I'm heading to Kingfisher in case you're wondering." Brody kicked his horse and started off.

"Hey, do you know a man by the name of Rosco?"

Brody dropped the lead rope and wheeled his horse around, ready for a fight. "I did know a man by the name of Rosco in Wichita. He's dead now, so what's your point?"

The men threw up their hands. "We ain't looking for trouble. We heard that you killed Rosco and a few more men that crossed you some time back, is all."

Brody never said anything back to the men, it wasn't necessary. Instead, he reached out and took hold of the lead rope of the mule and took off south. He would cross the Cimmaron River and go on to Kingfisher tonight.

Chapter Fourteen

A HERD OF CATTLE WERE SCATTERED OUT ON the sides of the trail for a quarter of a mile to the east and west. They had crossed the Cimarron River earlier and were filling their bellies with grass. Even though only a few of the cows were in the trail since the grass was beaten down, he didn't know if it was a good decision to ride through. As he approached the herd, a drover came over and cut him off.

"Where do you think you're going?"

"I'm heading right through there, and I'd appreciate it if you would move out of my way or clear me a path threw them cows?"

The man pointed to the mule. "Are you packing food on that mule?"

"No. I'm a doctor, and I'm packing medical supplies and books. Where is this herd from?"

"What business is that of yours?"

"I'm going to see a young woman whose family has a ranch somewhere close to Waco. I don't know where they live or how to get there. All I know is their names are Jennifer and Big Joe Bernie."

"We ain't too far away from Waco, but looking for a woman in that part of the country is like looking for a needle in a haystack. That's a big area to cover and not many towns around. There's also a lot of raids by Comancheros in that part of Texas. They're hitting the smaller spread, killing most of the ranchers and running off their stock. I've heard of instances where they've taken young women with them."

"I don't know who Comancheros are. Are they Indians?"

"They're originally traders from New Mexico, and they're of Mexican descent. But over the past years they've been trading with the Comanches, Kiowas and other plains tribes. Supposedly, they crossbreed with the Comanches and that's where they got their name. Now, a lot of them are raiding ranches and stealing cattle, horses, and women and either selling or trading what they steal, to the Indians. Sorry, I can't help you more with where your friends live. Follow me and I'll help you through the cattle."

"Much obliged."

The drover started through the cattle and slapped some of the longhorns with his rope to make them move so they could pass. When they made it through and with the river up ahead, the drover pointed west. "It's not as muddy over there."

"Thanks again, and you all stay safe out here."

The man was right about the mud. Scalpel and Forceps made it across with the water only coming up to their bellies. On the far side, he waited long enough for his animals to get a good drink before urging them to go faster.

When the road that would take him to Kingfisher crossed the Chisholm, he turned west and continued on until he could see the town in the dusk of night. Some businesses and a few houses were already lighting lanterns and lamps.

The town was mostly in darkness by the time he pulled up in front of the open livery stable doors. Brody could see a lantern lit in the tack room, and called out, "Hey, anyone here?"

The tack room door came open and out walked the same man who was here before. Only this time, he didn't have on a shirt, only his britches suspended by suspenders and no shoes.

"You looking to board your horse and mule tonight?"

"Yes, sir." Brody dismounted and walked up to the man and stuck out his hand. "I'm Dr. Brody Connor and we've met before."

The feller grabbed his hand with a strong grip, shook it up and down. "I'm mighty glad to see you, Doctor. If I recall, you went off to doctor school sommers."

"That's right, and I'm now a real doctor. I'll help you with the packsaddle since it's too heavy for one man."

"No sir, Doctor. I have a block and tackle that will take it off, and I'll leave it hanging until you need it."

"Thanks, I need to grab my clothes bag really quick before you remove the saddle."

With the bag in hand, Brody patted the man on his shoulder. "It's good seeing you again. I'm tired, so I'm going to the hotel and get a room. I'll let you know when I'm ready to leave town." Brody handed the man money for the animals and walked toward the hotel.

When he walked up to the counter, the man working took one look at him and pushed the ledger over. It's good to see you back Dr. Brody. How long are you staying?"

"I'm just passing through but I would also like a hot bath in a little while. I'm going down to the diner for supper and then coming right back here, and I'd appreciate it if I could have that bath then."

"Your bath will be ready when you return. You'll be in room eight down the hall on the second floor. It's got two windows, so hopefully you'll get a good breeze."

Brody laid money on the counter and picked up the key. He didn't go to the room, but instead set his clothes bag at the end of the counter where it would be safe until he could have a good meal at the café. A few of the people eating spoke to him, but the waitress was someone he didn't remember.

After the meal, he went back to the hotel, soaked in the tub, and shaved for the first time since he left Wichita. He smiled at himself. Was he trying to look good in case he saw his ex-girlfriend, Betsy?

Back in the room with both windows raised, the young doctor laid down and didn't wake up until he heard noises out on the street. He got up and splashed water on his face before going to the window, where it was already daylight.

Men were riding by on wagons, and others were on the boardwalk, but were they shopping this early or going to work? For the past two or more years, he had to be up at dawn to get to work or attend class. Many times, he only had a few hours of sleep because of all the studying he had to do.

Finally dressed in clean clothes, he would go eat breakfast and then take his dirty clothes to Rosalie, who was Betsy's ma. After that, he wanted to go see Dr.

Stevens and find out if everything went well with Lilly having her baby and giving it to the Purdy family.

The café wasn't busy since it was almost eight in the morning and everyone was already working. He ate his breakfast without having to talk to anyone as he sat at the window watching people. A few townsfolk came by that he recognized and then he spotted a couple coming down the boardwalk on the far side of the street.

He sucked in a deep breath and watched as Betsy, who had a baby in her arms, was walking beside a man who was holding the hand of a little boy. From what he could tell, Betsy was as pretty as ever and looked nice in her dress. They stopped in front of a store with a sign that read: *Alteration, Laundry, and Ironing.*

The man unlocked the door, and the family went inside. Brody got up and laid money on the table before walking outside. He started across the street and then changed his mind on where he was going.

Betsy was married and had a beautiful family, and he had no business even talking to her. He had his time with the young, playful girl, and he chose medical school over her. No sir, he would not interfere in her family.

It was then that he made the decision to tell the hostler to get his horse and mule ready while he went to the mercantile for supplies.

The man and woman who owned the store remembered Brody and were under the impression that he was back to open his medical practice there. He had to politely explain to them that he stopped by to sleep, buy some food, and head on to Texas. He didn't mention Betsy, Emeral, or Lilly and her baby.

When he left the store, he decided not to talk to Dr. Stevens and find out how it turned out with Lilly and her baby. He would ride by the Purdy place when he leaves Kingfisher.

Chapter Fifteen

THE HOSTLER HAD THE MULE TIED UP OUT front and was leading the horse out when Brody walked up with his sack of supplies.

"You want me to help you with that tarp so you can stow your things on the mule?"

Brody looked at the bag. "Nah, it ain't that much in it, so I'll hang it off my saddle. Thanks for taking care of my animals." Brody flipped him a silver dollar.

He mounted up and headed south down the dusty street but couldn't help glancing at the business that Betsy and her husband owned. Betsy was standing in the window watching him as he rode by. Their eyes met, she smiled at her former boyfriend, and waved at him.

Brody smiled back and touched the brim of his hat. Out of respect to her husband, he turned his face south and rode on out of town. He couldn't help but wonder what it would have been like to have spent more time with Betsy. That was water under the bridge now, and they had both moved on.

He remembered the way to the Purdy farm and was

quite surprised when he pulled into the yard and there sat Lilly holding a child, a little over a year old.

She jumped up and ran to the door. "Booker, come outside quick, you ain't going to believe this."

"Hello Lilly, it's good to see you and your baby."

She sat the baby on the ground and ran to Brody, where she put both arms around his neck and kissed his cheek. "It's so good to see you, Dr. Brody."

Booker came out of the house and also ran to the doctor hugging his neck. When Brody was free of their embrace, he looked around and asked, "Where's Susan?"

Lilly started back to pick up her daughter. Booker pointed out toward a big oak tree. "Susan got pregnant again, and it turned out really bad. Dr. Stevens couldn't save her, and she's buried over there under that tree. She wanted children so bad, and it wasn't God's will for her and me. Lilly was already living here with us, so it was fitting for the two of us to get hitched."

Brody looked at Booker with sincere condolences. "I understand, and I'm saddened to know that Susan passed, but I'm overjoyed to know that you and Lilly have a life together with that little one and probably more in the future."

Lilly came over with the little girl in her arms. "This is Bonnie, that's the closest name we could get to Brody. If it hadn't been for you, this loving child would not be here today."

With tears clouding his vision, he put his arm around Lilly. "I'm going to gloat a little bit here if it's all right. Bringing you together with Booker and Susan so you could have this beautiful child is the most important thing I've ever done. It put two people together, and you have a beautiful baby. I'm proud of that." He reached out and took the little girl from Lilly and kissed her cheek.

When he handed the child back, he opened his arms to Booker and Lilly. "I have to be going. I'm on my way to Central Texas to see if I can find someone that I'm wanting to get to know better. So, if I'm ever by this way again, I'll stop by."

"Brody, did you see Betsy?"

He looked at Lilly. "I saw her and her family walking to their business. I respect the bonds of marriage, and I chose medicine over her when I left here. But as I was leaving town, she watched as I passed by. We smiled at each other, and she waved to me."

"I knew when you wouldn't kill my baby that you were a good man. I know that Betsy loved you and would have talked to you if you had saw her, but I'm so proud of you for respecting her husband and not seeing her. Jefferson is a good man, and he loves Betsy more than anything."

"Thanks, Lilly. I have to go. Maybe the next time I come by, I'll have someone with me."

Booker walked up to Brody, sitting in the saddle. "Thanks for understanding. Some folks think we're terrible people around here."

"I'm not one of them. I think it's a wonderful marriage, and I hope you have a dozen kids together."

Lilly hollered from her chair, "Brody Connor, you get on out of here. A dozen kids, I swear, you men!"

Brody left out heading to the North Canadian River and Fort Reno.

THERE WAS STILL lots of daylight when he rode by Fort Reno and kept going. If he stopped at every place he came to, he would never make it to Central Texas.

Brody was bound and determined to get down to the Waco area and decided the night after leaving Booker's farm that he would only make one more important stop, and that was to see Emeral in Fort Worth.

The next six days were spent riding through a couple of rivers and numerous streams. The hot, humid weather made him go slower than he wanted, but on that sixth day, he pulled into Fort Worth, Texas and was astonished at the size of the place.

Finding a livery stable was easy since he saw three as he rode into town and was told that there were more on the south and west sides of the city. The same went for hotels, and they all had a variety of accommodations, like running water in the rooms where a man could bathe anytime he wanted. Although, that came with a price to go with it. His room was six dollars for the night, and after getting into his room and opening up his bag, he remembered that he still had dirty clothes from when he changed in Kingfisher.

After a hot bath and sporting his last change of clean clothes, he took his dirty clothes with him to the lobby. "Excuse me, do you have a clothes washing service here at the hotel?"

"Yes, sir, we do. Follow me and I'll show you the lady who takes care of laundry for our guests."

The lady took his clothes and assured him that they would be ready by the time he left in the morning. The city seemed to have a lot of places to eat and that was where he headed.

Fort Worth was experiencing an economic boom from the Texas and Pacific Railroad completing the line through the town. With the railroad came people, and the city grew to around four thousand, in part from all the commerce of cattle coming through on the Chisholm Trail.

The railroad came with cattle pens for shipping cattle to the eastern markets instead of cattle drives. The Texas ranchers could now take their cattle to the shipping pens and have the cattle loaded onto railcars. That improved their profits and they didn't have to make long cattle drives up into Kansas anymore. The cattle business grew so large in Fort Worth that it was nicknamed *Cowtown*.

Along with the drovers, cowboys, outlaws, gamblers, and people coming with the railroad to stake out their fortunes, brought with them the saloons, dance halls, and brothels. The area where all the less desirable businesses were located became known as, *Hells Half Acre,* or as some called it *Paris of the Plains.*

This area was known for the fights, stabbing, and of course, a gunfight over a saloon girl or poker game wasn't out of the question. The lawmen didn't last long in Fort Worth because of the retaliation when men were arrested and put in jail.

Even though it was becoming a hub for commerce, the criminal element was there all the time, and a man had to watch his back when patronizing one of the saloons where gambling was going on.

One of the biggest challenges had to do with the growth and migration of people coming west. These newcomers had sold everything they owned back where they came from and brought that money with them. Most were good, hardworking folks wanting to carve out a better life for their families. The influx of pioneers also brought with it another element of people, robbers, murders, and rapist who fed off the weak and vulnerable.

Lawlessness in the cattle towns and the exploding

population that came with the railroad, put a strain on the law that was spread too thin to protect the average citizen. The local city and county law didn't have the resources to hire enough men to patrol the streets, let alone the county.

The Texas Rangers had their own problems with internal conflicts and grappling with the changes to the frontier. The South Texas area was one of utmost importance for the Rangers combating outlaw gangs along the southern border, who were stealing cattle, and investigating border raids where people were murdered. Many of the Rangers' resources were assigned to South Texas.

The other major assignment was with the Frontier Battalion, which was assigned to protect the frontier from hostile Indians and Comancheros from New Mexico.

Then there were the bloody feuds between opposing ranchers. The feuds and range wars were some of the most deadly circumstances the lawmen had to deal with.

Chapter Sixteen

THE SUN WAS ALMOST OUT OF SIGHT WHEN DR. Brody left the café where he had a tasty meal. It was still early, and he needed to let his stomach settle before going to bed for the night, so he started walking south down the street.

A few blocks went by before he heard the music up ahead and kept going out of curiosity. He had overheard talking about the seedy side of town that was called, Hell's Half Acre, and wanted to see what it was. Brody wasn't a stranger to the rougher sides of a city. In fact, he had even smiled while eating when he heard that Fort Worth had a section called, Hell's Half Acre.

While attending medical school, he would go to the West Bottom area where the Kansas and Missouri Rivers meet. That area was also called, Hell's Half Acre, because of the numerous brothels, Gambling houses, and the constant gun battles and lawlessness along a subsection called, *Battle Row*.

Emeral taught Brody how to play poker when she was laid up under his care. He often visited the seedy side of

Kansas City and made some spending money when he wasn't studying or working at one of the local hospitals. This trip hadn't cost him much of his savings so far, and the money he won after Wichita hadn't been spent yet.

The young man crafted habits over the past two years when going into saloons and gambling halls. The men or women sitting at the table were his adversaries and he wanted to see them in action before he joined in their game of chance. The first thing he did while looking for a table to watch was remove the safeties from his guns.

He watched facial expressions, the way they wetted their lips, the little twerks of rubbing their fingers together. Most men did something or changed something when they had a good hand or if they were bluffing.

The first table he observed happened to be a poor man's game, where the men didn't have enough money for him to even consider sitting down.

As he made his way through the crowd, a table with only three men caught his attention, as well as more patrons in the room. This was the table that had money, and his first impression of the men playing cards was not favorable for one of the men. He was probably a rancher who had a compulsion to gamble.

The other two men were professional gamblers, and the evidence was in the way they handled a deck of cards. The man dealing cards set the deck to the right of his hand and picked up his cards. He looked at his cards and extracted two and discarded them.

The other gambler did the same but discarded three cards. The feller who was trying to be respectable at cards, discarded three cards. Then he did something that got Brody's attention—he rearranged his remaining two cards. That meant he didn't even have a pair, and the two cards he had were probably two face cards.

This was the critical time for Brody to pick up on what the other two players drew. The dealer dealt out three cards to the man on his left. The man picked up the cards to see what he drew and then put them down. He uses his thumb to roll the ring on his right hand. Brody would have to wait and see if rolling the ring meant he had a good hand or a bad hand.

The rancher picked up his three cards and made no expression, but he didn't have to. Brody already knew the man didn't have anything.

The dealer gave himself two cards, glanced at what he drew, and then looked to the man to his left. "Are you making a bet?"

"I check."

The rancher picked up twenty dollars. "I bet twenty."

The dealer picked up two twenties. "I see your twenty and raise twenty."

The man to his left threw in his money. "I call."

The rancher threw in his cards. "I'm out."

The dealer flipped over his cards to show a pair of tens.

The man on his left turned his over to show a pair of kings.

The dealer slid the cards to the man on his right. "Nice hand."

Brody had seen enough. "Would you fellers mind if I joined in on your game?"

The man shuffling pointed to the empty chair. "If you got money, the chair is empty. Help yourself. What's your name?"

"I'm Dr. Connor, and I appreciate you letting me play."

The man who was shuffling the cards and had won the last hand said, "I'm Richard Whitmer. He pointed to the rancher. He's Luther Miller, and this feller is known as St. Louis, but you can call him Louie."

"Nice to meet you all." Brody pulled out his money and threw in a five-dollar bill as an ante. Louie smiled at the young man, thinking he was either a good player or a real tenderfoot.

Brody lost the first three hands while continuing to study the other three men. The fourth hand was the turning point as he drew three sevens, an ace, and a king. Brody threw in a forty-dollar bet and asked for one card, and he discarded the ace.

After the bets were called, his card was another king and that made him have a full house. He checked the bet and that was all Louie needed—he bet sixty dollars. Luther called the bet and so did Richard, but Brody knew that he now had them in the palm of his hand.

"I see your sixty and raise you one hundred dollars."

The rancher threw in his cards. Louie put in his hundred and was trying to stare a hole through the young man.

Richard picked up his money and threw it in the pile. "I call."

Brody slid his right hand closer to his shoulder holster gun and used his left hand to flip over the cards. "I'm full with sevens over kings."

Both men threw down their cards. Brody waited, but no one said anything. He pushed the cards back to Richard. "You shuffle and deal in my place."

When all the bets had been made and the discarded cards replaced, Brody had two pair, Queens over threes. He again bet twenty, and by the time the bet was back to him, he had to throw in another forty, so he made it an even one hundred. This time, all three men called the bet, and once again, he had his hand close to his gun before he flipped over the cards.

Louie slammed his cards onto the table and was standing up when Brody's hand moved like grease lightning and produced the short-barreled .45 caliber gun pointed at Louie. The man froze in a half stance.

Calmly, Brody said, "Louie, I beat you fair and square. Don't let a friendly game of poker put you six feet under."

Louie raised both his hands. "I ain't goin' to draw on you."

Brody put his gun back into the holster and used his left hand to gather up his money, never taking his eyes off Louie. When he was finished and put the money in his pocket, he turned to the other two.

"Thanks for letting me play at your table. I'm sorry we had to end it this way, but I think my welcome is over and it's time I left."

Brody backed away a few steps, where he had enough room to turn and put some of the men inside the room between him and Louie.

Back on the street, he walked as fast as he could back toward the hotel before ducking in between two buildings to see if he was being followed. There were others inside the saloon that saw him win over five hundred dollars, and that was enough to get killed over in a lawless town like Fort Worth.

After five minutes of hiding in the darkness between the buildings, and he was satisfied that no one was following, he continued on to the hotel and called it a night. Winning at a poker table in a strange town was always dangerous, especially when you took the money off a professional gambler like Louie.

Tomorrow, he would stay clear of Hell's Half Acre and

go see Emeral. After that, he would ride south by going around the section of town where he just came from. It wouldn't be out of the question for someone to take a back shot at him, especially now that he had money.

He was almost to the hotel when he crossed the street and started back toward the saloon. On that side of the street was a dance hall with the music blasting out of the open windows and doors. Girls were inside dancing with the men for a small fee, of course. That wasn't something he had ever done, and that wasn't the reason he was standing out front watching the saloon where he played poker.

Brody walked across the street and looked through the window on the right. There were too many men standing in his view to see if the men were still at the table playing cards.

He walked to the door and stepped inside, stood still for a few seconds, scanning the room before he made his way to the opposite side of the room where he had previously been. The same three men were playing cards, but now there were two other men at the table.

With confidence that no one would try to come after him tonight, Dr. Connor walked back out and went back to the hotel.

Chapter Seventeen

THE ROOM HE WAS IN FACED THE NORTH AND didn't let in an abundance of early sunlight, which let the young doctor sleep in for a change. The soft bed did wonders to his tired body after sleeping on the ground for the previous six nights.

The opportunity to take another bath was all it took for him to soak in the water until it began to cool. He shaved, dressed, and headed downstairs with his bag so he could collect his clean clothes.

"Good morning, Dr. Connor. I hope you enjoyed your room."

"The room was great and I especially loved the bathtub in the room. Are my clothes ready?"

"Yes, sir, they're right over there." The clerk pointed to a table where there were three bundles of clothing.

"I have to go see someone at the train station. Can I leave my bag over by my clothes for an hour?"

"That'll be fine. You go do your business, and I'll make sure your things are safe."

The walk to the train station took him by the livery stables, which was good.

"Morning, you coming after your horse and mule?"

"I'm stopping by to tell you that I'll be needing them within the hour, so I'd appreciate it if you would get them ready to travel."

"Sure thing, Doctor."

"Thanks."

His next stop would be at the train station, although he didn't know where exactly Emeral worked. The station was busy with people waiting for the morning train to arrive. Some were waiting for guests or relatives to come in by rail, and others were waiting to leave town.

Brody heard his friend before he saw her and walked toward the sound. She was in the ticket office, sitting at a desk, shuffling through slips of paper and writing in a ledger book. Two men were at the ticket windows selling tickets up and down the rails. The third man was writing down arrival and departure times on a chalkboard.

Brody assumed the man at the chalkboard was Emeral's husband since she was at the desk working and the two ticket men were much older.

Brody saw an opening by the ticket window and called out, "Emeral, is that you?"

"She turned her face toward the window, rose from her chair, and ran to the window. "Brody, is that really you?"

"It's me all right." Can we talk?"

"Of course. I want you to meet my husband. Go around to the back side and we'll come out that door."

Emeral and her husband were waiting when Brody came around the corner. Emeral came to him and wrapped her arms around his neck. "I'm so glad to see you. I suppose you're an educated doctor now, ain't you?"

"I sure am. I even have a diploma stating that I'm Dr. Brody Connor."

Emeral turned to her husband. "Larry come here. This is the man who saved my life. This is Dr. Brody Connor, and this is my hubby, Larry Hunter."

"It's really good to meet you, Larry. Me and Emeral have had our moments, and she's one of my dearest friends and patients."

"I want to personally thank you for what you did. That took a lot of bravery and grit to put your life on the line for a stranger."

"I'm sure she told you of my childhood, and I'll never stand by and let some man beat a woman. I'll fight until my last breath before I let that happen. It just so happened that I was the better man, and Emeral pulled through in flying colors. I was so emotionally moved when I was told that the two of you were married and working here at the station."

"Larry is the station manager, and I'm the assistant manager. We hope to buy a house and start a family soon. Brody, why are you here? I'm sure you've had way better offers for work than Cowtown."

"I'm passing through on my way to Central Texas. After I left Kingfisher, I hooked up with that herd, and when I got home, I found out that the brother to the man I killed stole the tavern from my mama. Long story short, I killed some men in self-defense and met a rancher's daughter from Central Texas. We were writing each other about once a month, and then about six months ago, the letters stopped. So, I'm on my way to find her and see why she stopped writing me."

Emeral smiled. "Dr. Brody's in love. What's the girl's name?"

"Jennifer Bernie."

Emeral lost her smile and looked at Larry. "Brody, I'm so sorry, but Jennifer may not be there anymore. Her pa was Big Joe Bernie and owned the Dry Creek Ranch. About six months ago, his ranch and three more were raided by Comancheros. Big Joe was murdered along with the men who were at the ranch house. It's rumored that they stole his daughter, and the same for the other ranchers they hit. There has probably been ten or more raids on ranches in the past eight months. You may want to talk to someone at the Texas Ranger station in Cleburne, Texas, or at the local newspaper office. It's been in the papers and was the talk of the town for a while."

"Thanks, I'll do that when I leave here."

"Did you stop at Kingfisher on the way here?"

"Yes, I spent the night there, and if you're wondering, I didn't talk to Betsy. I saw her from a distance and we kind of waved at each other. She has a husband and two kids now, and I'm not getting involved with that. I did talk to Lilly, though, and she's doing great and so is her little girl. Did you know that her and Booker got married after Susan died?"

"Yes, she wrote me that they were hitched. It's sad about Susan, but I'm glad for both Lilly and Booker. He loved Susan, but he loves Lilly also."

"I'm glad everything has worked out for you. I'm getting ready to leave town, and I don't know when I'll be coming this way again, so give me a hug, and I'll be on my way."

She walked up and put her arms around him and kissed him on the cheek. "You don't be no stranger and stop by whenever you're in town. I can never repay what you did for me, and I love you for it."

He smiled, "I love you too Emerald. Tell Larry bye for me."

"Bye, Brody."

He walked out of the station and wiped a tear from his eye, not from sadness but from the joy of knowing that he had a big part in the ex-saloon girl's future. He had spared her life and treated her wounds, but she had helped him also. He was a boy on the run, and she taught him how to play poker and drink alcohol, which he didn't do anymore.

The newspaper building happened to be on the way to the livery, and that's where he stopped. A bell rang when he opened the door, and a man wearing a fancy suit came into the lobby area.

"Good morning, what can I do for you?"

"I'm Dr. Brody Connor and I'm a friend of Jennifer Bernie and was told you may have some information about a raid on her ranch that killed her pa, Big Joe Bernie."

"I seem to recall the name. Do you know the name of the ranch and how long ago it was?"

"I believe it was the Dry Creek Ranch, and it was about six or seven months ago."

"Wait here and let me go in the back to see what I have."

Brody waited for a long time, and the man finally came back with three papers in his hand. "I found the papers where we reported those horrible raids where numerous people were murdered. You can have the papers for five cents if you want to read them."

Brody gave the man a nickel and took the papers. "Do you know if there's any Texas Rangers in Cleburne?"

"There's not an office there, but there are like five Rangers that work out of there on a daily basis. You can usually find them in the saloon."

"Thanks for the papers and information."

Brody left the paper office and walked to the livery stable. It was time to ride.

Chapter Eighteen

THE RIDE TO CLEBURNE, TEXAS, WAS MORE than Brody could manage with a pack mule in tow. The thirty-two miles from Fort Worth didn't seem that far, but in the conditions of summer and not many water holes in between, it was well after dark when the town finally came into view.

He didn't have to rein the horse to the water trough, it turned on its own to the first one they came to. Brody sat in the saddle, looking down the street, trying to locate a livery stable for his animals and a hotel for himself.

The growing town had originally been an Army post called Camp Henderson and then the name was changed to Cleburne. After the Civil War, the small town was full of unrest and had a turbulent past. Now it was the beginning of commerce with a growing population of emergent and people settling here from Missouri.

Cotton, grain, and corn raised in nearby fields, along with many acres of cattle ranches, created the need for a better way to transport goods. The railroad was building tracks to Cleburne so the goods could be transported out of the area. The building of the railroad also brought in a flux of workers and their families.

When there's a deluge to the population of a town, more businesses start and that means more jobs. Housing becomes a booming business in a growing town with skilled craftsmen. Then there is the other element that comes with growth and that's the criminals who pry off the hardworking people.

The Texas Rangers didn't have a headquarters in Cleburne, although five Rangers were assigned to the area in and around Central Texas because of all the raids on ranches.

Brody saw the livery stable with no lights on inside the barn, although the doors were open, and that usually meant he could go ahead and leave his animals there for the night. The packsaddle would have to be unloaded before he could remove it and that would take a little time.

He stopped at the door so he could have more light and was undoing the girth strap when he heard a faint noise to his left and immediately pulled his gun and spun around to see a man startled by his movement.

"Hold on, mister. I ain't armed."

"Do you work here?"

"Yes, I'll go light a lantern so we can see."

"Thanks, that'll help. I'll also need you to help with my packsaddle."

The man lit two lanterns and hung one on the door and another one inside on a post. He came out and led the mule inside, where he tied him to a ring bolted to the post and untied a block and tackle. Brody came over, and the two of them were able to use the ropes to lift the pack off and tie it high enough where it wouldn't interfere with any animals or people walking under it.

"I appreciate your help and for boarding my animals tonight. I'm Dr. Brody Connor."

"I'm Henry Ivers and I'll grain the animals and turn them in the corral for the night. I charge a dollar a day per horse."

Brody handed Henry the money. "I'm needing to talk to a Texas Ranger. Do you happen to know where one might be at this time of night?"

"If any are in town, they're either at The Greasy Spoon or at one of the saloons."

"Thanks."

Brody took his clothes bag and headed to the nearest hotel. The desk clerk assigned him to a room where he left his clothing and then walked to the café called The Greasy Spoon.

He was hoping to find a Ranger eating supper but that didn't happen. The waitress served the young man a steak that was tough as boot leather and potatoes that weren't quite done in the middle.

Brody had a lot on his mind, and chewing on the meat wasn't helping him any. He wanted to talk to one of the Rangers and see what they knew about Jennifer. He finally pushed the half-eaten meal away, laid money on the table, and left the café.

Piano music accompanying a woman singing off-key filled his ears from across the street. As he started crossing the dirt street, two men running their horses came toward him. They reined the horses around and jerked back on the bits, causing the mounts to come to an abrupt stop in front of the saloon.

Brody wanted to go over and take a fist to both men for treating their horses that way and for almost hitting him, but he had other things to do tonight. After stepping inside, he stood to let his eyes get adjusted while also scanning the room for a Ranger.

Not seeing one from where he stood didn't mean one wasn't here, it meant he couldn't see the lawman from where he stood. It was time to mosey around the room and that's when he saw not only one lawman, but three of an elite group of state lawmen.

Brody walked to the table where the three men sat with a bottle and shot glasses.

"Evening, fellers, I'm Dr. Brody Connor and I was wanting to talk to you about a woman whose ranch was raided about six or seven months ago."

One of the Rangers pushed out a chair with his booted foot. "Have a seat, Doc."

As Brody was sitting down, one of the saloon girls came over. "You want a glass or something else?"

"I'll have two mugs, and if any of these men want some, get it for them."

The lawmen shook their heads to the girl.

"I'm on my way to the Waco area to see a young woman I'm sweet on. I just graduated from medical school and haven't heard from her in six or seven months. I heard in Fort Worth that her pa's ranch was raided and he was killed along with some of his men. No one knows where the girl is, and I was told you may know something."

The older Ranger drained his shot glass. "Son, the first thing is, we need to know her name and the name of the ranch."

"I'm sorry, it's Jennifer Bernie, and her pa is Big Joe Bernie. They own the Dry Creek Ranch and that's all I know."

"Well, you're right. The ranch did get hit by raiders

about six months ago. By all accounts, they hit the ranch well after daylight and caught the place shorthanded since most of the hands were off chasing cows. It was a bloodbath without much retaliation. Big Joe, along with four of his ranch hands were murdered, but there was no female in the destruction. One common thing with all the raids that have taken place is the women are taken for who knows what. So far, we know of fourteen women that have been abducted."

"So, they attack and kill the men so they can take the women? That don't make sense."

"It does if you're selling them for a lot of money."

"What about the cattle and horses on the ranches that they raid?"

"Most of the time, they drive the cattle off for a few miles to cover their tracks so no one can track them. Then they leave the livestock alone."

Brody sat pondering on what the men had told him. "So, if they have a buyer for the women, where do you think the buyer would be located?"

"If we knew that, we wouldn't be sitting here talking to you. We believe the buyer is in a different country and whoever is stealing the women are putting them on ships to wherever the buyer is located."

"I assume the ships would be south in the gulf then."

"Not necessary, they could transport the women into Mexico and then put them on a boat or they could go about any direction and do it. Right now the Rangers, along with the Army, are working day and night along the border of America and Mexico. Bandits have also been coming up from Mexico, stealing cattle and making raids. Then you have outlaw gangs here committing crimes and running off south to hide."

"I'm sorry, I wasn't thinking clearly. Could I have your names?"

"Sure, I'm Winford Lewis, this feller is Theo McDonald, and the pretty one here is Bill Mackey."

Brody shook hands with each one and finished off one of his beers. "I'm going on in to Waco and get a job at the hospital, I reckon. If I get any information, how can I get in touch with you?"

"You can send a telegram here and have it addressed to the Rangers. We all check on messages daily."

Brody finished off his beer and stood up. "Oh, I almost forgot. Can you tell me how to get to the Dry Creek Ranch?"

"It's about fifteen miles northwest of Waco. North of Waco is a dry creek with a bridge over it. North of the creek is a road going west. Take it until you see the burned-out house. There could be some of the cowhands still there, so be careful if you ride out that way."

"Thanks a lot, and it was nice meeting you all."

Brody walked back to the hotel where he would read the newspapers he got in Fort Worth.

Chapter Nineteen

THE NEWSPAPER ARTICLES DIDN'T GIVE THE doctor any more information than he already knew. Tomorrow he would head out to Waco with the hopes of getting there in two days but it could be three to make the sixty-three-mile trip. It wouldn't be a problem with his horse, but leading the mule slowed him down.

It was late by the time he finally finished up with the papers, took a bath, and climbed into bed. Not knowing what happened to Jennifer made him think about his future when he arrived in Waco. Of course, he wanted to go out to the ranch and talk to the hands there, but he was at a loss as to what else he could do, as he was a doctor, not a tracker.

THE FOLLOWING MORNING, Brody didn't go back to The Greasy Spoon for breakfast. He walked farther down the street, carrying his clothes bag and had breakfast at a little café not far from the livery. When he finished his food, he started a conversation with three men at another table.

"I'm heading to Waco and I'm leading a pack mule. Do you fellers have a suggestion on how far I can go where I can have a place to eat and sleep tonight?"

One of the men finished chewing a piece of ham. "I reckon you can make it to Hillsboro by tonight. The road is mostly level with some rolling hills and plenty of water in the creeks and rivers."

"Thanks."

Brody went to the livery and helped the hostler finish up with his horse and mule. The animals were rested and ready to hit the trail. Brody liked the level ground, which was mostly prairies covered in Big and Little Bluestem, Buffalo Grass, Switchgrass and other native varieties. This area was part of the Blackland Prairie and the Grand Prairies.

Brody had a lot on his mind and was thinking of all the ways he could help find Jennifer, but it still came down to gaining as much information as he could from the ranch hands and others in the area. The Rangers had said that fourteen women had been taken.

Waco was a large place, and he knew there was a college in town, and it may be hard to get work. He had to find work, and a doctor came across a lot of people each day, and maybe, someone would know something more about what happened.

His skill level was better than most when it came to fighting with fists or guns, but going up against a large group of Comancheros, Indians, or Mexicans was another matter. He would have to have help to solve the disappearance of Jennifer and hope she's still alive somewhere.

The terrain around Hillsboro was similar to that of

Cleburne. Farming and raising cattle seemed to be what most of the people did with their land. The rolling hills with its rich soil and rain in the spring, provided enough moisture to grow enough grass for the livestock. Now that it was hot, the grass was beginning to change colors, but it was still tall enough to give the cattle substance.

The town was coming into view with a couple of hours of daylight left, and this would be a swell time to visit the local law and see if there was any information about the raids he didn't already know about. The county courthouse could be seen taking up the center of the square and that meant there was a county sheriff.

His first stop would be to have his horse and mule taken care of, and then he could go about the business of seeing what he could find out. The livery happened to have two men working in it, an older man and a teen boy.

Brody addressed the older man. "Evening, I'd like to leave my animals here for the night to be fed and watered."

The man called out to the boy, "Delbert, take the man's horse and mule inside. We'll help you take the packsaddle off."

"Yeah, it's heavy. But the three of us can remove it easily." Brody dismounted and followed them inside, where the three of them removed the heavy load off the mule.

Brody stuck out his hand. "I'm Dr. Brody Connor, on my way to Waco to see a lady friend. I recently found out that her pa's ranch was raided by Comancheros who killed him and his men. The story I'm hearing is that they took her with them somewhere, along with a bunch more women, and I'm trying to find out as much as I can. Do you hear much about what's going on with the raids?"

"Them raiders are suspected to be coming out of New Mexico and hitting the ranches all along our western borders. I do know they are a bloodthirsty bunch that don't let anyone live, not even the children. I should refrain from saying that. They have killed the male kids and stole the girls. Some of those girls are as young as twelve years old."

"Do you have any idea who's behind all this?"

"Nope, and neither does the Rangers or the sheriff. By the rumor mill, they don't leave any tracks on which way they go. Which, around these parts, with the ground as hard as rocks, it's hard to track anything."

"I'm not a tracker, so I understand not being able to find out which way they went. I thank you for talking to me. I reckon I'll go see the sheriff and see if I can get any information from him."

"Do you want Delbert to have your animals saddled early tomorrow?"

"Sure, I'd like to get an early start."

Brody walked toward the courthouse with the hopes that he could obtain more information about the raids, even though he didn't know what he would do if he did find out anything important. He was only one man looking for a needle in a haystack.

The sign on the wall read, *County Sheriff Miles Walton*. Brody opened the door and there sat two men with badges pinned to their shirts.

"Hello, I'm Dr. Brody Connor and I'm looking to talk to the sheriff."

The man sitting behind the desk motioned to an empty chair. "I'm Sheriff Walton. Have a seat. This is my deputy, Lars Wise. What can we assist you with?"

"I'm on my way to Waco to see a lady friend of mine. I just finished medical college and she and I were writing each other monthly. I stopped getting letters from her about six or seven months ago, so I came west to see why. I've been told that she was taken by raiders and no one seems to know anything. I'm hoping you can shine some light on the situation. Her name is Jennifer Bernie, and her pa was Big Joe Bernie, and they owned the Dry Creek Ranch."

"Now, mind you, that ranch is not in Hill County, so I don't know any particulars of that crime, but I do know a little bit of what's happened in my jurisdiction. They raided the Lazy M about that same time and killed a family of four and took two teen girls. We followed the trail of stolen cattle and horses west for about five miles before they let the livestock scatter and that covered up their tracks. We rode in a half circle west of where they abandoned the cattle and never found one clue they went that way. Not only that, but no one seems to see them come or go, which is kind of strange."

Brody asked, "Is the Lazy M the only ranch that's been raided in Hill County?"

"No, there was one more incident where they tried to attack Samual McComb's place, but him and his men were up early that morning, and his dogs warned them of the riders. The McComb hands started shooting with rifles before the riders were in pistol range and shot two out of the saddle. The varmints picked up their men and skedaddled out of there and never came back."

Brody sat thinking and then scooted to the edge of his chair. "I'm confused about something. You said they ran off the livestock and then let them scatter. I heard that the same thing happened at the Dry Creek Ranch. Why would they drive off the livestock and not take them with them. The horses would be easy to sale and they could trade the cattle to the Indians."

"We believe they scattered the cattle to cover their tracks."

"If that's true, then the only reason they're raiding the ranches is to take the women. That don't make sense."

"I've heard they also take what valuables they can find before they torch the houses. So, that along with the women is all that I know."

Brody stood up. "I reckon whoever is buying them women are paying a great deal for them. I just don't understand why. Well, I best be going. It was nice meeting the two of you."

"It was nice meeting you, too, Doctor."

Brody left the sheriff's office and headed to the café to eat.

Chapter Twenty

BRODY STRUCK UP A CONVERSATION WITH TWO men at the café, and they invited him to join them at their table where he told them the reason why he was going to Waco.

One of the men, whose name was Chester, said, "I was with the posse that went after the raiding party, and we totally lost their trail. It was like they vanished into thin air. But then again, unshod horses are harder to follow than ones with shoes."

Brody swallowed a mouthful of food. "You just said unshod horses. No one had said that to me before."

"Yeah, they were unshod horses."

"So, it could be hostile Indians doing the raiding? Is that a possibility?"

Both men looked at each other and then the man doing all the talking said, "I never thought about that since everyone were saying Comancheros out of New Mexico. But yes, they could be Indians or Mexican bandits, for that matter."

"That's interesting," said Brody, and started eating

again. He then looked up. "Do you know where the Dry Creek Ranch is located?"

"No, can't say that I do."

"That's fine. I'm sure someone in Waco can give me directions. I have to also find a job there with another doctor or a hospital."

"There's a good doctor on the right as you come into town. He's in a white house with blue trim. His name is Dr. Wilks and he has a lot of patients that use him."

"I'll stop in and see if he needs help," said Brody, and cleaned his plate with the remains of a biscuit. "Thanks for inviting me to sup with you fellers. I'm paying for your food, and maybe I'll see you around."

"That's not necessary, but we really appreciate it."

Brody paid the waitress and headed to the hotel when, out between two buildings, came a man holding his arm with blood all over his hand. He took one look at Brody and fell to the ground.

Brody ran to the man and saw that he had a deep gash on his arm. "I need help over here," he called out, as he removed the handkerchief from around the man's neck and was tying it in place when a man and woman stopped.

"This man is cut really bad and needs to be taken to the doctor's office. Can you flag down some help to get him to the doctor?"

The woman took off, and the man asked, "What can I do?"

Brody saw that the injured man had on a belt. "Remove his belt so we can put it on his arm to slow down the flow of blood."

With them working as quickly as possible, the woman came back with three more men. "I have a wagon coming that can take him to Dr. Williams's office, although I don't believe he's there. I saw him leave town earlier on a house call."

"That's fine as long as I can get to his supplies," said Brody. "I'm a doctor and I can take care of his wound. We just need to get him where I have things to work with."

The wagon pulled up, and the men picked the man up and placed him in the bed. Brody got in and rode to the doctor's office, which was only about two blocks away. While the men were unloading the injured man, he started to come awake and tried to wrestle free but one of the men started talking to him, and he settled down.

Inside Dr. William's office, Brody found needles, thread, and chloroform to put the man back out while he sewed up the laceration. With the man unconscious, the doctor was able to examine the cut to make sure valuable ligaments or nerves weren't cut. He then cleaned the wound, sewed it up, and placed a bandage around the man's arm.

The man was beginning to wake up, and Brody was cleaning up the mess he made when the door opened and in came the doctor.

"You must be Dr. Williams. I'm Dr. Brody Connor and I had to sew up this man's arm. I'm sorry that I made a mess, but I'm afraid he would have bled to death if I hadn't helped him. I'll finish cleaning and be on my way."

The doctor set his bag down and took a look at the bandage. "Are you really a doctor or just someone out doing doctor work?"

"I graduated from the Kansas City School of Medicine. So, yes, I'm a full-fledged doctor passing through on my way to Waco."

"Well, Doctor. I reckon it's all right for you to come in and use my place. That's one of the reasons I don't lock the door. If someone needs help, there may be something here to help them. Do you have a job when you get to Waco?"

"No, sir, but I'll be seeking employment at the hospital or a doctor's office."

"I could use a good doctor here if you're of a mind to stay."

"I appreciate the offer, but I came here looking for a lady friend who was taken in one of the raids. I'm going to do everything I can to find her."

"Good luck with that. Them raiders must be some smart people to disappear the way they have. As far as I know, no one has seen hide nor hair of them on the prairie."

Brody stuck out his hand. "It's nice meeting you, Dr. Williams. The patient is now yours, and I best be going to the hotel. I have a far piece to ride tomorrow and I want to get an early start."

"If things don't work out for you in Waco, my offer still holds."

"I'll remember that."

Brody walked to the hotel where he bathed and then laid on his bed thinking about what he knew and what he could do about it. Jennifer could be dead, or in another country by now. All his efforts of trying to find out where she was could be for nothing. What if he finds her alive but in such a bad way that she can never put the terrible ordeal behind her?

Helping the man that had been severely cut with a knife was what the young doctor enjoyed. He wanted to help people, and the only way he could do that was at a hospital or doctor's office. He knew that fighting and gunplay were second nature to him, but being a healer to his people was a great blessing. All those sleepless nights studying prepared him for what his future would be.

Tomorrow, he would ride to Waco with the intention of finding a good job where he could treat people. Who knows, he may find out more about Jennifer as he treats the sick and wounded.

When sleep finally overtook Dr. Brody Connor, he dreamed of the time when he was caring for the lovely Jennifer in Wichita. They had grown close when she had an attack with her gallbladder, and he and Dr. Milrose cut it out. He still remembered that day when she came into the doctor's office wearing black leather britches, a black shirt, black boots, a black hat, and the six-shooter on her right hip.

It was love at first sight, but he didn't let that strain his judgment as he and the doctor operated on the beautiful, mysterious woman.

The dream turned out to be weird—one second he was dreaming of them at the doctor's office and then he was dreaming about riding across the prairie heading between twin plateaus. Then he woke up glazing at the ceiling, wondering if this was another dream from the Great Spirit.

Not knowing what time it was, he got out of bed and went to the window, where the town was still dark and not a soul was out on the street. Brody sat on the edge of the bed and closed his eyes. What did that dream have to do with him and Jennifer? He wanted to continue the dream, but knew it was over with tonight. Lying back down thinking about where he would look for a job tomorrow, he went back to sleep, but this time he didn't dream about Jennifer. He saw the twin plateaus and was riding to them when he saw buildings up ahead. Then the closer he got, the farther they seemed to be. What was happening? Why wasn't he gaining on the buildings? The darkness overcame the dream, and he opened his eyes to the light coming in through the window. What was the meaning of the dream he had?

It didn't matter right now, as it was time to get dressed, eat breakfast, and head to Waco with the hopes of finding a job.

Chapter Twenty-One

THERE WERE NO EMPTY TABLES IN THE CAFÉ, but two men he had never seen before pointed to an empty chair at their table. Before sitting down, he stuck out his hand.

"I'm Dr. Brody Connor, and I appreciate you letting me join you for breakfast."

"Have a seat. You can call me Slick," said the man who offered the seat.

The other feller shook hands with Brody. "I'm Henry Miller. Are you going to be our new doctor in town?"

"Not right now. I'm on my way to Waco looking for a lady friend of mine who was taken in one of the raids a while back. Are you familiar with the raid on the Dry Creek Ranch?"

"Oh yeah," said Slick. "That's Big Joe's ranch, and they took that hell raising daughter of his with them, I hear."

"Well, she's a good friend of mine, and I'm trying to find out where they may have taken her."

Henry picked up his knife and commenced to smear

butter on his biscuit. "If you want my opinion, I'll tell you what I think."

Brody sat there waiting on the man to tell him what he thought. Finally, he said, "I would like to know what you think?"

With half the biscuit in the man's mouth, he said, "Over the past year, I've heard of seven different ranches that have been raided." He swallowed. "At every ranch that was raided, I hear the same thing—they kill everyone there and steal the young girls and women. They run off the livestock but abandon them after a few miles. That makes me think the only thing they're after is what loot is at the place and the women. The other thing that sticks out to me is they have never raided a farm or ranch where there were no females."

Brody was intrigued with what the man was saying. "Go on and tell me the rest of what you think."

"Well, I'm not sure it's who they say it is that's taking the women. I've heard that they ride unshod horses, and I know for a fact that some of the people had their throats cut, and most of them were shot while still in their beds. That makes me think that whoever is doing this happens to work for the outfit, so they know the lay of the house and bunkhouse."

Slick finished his food and pushed his plate away. "Look, this old fool is just speculating and don't know what happened. He used to be a lawman and comes up with all kinds of nonsense."

Brody only smiled, but deep down, he took in every word that Henry had said. This was the most believable explanation that he had heard so far. He didn't want to ask any more questions in front of Slick so he finished his food and left the café, only to go outside and wait until Henry left.

It was less than a five-minute wait until Slick and Henry exited the café and walked off in different directions. Brody stayed where he was and watched as Henry crossed the street and went inside the hardware store.

Brody waited a couple of minutes to see if he came back out, and when he didn't, Brody crossed the street and entered the store to see Henry stocking a shelf with boots.

"Henry, would it be all right to talk to you a little more on what you think has been happening with the raids?"

"Sure, let's go over there so we can talk in private." Brody followed him to the wall he had pointed to. "So, what else do you want to know?"

"Who do you think is taking the women if not the Comancheros?"

Henry looked around like he didn't want to be heard. Then, in a quiet voice, he said, "I think it's White men that's hiring on with the ranches and then orchestrating the raids once they know where the money is kept and earn the people's trust. I heard similar things after the war, and they would steal the women and keep them locked up until they had enough to put on a ship. Then the kidnappers would sell them across the ocean for a lot of money."

Brody was taking all this in, and his mind was working overtime trying to process all this and come up with more questions. "How would a man go about finding out where the women were being kept?"

"If I knew that, I wouldn't be working in a hardware store. The Rangers have been looking into every clue and have come up short. So, I don't know."

"Thanks for giving me your opinion. I think you have

probably given me more to work with than anyone. I best be letting you get back to work. Thanks again."

"You come back anytime, young man, and I hope you find her alive."

Brody walked out of the hardware store and went to the livery stable where his horse and mule were tied in the shade. When he was within fifteen feet of the double doors, out stumbled the hostler, as a man with a mustache pushed him from behind so Brody would have to reach out and catch the stable worker, but instead, Brody immediately turned sideways, where the man doing the pushing couldn't see him removed the safety from his gun. The hostler fell to the ground, and that's when Brody went down onto one leg and used the leg sweep he learned from William to take the man down.

Brody propelled himself back to a standing position and waited to see what the man's next move would be. The man was so surprised by having his legs taken out from under him, he was still dazed when he stood up. He pointed a finger at the doctor and said, "Mister, you been poking your nose into my business, and if you ain't careful, you'll get what I gave Earnest yesterday."

Brody thought the man was being comical. "Are you referring to the man I sewed up with the cut arm?"

"Yeah, and if I had wanted him doctored, I would have taken him to the doctor."

Brody didn't have time for the man and his nonsense. "Look, mister, I'm here ready to get this started if you're brave enough. We can have a fistfight, a knife fight, or draw on each other, the choice is yours, but you'd better know that if you come at me again, I won't have any mercy on you."

The man was still a little dazed from being knocked down. "I don't feel like it today but you better believe that the next time you stick your nose in my business, that I'm coming for you."

Brody smiled at the man and shook his head. This man was an idiot and needed to be taught a lesson in manners. Brody took two quick steps and came around with a haymaker that landed on the man's chin. His eyes rolled back in their sockets, and his legs turned to noodles, causing him to fall to the ground out cold.

The hostler was still sitting on the ground watching everything that went on. "Dr. Brody, I'm impressed. You're a fighter, and most men are scared of Sid. He's been known to use a knife on more than one man."

"Well, I reckon it wasn't his lucky day. I'll be seeing you."

Brody mounted up and had started down the street when Henry hollered from the hardware store, "Hold up, I thought of something else."

Brody reined his horse toward where Henry was walking out into the street.

"I been thinking, and I drew on this paper the locations of the ranches in Hill County where the raids took place. If I was you, I'd map out where all the raids have taken place to see if there's a pattern on where they came from or where they may have went to. It may also tell you the next place they're going to hit."

"That's a good idea. Thanks, Henry."

Brody took off with the hopes of making it the thirty-three miles to Waco before dark.

Chapter Twenty-Two

THE WEATHER WAS HOT AND HUMID AS HE RODE through the rolling hills covered with grass, weeds, and mesquite trees. He stayed on the roads as much as possible since the mesquites had thorns on them that could cause a man severe pain.

The doctor changed into his short-legged britches and sleeveless shirt two hours out from Hillsboro. The horse and mule were both lathered up, and he hadn't seen a waterhole since he left the livery stable. One canteen was empty, and the second one wouldn't last long with him taking sips from it. He had to control his drinking and slow his animals down so they could cool off.

By late afternoon, he was still on the road and had no town in sight. Riding in the heat of day wasn't the best choice he had ever made, but they would arrive sometime later in the evening. The possibility of finding shade and waiting until the sun goes down was a good option but that would put him getting into Waco way after dark.

The more he thought about resting until sundown, the more he liked the idea. What did it matter when he arrived in town? He could clean up tonight and seek a job tomorrow.

Off to his left, about fifty yards, were three larger trees and that's where he would hold up until the sun went down. It so happened that among the trees were enough grass for the horse and mule. He loosened the saddles and put hobbles on their front hooves and let them graze.

Using his clothes bag as a pillow, the hot, tired young man sat down with his back to a tree and in a few minutes was sound asleep with sweat droplets rolling off his face.

He suddenly opened his eyes as something touched his right leg. It was dusty and dark with the day fading away, but it was still enough light to see a Western Diamondback Rattlesnake slither across his booted foot. Brody wanted to jump up and run but that could be a deadly move. Instead, he stayed still and let the snake slither off. That was a close call, and it was time to get away from here.

Brody couldn't hardly tighten up the saddles for looking at the ground, no way did he want to encounter another rattlesnake today. When he was confident the packsaddle was secure, he mounted up and started off. The horse and mule were in much better shape now that they had rested and grazed.

It just so happened that he was only an hour from Waco when he stopped to rest. The city was coming into view, and as he entered town, a situation caught his eye. In front of a large white building were more than a dozen people lined up along the porch. The sign on the building read: *Dr. Hermon Wilks*.

This would certainly be someplace he would apply for a job. If the doctor's patient allegiance was this demanding, it was a good chance that he would be hired.

The Brazos River runs through Waco and goes southwest. To the west is Edwards Plateau, and to the east is the Post Oak Savanah, which is the transition between black land prairies to the west and Pineywoods to the east, and in the middle of all that is the Post Oak Savanah, a large area covered in post oak trees, native grasses, and wildflowers.

Edwards Plateau is known for its limestone hills, an abundance of springs, and deep canyons. It's commonly referred to as the Texas Hill Country and the crossroads of Central, South, and West Texas.

Brody found a livery stable that was still open. "Howdy, can I board my animals here for a few days?"

"Yes, sir. I'll remove the saddles, curry comb them, and feed each a bucket of oats for two dollars a day."

"That sounds reasonable." Brody pulled out some money and paid the man four dollars. "That's for two days to start with. Which is the best place in town to eat?"

"Down the street is the Best Café. Beverly Best is a great cook."

"Do you need me to help you remove the packsaddle, it's heavy?" asked Brody.

"No, Mr. Weaver is inside and he'll help me."

Brody took his clothes bag and started toward the Best Café. A few doors down the street was a nice-looking hotel, so he went there first.

"Good evening, sir. Would you like a room?"

"Yes, and I'd like to bathe," said Brody, and picked up an ink pen. He signed his name as *Dr. Brody Connor*. The clerk was watching and then handed him a key.

"Your room is down that hall, and it has all the modern conveniences for only three dollars a night."

Brody handed the man enough money for two nights, picked up the key, and walked to his room, where he took out his clothes and saw that everything he had was dirty. Maybe he should buy a new set of clothes to wear tomorrow when seeking a job.

He gathered up his soiled clothes and went back to the counter. "Excuse me, do you have someone who can do laundry for me?"

"Of course, we're a full-service hotel. Leave them with me and I'll see to it that they're ready by noon tomorrow."

"Thanks." Brody walked outside and stood there taking in the sights of the city. Waco was having an economic boom mainly because of its location along the Chisholm Trail. But there were other contributing factors to its growth. The suspension bridge built in 1870 across the Brazos River and the Waco and Northwestern Railroad built in 1871, made it a major point for settlers going west.

The city had numerous businesses such as furniture, clothing, grocery, and drugstores. Most of them were doing business around the square with the county courthouse in the middle.

The numerous saloons and gambling halls brought in not only cowboys from all the cattle drives but crooks, outlaws, and professional card sharks. There was a lively atmosphere in the drinking establishments, where gunfights contributed to the town's nickname of *Six-Shooter Junction.*

There was one more part of town that most God-fearing citizens didn't care to discuss. It was called *The*

Reservation, where prostitution was legal and regulated by the city.

Brody walked to the square in hopes that he could catch the county sheriff in his office. After inquiring where the office was, he walked to the back of the courthouse and went inside to find three men with badges on, in the little office, drinking coffee. "Howdy, I'm Dr. Brody Connor and I'd like to talk to the sheriff about Jennifer Bernie."

One of the men stood up and stuck out his hand. "I'm Sheriff Tillman Spencer. There ain't much to tell except her pa, Big Joe, and three of the ranch hands were murdered and Jennifer went missing."

"Sheriff, I already knew all that," said Brody. "I was hoping you could tell me about any more raids that have taken place in your county."

"I've had that one, and two more. There's been two north of here in Hill County, and I know of three south of here. Why do you want to know about them?"

"I don't know yet. I'm hoping I can see a pattern where they come from or where they go. I'm new at all this and don't really know the questions to ask or how to go about finding her."

"Well, at least you're honest about it."

"Can you tell me how to get to the Dry Creek Ranch? I'd like to see for myself what happened."

"Sure, that's easy. Go across the river and turn west along Hogg Creek. Follow it until it ends, and you'll be on Big Joe's spread. I must warn you that there's still a few of their ranch hands out there and they may not take kindly to you."

"Thanks, Sheriff."

Brody walked around the square looking for a

clothing store where he could purchase a new change of clothes for job hunting tomorrow.

Chapter Twenty-Three

DR. BRODY CONNOR WAS PROUD OF HOW GOOD he looked decked out in a new cream-colored shirt with a black string tie, and sporting a vest of gray and black material so he could hide the shoulder holster gun under his left arm. The britches were gray, and he even stopped in the cobbler's store and had his boots shined.

Now all he needed was a shave and haircut at the barbers' parlor before he walked to Dr. Hermon Wilks' office. The barber shop was open for business, but inside sat three men who were probably telling stories because they stopped talking when Brody walked in.

One of the men stood up. "You need a haircut, young man?"

"Yes, sir, I need a shave also."

"Have a seat, and I'll get started. Don't pay these fellers no mind, they're telling stories and mostly lies."

Brody nodded his head at the men. "I'm Dr. Brody Connor and I'm new in town."

"Are you going to start doctoring on folks around here?" asked one of the men sitting.

"That's my intention, but the real reason I'm here is to see if I can find out what happened to Jennifer Bernie. I assume you have all heard about the raid on the Dry Creek Ranch."

The men were all nodding and making facial expressions like it was bad. The barber put his hair-cutting drape across Brody's chest and fastened it around his neck. "That was the talk of the town a few months ago, but nothing's been done about any of those raids."

One of the men got up and walked to the window. He turned back and pointed a finger at Brody. "You watch who you talk to about those raids. I have a suspicion that with all the newcomers coming here to live, along with all them drovers that stop by, it could be someone we know doing the killing. It just don't make sense that all they do is steal the young women."

The barber wiped hair and shaving cream off his straight razor. "Now, Lester, that's been talked about so much that no one in their right mind believes that. We all know it's them outlaws coming into Texas from New Mexico."

Brody let the barber finish on his face before he said anything else. "If it was you and you didn't want to be seen, where would you keep those women?"

The men all went quiet for a little bit. Then Lester said, "Iffin it was me, I'd have a place in the Edwards Plateau area. Maybe in one of them boxed canyons or a man could keep them at one of the ranches that's out in the middle of nowhere."

The barber was snipping off hair with his scissors and said, "That's the kind of speculations that could get a man shot. The law don't even think like you do, you old coot."

The men started talking about all the travelers

coming through on their way west and using the bridge to cross the river. They were making a suggestion that the city should charge travelers to cross but keep it free for the people in the county. Brody paid for his haircut and shave, then asked, "What do you fellers think of Dr. Wilks?"

The barber spoke up, "Hermon is a fine doctor. He delivered all six of my youngins."

"He's been treating my ticker for years, and I'm still here, so I agree with Roy for once."

"Thanks, men, I'll be on my way."

Brody walked down the boardwalk which seemed like a half mile, until he could see Dr. Wilks's office. Sitting on two benches were four people, and he wondered if they were patients waiting to see the doctor.

Brody walked up to the door and was about to go in when a man sitting on the bench said, "Hey, you can get in line like the rest of us. We were here first."

Brody looked at the man. "I'm Dr. Brody Connor and I'm going in." He opened the door and walked into a room that had five more patients sitting in chairs. To his right was a door that had a sign that said: *Patients Only.* Brody opened the door and walked in to find the doctor and a nurse putting plaster on the arm of a boy who was maybe ten.

"I'm sorry to barge in on you, Dr. Wilks, I'm Dr. Brody Connor, and I recently graduated at the top of my class from the Kansas City School of Medicine. I see you have a lot of patients waiting to see you and I'm here needing a job."

Dr. Wilks stood where he was, looking at the strapping young man who claimed to be a doctor. Wilks was in his late sixties or early seventies, sporting a gray goatee and mustache. He was only about five foot eight but weighed close to two hundred pounds, and the one thing that seemed odd was the hat on the man's head. Brody figured the older doctor was totally bald and didn't want people to see his head.

With plaster on his hands, the doctor pointed to a chair. "Go have a seat and tell me more about your experiences with medicine."

"I worked for Dr. Milrose in Wichita for two years before going off to school. While working there, I assisted in ten childbirths, bandaged lots of cuts, broken bones and even operated on Jennifer Bernie, who you may know."

Dr. Wilks stopped what he was doing. "So, you're the doctor who operated on Jennifer when she was in Wichita?"

"Yes, sir. She's the reason that I'm here in Waco. We were writing each other, and about six or seven months ago, I stopped getting letters, so when I graduated, I headed here. I've since learned about what happened, and I'm still going to look for her."

"I've been treating the Bernie family for might nigh fifty years. I saw where you operated on Jennifer, and if you want a job, put what you have in the way of books and instruments in the room across from the waiting room. I'll pay you fifty cents for each patient you see, and we'll work out how much for delivering babies, surgeries, broken bones, and gunshots."

"Thanks, Dr. Wilks, that sounds good to me. I'll go to the livery stable and bring my things over here so we can get some of these folks that's waiting to be taken care of." Brody walked out and went to the examination room where he would work out of. It had a desk, three chairs, an examination table, and a stand-up glass door cabinet. Along the wall were shelves and a counter with a few instruments on top of it. The room and furnishings look clean and in good shape. He could make this work just fine. All he had to do now was get all his stuff in here.

When Brody got to the livery stable, he told the boy who cared for the animals and mucked the stalls that he found a job and would need to take all the stuff on the packsaddle to Dr. Wilks's office.

The boy looked up and down the street for a second. "We could unpack the saddle and put everything in the back of a wagon. That would be much easier than unpacking that mule in the heat."

"I tell you what I'll do. If you'll help me get everything into my office, I'll pay you three dollars."

The boy stuck out his hand to shake. "It's a deal."

TWO HOURS LATER, Dr. Brody saw his first official patient. By six that afternoon, he had seen thirty patients and for the first time in months there was no line waiting to see a doctor.

Dr. Wilks came in, drying off his hands. "Well, Brody, are you coming back tomorrow?"

"Of course, I am. I've been wanting to help people all my life, and this is where I want to be. There is nothing like the feeling when you bring a life into this world or help save a life. It can be hard, demanding work, but I'm ready and trained for the challenges ahead."

"I can't help but notice that gun in the shoulder holster. Jennifer told me a little about you, and I like having someone that's not afraid to fight working here. All our patients are not kind, loving people."

"I know, but you also need to know that I won't stand by and let someone bully or beat another human, especially a man beating a woman. I have a tendency to get involved, and it may not turn out good for the man."

The older man patted Brody on the shoulder. "You did a fine job today, but I think we need to hire you a nurse. I may know someone who has some experience, and I can talk to her tonight to see if she's interested. Right now, I want you to go eat your supper and get some rest. It starts over in the morning, and I usually show up around seven, so here's a key in case you want to start earlier. My wife is always on me to slow down a little and get more sleep."

"Thanks, Doctor. I like the idea of having an assistant who can help out with the patients. I'm also a stickler on keeping my instruments sterilized and my workplace sanitary."

"Go on and have your supper. I'll see you in the morning."

Chapter Twenty-Four

It seemed that everyone in the café knew who the young man was who came in for his breakfast. They were speaking to him like he had been raised in Waco. Word gets around with the locals fast, and he even recognized one man that he had treated for his rheumatism yesterday.

No one was waiting in line when Brody used his key to open the door and go inside. He wanted to get his office ready to see patients and make sure he was stocked up on medications, bandages, and that all his instruments were clean.

By the time that Dr. Wilks arrived, Brody had already seen six patients and was taking a break to sterilize more towels after sewing up widow Martin's foot, where her knife slipped off the table and cut her foot. The cut was deep enough that it took six sutures to close up. Brody was pleasantly surprised to find that Dr. Wilks had a good stock of mast-produced sterile catgut and silk sutures. He used them in medical school but used boiled horse hair when he worked for Dr. Milrose in Wichita.

Brody had made himself at home in the back room where there was a cookstove and lots of pans for heating water. When Dr. Wilks entered what he called the kitchen, a middle-aged woman had come with him.

"Dr. Brody, this is Emma White, and she's agreed to be your nurse if you're in agreement."

Brody wiped off his hands and came to where they stood. He stuck out his hand and said, "Hi Emma. It's nice to meet you, and I assume that you've worked in a doctor's office before?"

"Yes, I worked right here for Uncle Herman. I had to quit when my last son was born, and now I'm ready to get back to work."

Brody looked at Dr. Wilks. "I told you yesterday that I'm a stickler for keeping my work area clean and all the instruments sterilized. I assume that you told Emma what I expect, or do I need to do that?"

"She's working for you, so it's up to you to give her directions and assignments. If there's a problem, then you can come to me."

"Fair enough." He turned to Emma. "I want to boil all these towels for fifteen minutes and then hang them up to dry inside here. I've already installed us a couple of lines. As for my instruments, there's Carbolic Acid and rubbing alcohol that we can put most of the smaller instruments in."

The woman looked inside one of the pots. "How do you expect me to get them towels out when they're in boiling water?"

Dr. Wilks started to laugh. Brody smiled and pointed to a pot of water. "I've already boiled that pot and it's cooled off, so you can take the tongs and transfer the hot towels from the hot water into the cold water. After that, it's fine for you to wring out the water and hang them up to dry. Be sure to wash your hands before handling them at all times."

"May I make a suggestion?" asked Dr. Wilks.

"Of course," said Brody.

"Emma, there's a couple of wash pans in that cupboard over there. Take them into the examination room and use one for hand washing and the other for rinsing off the lye soap."

"That's a great idea. Emma, if you'll get that set up then I'll finish the towels."

Emma had a pregnant woman in the examining room when Brody came back in. In fact, he saw all the expecting mothers that day because Dr. Wilks turned them all over to the younger doctor.

Word about Brody working for Dr. Wilks had already gotten around the town and both doctors were busy all day treating a variety of diseases, broken bones, and of course, the five pregnant patients Brody now had.

Emma turned out to be a big help with most of the non-serious patients and had skills in applying bandages. They had seen all the patients and were in the process of cleaning when the outer door opened, and Brody heard Dr. Wilks call out, "Brody, I need you in here."

Brody took off to the outer reception area to find the doctor helping a man to Brody's examination room. The man was holding his side with a bloody hand, and his face was twisted in pain. Brody knew immediately that the man had been shot and would need surgery to remove the bullet.

With him on one side and Wilks on the other, they maneuvered the man into the room where Emma had already gathered a stack of towels.

"Sir, we're going to put you on the table, and I'm going to give you something to put you asleep while I remove that bullet. So turn where you can put your butt on the table and we'll lay you down."

"I don't want to be put out. I'm a bounty hunter, and I don't want anyone coming in here to shoot me."

Brody pulled back his vest to show the man his gun. "I'm very good with this gun, and I guarantee that no one will harm you while you're in my care. It's going to hurt really bad if you don't have some chloroform."

The man grabbed Brody by the wrist. "You do what you have to do and get this bullet out of me."

Dr. Wilks already had a rag with chloroform on it and applied it to the man's nose and mouth. Brody didn't waste any time cutting the man's shirt where he could clean the bullet hole.

"It doesn't look like it's deep, which is a good thing. Emma, I'll need those long-nose tweezers and the long-nose forceps." Brody had an instrument in each hand as he started into the wound to retrieve the lead.

"Wipe the blood off, please."

"There it is. Just a little more and here it comes."

He pulled the bullet out and dropped it in a pan, then started to clean the wound with iodine.

"Emma, hold a towel on the wound while I get a couple of needles and sutures. I'm going to put a few sutures inside the hole and some on the outside so it will heal faster."

Brody went to work on the wound, and when he finished the last stitch, it was Emma who was the first to say anything.

"Dr. Brody, you do excellent work with that needle. I can tell that you've had a lot of practice."

Dr. Wilks put up the bottle of chloroform and threw the rag in the dirty clothes basket. "That was some fine work you did with that bullet wound. I think you're going to be really popular around here real soon, if you know what I mean. We may have to remodel and have a surgical room added on."

Brody went to the wash pan. "That wouldn't be a bad idea and also add a ten-room hospital along with it."

Dr. Wilks started to laugh. "You'd better get cleaned up. This bounty man will be waking up soon, and I don't know what you're going to do with him."

"I may have to stay here with him tonight."

"You may not know it, but there's three rooms behind the kitchen with beds in them, and I would suggest that you move him in there where it's more comfortable. You can either stay the night or go to your hotel room. It's up to you."

"Thanks, Dr. Wilks. I'll decide after he's regained consciousness. You go on home, and I'll see you tomorrow."

Brody cleaned up in his work area and took his dirty towels to the kitchen where they could be cleaned and sterilized tomorrow. When he returned to the room, his patient was regaining consciousness.

The doctor had enough experience to know the man would be a little panicked waking up from the chloroform. At the first sight of the man's eyes opening, Brody began to talk and reassure the bounty hunter that he was going to be fine.

"Mister, can you tell me your name?"

The man closed his eyes and took a deep breath.

A second time, Brody asked, "What's your name?"

The man opened his eyes and looked at Brody. "It's Dash Patterson. Doctor, my side is really hurting."

"Dash, I'm Brody Connor, and I wish we had met a different way. I'll get you something to help with the pain and then I'm moving you to a bed where you'll be more comfortable. This table is hard and no bigger than it is, so you'll probably fall off to the floor if you try to turn over."

"Thanks, Doc."

Brody gave him a small amount of laudanum, then went to the rooms that Dr. Wilks told him about. The room he chose for Dash would be across a hall from the one he would use for the night. After turning down the covers, he went back and assisted Dash to his bed. It was painful to the bounty hunter getting his boots and britches off, but with Brody's help, he managed to get in bed and have another dose of laudanum before going off to sleep.

Brody went to his room, laid on top of his bed, and fell off to sleep.

Chapter Twenty-Five

THE YOUNG DOCTOR WAS IN A DEEP SLEEP, seeing images of plateaus, hills, and gullies covered in grass, wildflowers, and scrub mesquites. The sun was overhead, reflecting off of boulders protruding from the sides of the mesas with a brilliance of color. "Help, help, I'm hurting."

Dr. Brody came awake, rubbing his eyes when he heard Dash call out his name. He stumbled into the patient's room, still rubbing the sleep from his eyes.

"Dr. Brody, I'm hurting. Can you give me some more of that stuff to ease the pain?"

"Sure, I'll be right back." The clock in the office showed that it was ten after five. Brody administered the laudanum and took a look at the wound. It was red and a little inflamed to the point that he would need to clean it again when Emma arrived.

Brody sat down in the chair by the bed. "Dash, what do you know about the raids where women are being taken?"

"I haven't been involved up until a couple of days ago,

when I came looking for Porkchop Smith. I usually work in North Texas and Southwest Arkansas, but when I started after Porkchop, the trail brought me about ten miles south of here and that's where I ran into four men that didn't want to be seen. I never had a chance when they started shooting at me, so I hightailed it out of there mighty quick, and I'm sure that they are involved in some sort of criminal activity."

"Did you get a look at them?"

"Not really, they were pretty far away, and with rifles being fired at me, I didn't take the time to see what their faces looked like. I can tell you that they were all riding those wild mustangs that run wild. They must have captured some and broke them to ride."

"Would you describe the men as being Comancheros?"

"The men I saw were all White men, although they were a scruffy-looking bunch with soiled clothing, long hair, beards, and sporting Henry rifles. My professional opinion is that they work for someone that's supplying them with nice guns and wanting anyone that sees them on those mustangs to think they're Mexicans because each one of them wore those wide-brim sombreros."

"That's interesting. That may be why everyone thinks it's the Comancheros that's doing the raids. It makes sense when they're riding unshod mustangs and they look like Mexicans and Indians. When you're well enough to ride, are you going back after Porkchop?"

"I don't know. It depends how I feel and where he's off to. I'm not certain he'll stay in this part of the country, especially if he gets wind that I'm hunting him. Why do you ask?"

"I came here to find out what happened to a woman that I care deeply for, and I may need help since I don't know anything about tracking someone down. She was taken in one of the raids about six months ago, and no one knows much about what happened or where they have taken her. I can hold my own with fists or guns, and I've killed men before, but finding her is more than I may be capable of."

"Let's see how things go and how much I'm going to owe you for treating me. I don't know if I can locate them either. It doesn't seem like the Rangers know much or they would be arresting someone."

"Fair enough for now. I'm riding out to her ranch as soon as I can take a day off and talk to the hands that are still there. I've already talked to the Rangers, the local law, and some of the people around here. No one knows who or where they are taking the women. I'm hoping the men at the ranch will have more to tell me."

"Yeah, that would be my first place to get information, but remember that it's been a long while, and people seem to forget important information over time or they may have their own ideas on what happened. You have to take those with a grain of salt since they may not be true."

Brody stood up. "I need to get busy. I'll check on you later."

He went into his room and made his bed and got ready to go eat breakfast and would bring one back for Dash. He would also talk to Dr. Wilks and see if he could continue to sleep in the room he used last night. The hotel room cost money, and if he could save up enough, he could buy his own place soon.

Dash was asleep when Dr. Brody returned with a plate of food. He didn't want to wake the man up so he put a towel over it and started getting prepared to see patients. The morning was slow, and he had only seen one man to remove a splinter from his hand when Emma came to work.

Brody was in the kitchen putting wood in the stove when she came in.

"Good morning, Dr. Brody. Are you wanting to wash towels this morning?"

"Yes, it's been slow so far today, and I needed something to do. If you would make sure the examination room is ready, I'll get the water boiling and start gathering up all the soiled towels from both offices."

By ten that morning, Brody had seen a total of four patients and Dr. Wilks only two. Brody knocked on Dr. Wilks's door and stepped inside. "If you don't mind, I think I'll ride out to the Bernie place and talk to the hands about what they remember about the raid."

"I don't have a problem with that at all, in fact, I have a patient that you can stop in on out that way if you don't mind. You ride by their place on the way, and it would help me out if you checked on their little daughter. She's had different issues since birth, and I keep tabs on her well-being."

"I would be delighted to, Doctor. Just give me the directions."

"You gather your things and I'll draw you a map and put down the directions. Brody, you be careful out there on the ranch. Those hands are a might protective of the place and they all thought a lot of Jennifer and her pa."

"I understand. I have actually met a few of the hands and hope those men are still there so we can have a good conversation. I really want to know what happened."

"Just be careful. I don't want to lose my best doctor."

"Oh, one other thing. Would it be all right if I continue to use the room where I slept last night? I'm wanting to get out of the hotel."

"Sure, use it as long as you want and don't worry about your patient, I'll keep a check on him until you get back."

"Thanks, Doctor."

Brody went into the room where he slept and put on his other gun, grabbed his hat, and started to the livery stable. The hostler saw him coming, put down the pitchfork, and started out to meet him.

"Morning, Doctor. Do you have another job for me?"

"Yeah, would you get my horse saddled? I need to go on a ride. I'll be back for him in a few minutes."

"Sure thing, Doctor."

Brody took off toward the hotel so he could get his clothes that were washed and the bag from his room. He would take them to his new room and bring his black doctor bag with him to the Dry Creek Ranch.

———

WITH HIS DOCTOR bag tied onto the saddle, Dr. Brody walked his horse down the middle of the street under the watchful eyes of the people on the boardwalk. He was still the talk of the town, and most folks were nosy and wanted to see what he looked like.

He didn't know what to expect when he arrived at the Bernie place and decided to stop and check on Kathy Prichard. She was the daughter of Mallard and Patty Prichard, who ran a little spread east of the Bernie ranch.

Two hound dogs came out to meet the doctor as he rode up the wagon road to the main house on the Prichard land. A woman was standing on the porch wearing a bonnet to cover her head, and a child of maybe five was standing beside her.

"Howdy, ma'am, I'm Dr. Brody Connor, and I work

for Dr. Wilks. I'm on my way to the Bernie place, and the doctor wanted me to stop in and see how Kathy was doing."

"Well, come on in, and I'll ring the bell so my husband will come to the house. I'm sure he'll want to meet the new doctor we've heard so much about when we were in town yesterday."

She walked to where a bell hung off a porch rafter tail and rang the bell four times. He wondered if they had a system for what each amount of rings meant.

"Please come on in, and I'll get you a tall glass of water. You can examine Kathy in the living room."

Mallard came in and after a few minutes of conversation and getting to know each other, Brody started talking to the child and after a series of questions, he examined her ears, eyes, throat, and listened to her heart, lungs, and stomach.

"I don't find anything wrong with her right now. If she starts having any problems, come for me. I best be on my way, and it was so nice meeting you all."

"You come back anytime, Dr. Connor."

"You can call me Dr. Brody if you want. That's what most people are calling me now."

Brody left the Prichard's place with questions he would have to get answers for when he returned to Waco. During the examination and listening to Kathy's heart, he heard it skip a beat on a regular basis. He would have to discuss this with Dr. Wilks and see if there was a way to correct the rhythm.

Chapter Twenty-Six

AFTER LEAVING THE PRICHARD LAND, HE followed the directions on the map, and he was soon riding the road through a range covered in grass, weeds, and small clumps of brush. The thing that caught his attention was the lack of mesquite trees. Every once in a while, he could see where a mesquite had been cut down. That meant that Big Joe or his foreman wanted to get them off the prairie.

Brody enjoyed the freedom to ride his horse and not have the mule tagging along. There was something calming about riding across the land, looking at cattle grazing, and thinking about how he was going to find Jennifer.

The barn was the first building that came into view, and after riding a little farther, he could see the bunkhouse and the burned-out residents where Jennifer once lived. The two chimneys and the southeast corner of the structure were all that was still standing.

Brody pulled one of his pistols and fired a shot into the ground to let the men at the ranch know they had company. After the shot, he replaced the spent shell and walked his horse toward the barn with his hands in sight so the men there would know he wasn't there to cause trouble.

Two men with rifles came around from the back of the barn and took up positions behind a wagon. Another man stood in the doorway of the bunkhouse holding a rifle.

Brody was almost at the burned-out house when he heard horse hooves pounding the hard ground. Two riders were coming toward him with their pistols drawn. The doctor stopped his horse and raised both arms into the air.

When the two riders pulled up within ten feet of the young doctor, one of the men grinned and holstered his pistol.

"Hello, Brody. I'm Manuel. You may not remember me, but I helped you out in Wichita when you rescued your mama."

"I do remember you. You were one of the men that came up that drainage ditch to the house and set the fire. You all pitched in and helped to kill Rosco and his gang of killers."

"This is Sam Roberts. Come on to the bunkhouse and let's talk over a hot cup of coffee."

"Hello Sam. You fellers can have coffee. I'll take a glass of water."

The three men rode on to the barn, where the men using the wagon for cover came into the open.

"Who do you have here, Manuel?"

"Shepherd, do you remember that young doctor that cared for Jennifer, and then we helped him kill those men that harmed his ma? Well this is Brody, and I'm thinking he's coming to call on Jennifer."

"Hello Brody, I do remember you, and I'm sorry to say that she ain't here. The Comancheros stole her when they killed her pa and burned the house."

"I heard about the raid and that's why I'm here. I'm trying to find out as much as I can, so maybe I can go find her. Let's go inside, and you can tell me everything you know about the raid."

Shephard pointed to the bunkhouse. "Come on, let's go to the bunkhouse and talk."

Once everyone was seated, a man who introduced himself as Sage poured coffee for everyone and gave Brody a glass of water upon his request.

He took a big gulp of the water. "I had coffee once and never liked the taste, so I now stick to water. Manuel, would you tell me where you were and what you saw when you first knew something was wrong?"

"Sure, all of us was about five miles to the east trying to make some cattle that wandered off to come back to our range. That don't happen very often, but that morning, a feller east of here came and talked to Big Joe. As soon as the man left, Joe came down here and told us to saddle up and go fetch the cattle.

"It took us to after the sun was high to get them bunched so we could drive them back. We never heard the shooting going on, I reckon the sound of the cattle and us hollering drowned the sound out. We was making good time when Shephard saw the smoke in the air and that's when we spooked the herd by shooting our guns and then we all came running."

"Let's stop here for a few minutes," said Brody. "Who was the man that came to the house that morning?"

"We don't know. Just a neighbor to the east, I reckon."

"Did you see what he looked like or what kind of horse he rode?"

Manuel shook his head, no. Shephard spoke up. "He was on a chestnut with a star in his forehead and two white stockings on his hind legs. I never got a good look at his face."

"You also said it took a long time to gather up the cattle. Why?"

"They were scattered out over a hundred acres or more."

Brody was thinking about that. "Could that have been planned and someone scattered those cattle so y'all wouldn't be at the ranch headquarters?"

Manuel's face got red. "You may have a point there. Those cattle were scattered more than usual. Most herds are social and seem to stay close together."

"Okay, now tell me what you saw when you returned to the ranch. Manuel, you go first.

"Well, the first thing I saw was the house on fire and Big Joe lying in the front yard. I went to him, but he was shot at least eight times. I ran around the house looking for others and found Curtis between the house and barn, dead. In the barn was Bronco and Billy. They had all been shot multiple times. After that, we all pitched in and buried the dead back in the little cemetery on that knoll south of the house."

"Is that about the same that the rest of you saw?"

The men were all nodding their heads.

"So none of you saw any shell casings on the ground? Did your friends have guns with them that had been fired? Were there any of the dead attackers on the ground anywhere or any of their horses shot?"

Sage cleared his throat and replied, "Yeah, there was one dead horse, and it was one of those spotted wild mustangs that roam the prairies. There was a lot of empty hulls by each of our men, and we picked up some more at different places. Our hands put up a fight and probably killed a few of them savages. I also saw where someone had laid in a pool of blood over by where Billy had been shot."

The other men then started to recall seeing blood and spent casings on the ground and even found a pistol that belonged to one of the attackers.

"The blood you saw was probably from some of the raiders getting shot and most likely dead. Does anyone know how many blood patches were on the ground?"

"I remember seeing two over in front of the barn doors," said Sam.

"I saw one in front of the house by that little tree," said Shephard.

When no one else had anything more to add, Brody changed direction in his questioning. "Okay, let's talk about what you did after the corpses were buried. I assume you tracked them as they left the house."

"Yeah, the ponies they rode were all unshod mustangs and they headed west, pushing a herd of cattle. It must have been a lot of them to raid the house and then drive those cattle so far away," said Manuel.

Brody sat thinking about what he had been told. "How many cattle are you talking about?"

"It was probably two or three hundred head that we found about five miles west of here. That's where we lost the tracks of the mustangs. They rode them through the cattle, and there was no way we could find their trail after that."

Brody was in deep thought. "Could the cattle have been moved the day or night before and no one knew it?"

"I suppose so. We don't usually check each herd, but

every few days. Someone could have moved them without us knowing it, I reckon."

"Did any of you go on west to see if you could pick up the trail?"

Shephard set his coffee cup down. "We rode for twenty miles west of here and never seen one clue. We even went north and south looking for any sign of the attackers."

"Well, I've learned a lot here today and when I figure anything out, I'll let you know. In the meantime, I think the person that came to the house that morning and talked to Big Joe is an important piece to this puzzle. Be watching for that chestnut in Waco and on the range. I have to get back and see some patients. It was good seeing you all."

"You come back anytime, Brody."

The doctor mounted up and headed back with some good information.

Chapter Twenty-Seven

THE RIDE BACK TO THE OFFICE GAVE BRODY time to think about all he knew about the raid. It seemed like at least three of the raiders were shot dead. The others must have loaded up their dead and taken them along. That created another speculation from Brody. Did the raiders really drive a herd of two or three hundred head of cattle with three dead members laid across the back of their horses?

No, they didn't do that. Those cattle were driven off before the raid with the knowledge that the ranch hands would come to where they were grazing. The same thing happened to the cattle that the hands when after the morning of the raid.

Then there was the man who came to the house that morning riding the chestnut. He was a key piece of the puzzle, and by what everyone said, he was a white man. That chestnut with the star in its forehead and two white stockings, would be the focus for the next few days. He would ask all his patients if they knew who rode the horse.

Dash would need to be informed of what he knew. The bounty hunter said that he saw four men on wild mustangs. He was pretty sure they were white men pretending to be Mexican or Indians.

Maybe the law was looking in the wrong direction for the missing women. The men responsible could be under the law's noses and they didn't see them. If it were White men stealing the women, then they would have to have buyers with lots of money. Maybe Dash could shed more light on where the men could sell the ladies for lots of money.

Brody stopped at the livery stable and left his horse before taking his doctor bag and walking to the office, where five patients were waiting to see one of the doctors.

His first patient was a young child with a stomachache and crying.

After talking to the child's mama and finding out the boy had been eating vegetables straight from the garden, he mixed up some baking soda with water and had the boy drink it. After a couple of burps, the kid felt better.

AN HOUR AND A HALF LATER, when all the patients had been treated and the waiting area was empty, Brody went to check on Dash, who was sitting outside the back door with his gun in his lap.

"How're you feeling, Dash?"

"Hello, Doctor. I'm really sore, but the pain is much better. I was tired of that little room, so I moved out here to get some sunshine."

"I think if you're still improving at this pace, you can leave here and go to the hotel or maybe a boarding house for a couple of weeks. I'll be honest, you're going to have some discomfort for a few weeks, and I'm not sure you can ride a horse for some time."

"At least me and you think alike. I had already thought about all that. How was your ride out to your girlfriend's ranch?"

"I found out some interesting information. The morning of the raid, a man who said he was a neighbor came by and told Big Joe that a herd of his cattle had wandered to the east onto his range. Joe sent his men to bring the cattle back."

Dash pointed to a chair. "Sit down, this may take a while. So, who was this feller that came by?"

"No one knows, and none of the hands saw what he looked like, but they did give me a description of his horse. He was riding a chestnut with a star on its forehead and two white stockings."

"That narrows it down some. What else did you find out?"

"They saw blood on the ground but no bodies, and all the horses were unshod. There was one dead horse, and it was a wild mustang. The other thing that don't make sense is the herd of cattle they drove off to the west."

"Why does that not seem right?"

"It was a herd of two to three hundred head. There is no way that the raiders could load up three dead bodies and move that many cattle in the amount of time they had. The other thing is those mustangs. They're not cow ponies, and there is no way the men on those horses moved those cattle west for five miles."

Dash leaned back in his chair and made a face from the discomfort of his wound. "Here's what I think. The man that came to the house that morning set up the ranch for the raid. We need to find out who he is and where he's from. I also agree that someone else drove those cattle west for five miles. I have a feeling that was done by cowboys that are used to herding cattle, and the other thing is the amount of time it took. I cowboyed for a while on a couple of cattle drives, and getting them bunched up and moving five miles probably took six or seven hours. The other thing I'm thinking is that the raiders didn't go west. I think they may have intersected with the herd closer to the ranch house and turned south while the drovers continued to push the cattle west."

It was Brody's chance to tell Dash his plan. "I'm in agreement with everything you said, and I'm going to start asking all my patients if they know who rides the chestnut. I'm also thinking about riding back out to the ranch and getting one of the hands to take me west where they drove the cattle and see if we can find where the horses turned south."

"That's a good plan. I'll move to that little boarding house down the street tomorrow or the next day and start asking around town who rides that horse. Dr. Brody, this may involve some local people, and they don't want to be found out, so you keep the safety off those guns and watch your back. These men have no problem shooting someone in the back to keep from getting arrested."

"Yeah, I've considered that also. Do you think it would be to my advantage to ask about the horse owner at the saloons?"

"That could be risky. Let *me* ask at the saloons."

"I'm a pretty good poker player, and I could bring it up during a few hands."

"That might work, but I think for now you ask your patients and let me ask in the saloons. Remember that I'm a bounty hunter who asks a lot of questions."

Brody nodded his head. "So, I take it you have decided to team up with me and find my Jennifer."

"I figure if we're out looking for her, I may get information where Porkchop went, and you can help me take him down."

Brody laughed. "I think that's a swell idea. I better go see if we're finished for the day and get my office cleaned up and ready to start over in the morning."

Emma was mopping the floor when Brody came back inside. "Is there anything you need me to do, Nurse?"

"No. There was only a few soiled towels, and I put them in the kitchen so we can wash them tomorrow. You can go eat if you want to while I finish up."

"Thanks."

Brody went back out the rear door where Dash was still sitting.

"Dash, do you think you're able to walk to the café for supper?"

"I can sure try. Let's go."

The two men walked through the backyard to the alley and then out onto the street. It was still early enough that the café wasn't crowded.

Chapter Twenty-Eight

BRODY AND DASH WERE ABLE TO GET A TABLE TO themselves in spite of the people who were eating their supper, greeting the doctor as he came in. Dash ordered coffee with his food, and the girl asked Brody, "Doctor, do you want water or milk?"

"Water is fine, and I'll have the same food as my friend."

When the girl had walked away, it was Dash's time to ask some questions.

"I have to ask, can I depend on you in a fight when the lead is flying?"

"You can depend on me. I'm not a tenderfoot when it comes to gunplay. I've been in more gunfights than I want to remember. Some were with me facing the feller face-to-face. I'm better than most when it comes to speed, and if you're concerned about what I can do, go out to the Dry Creek Ranch and talk to some of the hands. They saw me in action when they were in Wichita two years ago."

"I'll take your word on it. How far will you go to find that woman?"

"I'm not sure what you mean. I've already turned down high-paying jobs at prestigious hospitals to come here to find her. I plan on continuing my search until I know for sure where she is."

"What if we find that she's dead?"

"I'll cross that bridge when I come to it."

"Brody, I'm scared that whoever took her has already sold her to the highest bidder. That someone could be in a foreign country, and we may never find her. You have to be prepared for bad news."

"My stepfather beat me and my mama. I killed him so he wouldn't beat her anymore. I also killed a man in a gunfight for beating a saloon girl within an inch of her life. Dealing with death is also part of my job, and I respect the fact that we all will die someday. I was trained on how to fight with my hands and guns by an old Indian warrior. He taught me how to plan out an attack and how to have the element of surprise. The winner is nine times out of ten the one with surprise as a weapon."

"Who was the old Indian that taught you how to fight?"

"William Longtooth, the healer. I stayed with him for a few months, and he taught me many things about life."

"I've heard of him and of some of the battles he was in. Did you know that he was dead and that Porkchop and Twisted Nose killed him over some food?"

Brody's head came up, and he was looking Dash in the eyes. "I knew that he was dead. I found his remains and buried them at his camp. I didn't know who killed him. Are you sure it was Porkchop and that other feller?"

"Yeah, I'm sure. They killed him and then bragged

about it at Durant Station, down close to the Red River. I know the man that they told it to, and I believe him."

"Just so you know, I'm going to kill Porkchop and Twisted Nose when I see them."

"That's mighty big talk coming from a doctor."

"William was my friend, and I don't let anyone harm my friends or family. That's why I killed my stepfather and the rest of those men in Wichita. Porkchop will pay for what he did."

The girl brought out their food, and they had to stop the conversation since it wasn't something she needed to hear. When the two men finished their plates of food, Brody and Dash walked back to the doctor's office where Dash was ready for bed.

Brody was still processing all the information he acquired at the ranch and knew the man who came to the ranch that dreadful morning was the key to finding where Jennifer was. It was still early, and that's when he decided to go to the saloon and play some poker to see if anyone knew who rode the chestnut with the star in its forehead.

The first saloon he looked inside only had four customers, and no one was playing cards. Walking along the boardwalk revealed something else he could start doing. Horses were tied to hitch rails all along the street, and he needed to pay attention and watch for the chestnut. Then another thought came to him, and he veered off to cross the street and headed to the livery stable.

The boy who had helped Brody move his things to Dr. Wilks's office was still working.

"Can I pick your brain for a few minutes?" asked Brody.

"Oh, hi Doctor. What's on your mind?"

"I'm trying to locate a feller. Do you know who rides

a chestnut with a star in his forehead and two white stockings?"

"There's a few of them around and I'm familiar with a couple, but I don't believe any that I have seen has the star on their forehead. Where are the stockings, front or back or mixed?"

"I don't remember. I would appreciate it if you would let me know if you see that horse and I would keep this between us."

"Yes, sir, I sure will."

Brody started walking off but stopped. "I just remembered, the stockings were on its hind legs. By the way, what's your name?"

"It's Timmy, Timmy Rico.

"I'll be seeing you, Timmy."

Brody angled across the street to the Cattleman's Saloon and eased inside where he stood surveying the room. There were five cowboys bellied up to the bar. More men were at tables scattered throughout the room and then he saw four men playing cards with an empty chair.

Brody didn't like playing five-handed cards but playing tonight was for information and not to make a lot of money. It was difficult for him to read the table with four opponents as opposed to only three.

One of the men was shuffling the cards when Brody walked up.

"Evening, men. I was wondering if I could join in on a few hands?"

"Sure, Doctor, we have an empty seat."

The man sitting to the left of the empty chair stood up and put his money in his pocket. "I'm done for the night. Doctor, take this empty seat cause the one I'm in is unlucky, or these three crooks are ganging up on me."

Brody pulled out the chair and sat down. He placed a few greenbacks on the table and asked, "What's everyone's names? I'm Dr. Brody Connor."

The man shuffling the cards said, "I'm Martin."

The man to his left said, "I'm Afton Collins. I'm sure glad that you're here working with Wilks."

The third man stuck out his hand to shake. "I'm Lilburn, but most people call me Dip."

"Dip, that's a different name. I take it you dip snuff."

"Yep, most of the time."

The winning hands went back and forth between the men for an hour before Brody asked. "Do any of you know who rides a chestnut with a star on its forehead and two white stockings on its rear legs?"

Afton and Lilburn both shook their heads and said, "No."

Martin took a drink of his whiskey. "Why do you want to know?"

Brody wasn't expecting that question. "I happened to see the man sometime back and thought that horse was something I would consider buying. Now that I'm working, I thought I would try to see if I could buy it."

"Good luck in finding that particular horse. I doubt it would be for sale if you do find it." Martin then mouthed a cocky smile and started picking up his money. "I'm done for the night. It's been fun, fellers, I'll be seeing you." He left.

Brody also stood up and shook hands with Afton and Lilburn. "It was fun playing cards and meeting you men. What does Martin do for a living?"

"Don't rightly know. He comes to town about once a week to drink and play cards. Other than that, we don't know much about him."

Brody walked outside and didn't see Martin anywhere

on the street. The way he asked Brody why he wanted to know who rode the horse made the doctor wonder if the man knew more than he was letting on.

As Brody was walking back to the hotel, a horse and rider came from the livery stable. The man was Martin, who didn't acknowledge Brody watching from the boardwalk, or maybe he didn't see the young doctor. Brody let the man get a block down the street before he walked to the livery.

"Timmy, are you here?"

The boy came to the door. "Howdy, Doctor. Do you need your horse?"

"No, I'm wanting to know who Martin is? He just left here on his horse."

"I didn't know his name. He comes here about once a week and sometimes leaves his horse here if he spends the night. None of his horses have brands, and I don't know where he works."

"You said none of his *horses*. Does that mean he rides different horses?"

"Yep, occasionally, he'll ride a gray, but most of the time he's on a different horse."

"I wonder why anyone would do that?"

"Normally, it's because the ranch has a big remuda and the horses need riding."

"I see. So, he probably works on a large ranch somewhere close by?"

"Not necessarily close by. It could be one of those ranches down on the plateaus. There ain't a lot of places for those men to get whiskey or women. I know the man goes down to the Reservation District when he's in town.

"Thanks for the information."

Brody walked off but changed his mind about going

back to the office, and instead walked to the Reservation, hoping to see if Martin went there when he left the saloon. About halfway to the area of town where the prostitution houses were located, he really didn't think the man would collect his horse and go there. This was most likely a wasted trip, but since he was so close, he would see if the horse Martin rode was tied out front of one of the houses.

This was Brody's first time here, and he was surprised at how many businesses were open with working girls. At the third building he passed by, there stood the horse that Martin had rode from the livery stable.

Brody went to the window and peered inside to see Martin hugging a brown skinned woman with black hair. When they broke their embrace, he started to the door, and Brody took off down the street and hid in the shadows until Martin was out of sight. He went back to the office and started to his room when Dash called out.

Chapter Twenty-Nine

Dash was in bed when Dr. Brody walked in and sat down. "What do you need, Dash?"

"I been thinking about what you told me regarding the raid, and I have a new theory on what happened."

Brody leaned back and crossed his arms. "I'm all ears, go ahead."

"I think the herd was moved east two days before the raid and the other larger herd was moved west the day before the raid. We know that the man on the chestnut came there the morning of the raid so it would be less men at the house. I think the kidnappers killed everyone at the house, tied up your woman, and loaded up their dead and wounded."

Brody kind of shook his head. "I know all this. Is that all?"

"No, they then rode east and covered their tracks with the tracks of the ranch hands. They only used the cattle taken west to throw off everyone. I bet a man could ride east but not in the same path that the hands took, and he may still find where they turned south. I'm betting on them turning south and heading toward Edwards Plateau."

Brody stood up and started to pace the floor. "You just may have the best idea yet. I'm riding back to the ranch tomorrow and see if I can find their trail."

"It's going to be really hard to find, but it's doable. Look for damaged grass, torn up soil from the horses' hooves. Remember that a running horse will kick up dirt. Look for anything that one of the men or even Jennifer may have dropped."

"I'll take one of the ranch hands with me. I'm hoping that I can find her tomorrow."

"Doctor, don't get your hopes up too much. She may be halfway across the ocean by now. If you do find where she is, I suggest you go back to the ranch and take all the men you can find with you. It would be really nice if you got some of those Texas Rangers to come with you. They're more skilled than cowhands and less likely to get killed."

"Thanks, Dash. I'm going to turn in and head out as soon as I can tomorrow."

THE FOLLOWING MORNING, Brody was working when the first patient came in and had already seen five by the time that Dr. Wilks arrived.

There were no patients in the waiting room when Brody approached the elderly doctor. "I hate to do this to you, but I have some new information concerning Jennifer's disappearance, and I need to go check it out. I may be gone for a few days, but I'll be back."

"I understand that you want to find her, but son, you

need to let the law do its job. She may not be alive or in Texas anymore."

"I'm well aware of all that. I came here to find her or at least try. If you want me to clear out my things, I will."

"Oh, no! You go do what you need to do and take all the time you need. I've been taking care of this place for fifty years, and a few more days won't kill me."

"Thanks, Dr. Wilks. I'll be back as soon as I can."

Brody went to his room and packed one change of clothes, grabbed his skillet and then packed all the bullets he owned along with his sewing kit and bedroll. The rest of the items could be purchased from the store while the hostler saddled his horse. He was closing the door when he thought about the canteens and went back for them.

The hostler must have seen the doctor walking toward the livery carrying his bulging saddlebags and waved. "Do you want your horse saddled?" he called out.

"Yeah, I'm going to the store and will be back in a few minutes."

At the store, he purchased two more boxes of .45 shells and a sack of jerky. The small skillet in his saddlebags could be used if he had to kill a small animal to eat, otherwise, he hoped to eat with the ranch hands.

Timmy had the horse saddled and tied up out front when Brody walked from the store, and secured his saddlebags and bedroll. Timmy came out and said, "I been asking a few of my friends and they say Martin is a hired gun that works for some ranch northwest of here. They say he always rides west and then changes direction a mile or so from Waco."

Brody looked at Timmy, squinting his forehead. "How do they know all this?"

"Martin always has money playing cards and he has a

sporting woman in the Reservation. My friends were going to rob him but changed their minds after following him one day, and he caught them. I reckon he whipped them pretty good, cause they don't want anything to do with him now."

"Thanks, Timmy, here's a dollar for helping me."

Brody mounted up and headed out once again to the Dry Creek Ranch.

Today, the ride didn't take as long since he knew the way and had his horse loping. When he passed by the road that went to the Prichard place, he made a face of anguish. He had forgotten to discuss Kathy's heart problem with Dr. Wilks and that had to be done when he returned to the office.

There was only one ranch hand at the burned-out headquarters, who happened to be in the corral working with taming a colt. The hand's name was Manuel, who saw Brody coming and had picked up a rifle, but after recognizing the doctor, he put it back.

"Morning, Doctor. What brings you back so quick?"

"Hi Manuel, I have something I need to check out and I need your and the other hands help. I think the raiders went east when they left here and used the tracks of the men that rode after the cattle that had wandered off. I want us to ride in the same path as close as we can and try to pick up their trail."

"East, we never thought about that, but it does seem possible. Give me a few minutes to see if I can get the men in here. I'm going to fire off the double-barreled ten-gauge and they should come running."

Manuel went into the bunkhouse and came out with the big gun. He fired one barrel at a time, and the kick from the shotgun almost knocked him down.

Brody dismounted and took his horse to the water

trough and even splashed some on his shirt. It was already hot and would get hotter before the day was over. This was also a good time to refill the canteen he had been drinking from.

Manuel saddled a horse and had gone after his rifle and canteen when Shephard came into the yard with his gun drawn.

"Is everything okay here?" he asked.

"Yes, I'm waiting on the others to arrive. I have a new plan on locating the raiders and need all of you to go with me."

"I'm going to change to a fresh horse while we're waiting. They should be along directly."

Chapter Thirty

THE OTHER COWBOYS SHOWED UP, AND LIKE Shephard, Sam and Robert they also swapped out their mounts for fresh ones. Brody filled all of them in on his plan and emphasized the importance of riding close to the same way they had ridden after the stray cattle to the east. They were instructed to look for anything out of the normal, whether it was a broken twig on a sapling, or something someone may have dropped, like a cigarette butt or spat out a used chaw of tobacco.

The hands walked their horses away from the house, and of course, the wind, rain, and time had covered any tracks, even their own. The sun rays were already making the horses lather up, and all four men's shirts were soaked when Manuel stopped his horse.

"Look over there to the left. That brush looks like something rode right through the middle of it."

Brody dismounted and started walking toward the brush when suddenly, he drew his gun and fired one shot. Next to the clump of brush was a coiled-up rattlesnake.

"Did you kill it?" asked Sam.

"Yeah, it's dead, but that's not important." Brody leaned over and pulled something from the brush. It was a pearl-colored button attached to a small piece of faded cloth. "I think someone rode through here and dropped this to mark the trail."

He handed the button to Manuel. "Do you remember what Jennifer was wearing the day of the raid?"

"No, I don't know. Do any of you know if Jennifer was wearing something with this color of material and button?"

They were all shaking their heads *no*. Brody started back to his horse but stopped. He handed the reins to Manuel. "I'm goin' to walk ahead and try to not miss anything. You all stay back and keep your eyes peeled so we don't miss any clues."

Brody stopped walking and just stood looking at the terrain and thinking about where he would go if he was leading a group of men and a kidnapped woman. It had to be somewhere that wouldn't reveal their tracks and somewhere that most men wouldn't ride.

He knew they didn't ride west, or east. That left north or south. Everyone he had talked to seemed to think the raiders went west or south. But the young doctor kept looking to the north. Finally, he pointed to an area composed of shallow gullies, brush, and rocks.

"Let's go over there where the going is much more difficult. I think they went that way."

Manuel spoke, "Boss, why would anyone ride through all that if they were on the run?"

"That's actually why they rode that way. No one in their right mind would go through there unless you were raiders trying not to leave a trail. Let's go through here in single file, and everyone keep a keen eye out."

Brody took the lead, and it wasn't long before he pointed up ahead, where it looked like horses had disturbed the soil as they went down the side of a gully. The trail was still faintly visible where they could see small clumps of dead grass and slight indentations in the soft soil. The men stayed in the gully for a half mile until Manuel stopped his horse.

"Look up there. I think I see something." The ranch hand took off up the slope and dismounted. He picked up something off the ground and held it up so the others could see. It was a silver concho off of someone's saddle.

Brody was the next one to go up the embankment so he could see what Manuel was holding. Manuel handed it to the doctor, who was looking at it.

"Jennifer often wore black leather britches with these fancy conchos down each side from the knee to the bottom cuff. I believe she is leaving us clues."

Brody put the concho in his shirt pocket. "I'm thinking they rode this way." He took off with the others following. Another half mile and there was another of the shiny conchos, but this time they didn't know which way to ride.

Brody was looking at the terrain and thinking out loud. "They have been going in a northern direction. I don't see any reason they would change the way they were heading, so I'm thinking we continue on this way."

Sam spoke up. "There's a big ranch north of here that's owned by Colonel Musgrove. I had a partner that worked there for a short time about eight years ago."

"Do you think we're on the right track to be able to see it if we stay on this trajectory?"

"I don't know. I ain't never been there."

Brody sat on his horse thinking about his next move. The main thing was to make sure he didn't do anything to get the men hurt. "I think we spread out and walk forward and continue to watch for clues. If we happen to see a ranch up ahead, then we'll deal with it if needed."

The five men spread out and were climbing a hill when Manuel stopped and pointed up ahead. Brody couldn't see anything because of the hill and was about to move on up when Sam said, "Listen up. There's a lot of horses coming this way."

The men eased forward enough where they could see over the hill, and the sight caused them to look at each other. It was a herd of wild mustangs, and the leader was a magnificent black stud taking its herd away from the four riders swinging ropes over their heads.

The cowboys got close enough and threw the ropes, catching four horses in the rear. Brody backed his horse down the hill and motioned for the rest of the men to follow.

"We don't want them to see us. Sam, go up the hill far enough where you can see which way they go so we can follow."

Sam dismounted and went on up and laid on his stomach.

Brody started talking to the rest of the men. "I'm thinking we're close to finding the men doing the killing and kidnapping. Those men roping those mustangs affirm that as far as I'm concerned."

Sam came running down the hill. "They're headed northwest with four horses in tow. I'm almost sure those mustangs have been roped before. They ain't putting up no fight at all."

Brody pointed up the hill. "Let's head on out but stay back enough so they don't see us."

The five men started riding in the direction of the men with the horses, and when they came to a creek, they let their horses drink while Brody dismounted and walked to the far edge of the trees, where he could see the ranch buildings.

The ranch house was impressive, it was two stories with white walls and blue trim. The front porch went the full width of the house and must have extended fourteen feet with a number of chairs and two small tables.

There were two large barns and a corral that had fenced dividers between the structures. Next to the second barn was a long, narrow bunkhouse, and to the right of it, some fifty feet were three, two-hole outhouses.

Farther back behind the bunkhouse was another long, narrow building that resembled another bunkhouse. Then he saw something that got his attention. There was a clothesline between two trees with women's garments hanging to dry.

That was all Brody needed to see. He backed away and went to the others.

"I'm pretty sure this is who's been doing the raids, so we need to go back to Waco and notify the Rangers."

Manuel pulled his rifle from its scabbard. "I say we ride in there and fill them full of lead."

"No, we notify the Rangers and come here with them. Let's ride."

"Hold up," said Shephard. "Just assuming that this is where the raiders went ain't enough. We need to know more about this bunch before we come in here shooting up the place. We would be no better than the raiders if we came in killing people and they hadn't done anything."

Brody knew that he had acted in haste. "What do you suggest we do?"

"A couple stay here hidden out of sight and watch. A

couple of more ride around to the left and get into a position where they can see that bunkhouse in the back. From what I can tell from here, there ain't no place to watch on the right."

Brody thought for a few seconds. "I'll give you one hour to get into position and then I'm riding in, acting like I'm lost and ask for directions back to Waco. If they're the ones doing all the meanness, then I'm sure they'll want to get rid of me as quick as possible."

Chapter Thirty-One

Brody was antsy having to wait on the men to get in place before he rode out of the trees toward the house. Would whoever he talked to believe he was lost, or would they start shooting? Then he noticed that his once lathered horse wasn't wet, and that would let whomever he talked to know he wasn't telling the truth.

Brody mounted up and started to run his horse back the way they had come. It didn't take long until the horse was breathing hard and leathered up again. It had been enough time, so he rode through the trees and loped his horse toward the ranch house.

Not long after leaving the creek and trees, he could see a number of men moving around the barn and the first bunkhouse area. When he was within two hundred yards of the house, three riders came at him, running their horses.

Brody stopped and waited, as he didn't want to get so close that men with rifles could take a shot at him. What he did see was three men run from the first bunkhouse and go to the second one. He also saw four men with rifles come out of the house and stand by the porch post.

When the riders were close, Brody raised both his hands chest level so they would see that his hands were empty.

"Howdy, I'm Dr. Brody Connor from Waco, and I'm lost. Can you point me in the right direction back to Waco?"

One of the men put his hands on the saddle horn and took the makings for a cigarette out of his pocket. "So, are you that new sawbones we been hearing about in Waco?"

"I reckon so. I work for Dr. Wilks, and since he wants to stop doing house calls, it's up to me, but I'm not familiar with the area yet and get lost easily."

The man struck a lucifer off the saddle leather and lit his cig. "You need to be more careful where you ride. The way back to Waco is that way." The man pointed to the east.

"Thanks, I appreciate it."

Brody was turning his horse to the east when he saw a woman run from the second bunkhouse, and a man caught up with her and took her to the ground.

The doctor didn't let the men know he saw the woman and took off without looking back until he crossed through the stream. The men had turned and were riding back while Brody kept going so he could meet up with the cowboys. He was antsy to know what they saw and how many men they estimated were at the ranch. From where he was, he saw the three who came to meet him. Four were on the porch and probably another five around the barn and bunkhouse area. There were at least twelve and most likely more.

He could see the two men who had stayed in the

trees by the creek, and one of them was waving his hat and pointing toward the ranch. Looking back, two men were leaving the ranch and heading his way. Brody knew the men were following to make sure he left like he was supposed to.

He never stopped until he went over a hill and looked back to see the two men turn around and head back toward the ranch. Brody went on a little farther and found a shade where he could wait on all the Dry Creek Ranch hands.

It took almost an hour before the ranch hands finally showed up. Shephard was the first to talk. "You were right about storming that ranch. There must be fifteen or more armed men there."

"I counted twelve for sure. What did you see from where you were?"

"We had to hold up on that knoll east of the second bunkhouse and saw three men run into the place. While you were talking to those three men that rode out to meet you, one of the women ran out hollering, but we couldn't hear what she was saying. One of the men caught up with the woman and took her down. He laid on her until you turned and rode off. Then he picked her up by the hair of her head and drug the poor woman back inside."

"Were you able to tell if there were other women inside the place?"

"I believe there are, based on the clothesline behind the living quarters. You can't see all of the line from where you were, but I estimate by the amount of clothes hanging on the line, there are more than six people inside that house."

Robert, who was with Shephard, spoke. "We also saw

a guard sitting at the back of the house where the women were."

"So they have a guard on the building. That means they have something to hide," said Brody.

Manuel, did you see anything different?"

"Yeah, about a half mile behind the main house is another bunkhouse and a large pen with wild mustangs in it. There must have been twenty old saddles sitting on the rail fence. I'm betting that's what they use for the raids."

"Yeah. I still say we contact the Rangers and get their help in taking this place down. The odds are too one-sided for the five of us."

All the men were nodding their heads in agreement.

"Let's head on back, and I'll break off so I can go back to Waco and talk to the Rangers. Where would be a good place for us to meet up when we go rescue the women?"

"Where we came out of the rough land would be a good place to meet. All you need to do is give us an hour, and we'll be there ready to fight," said Manuel.

"Okay, I'll get word to you when it's time, and we'll teach them fellers a lesson in warfare."

Brody rode off from the Dry Creek hands and headed on to Waco at a pace faster than he should be going. The thought of finally finding Jennifer was on his mind, and he couldn't wait to hold her to him.

He hoped there would be enough lawmen at Waco to be able to charge the ranch and take the men before they did any harm to the women. They would need some wagons to bring the kidnapped women back to town or maybe use some from that ranch.

Brody didn't know where the Rangers operated out of Waco, so he would ride to the county sheriff's office and let him know he had found the kidnapped women and the men who had killed so many good men in Central Texas.

Leaving his horse tied beside the water trough, Brody walked into the sheriff's office to be met by an elderly man sweeping the floor.

"Howdy, the sheriff and his deputies are all out investigating a hog getting stole. Is there something I can do for you?"

"Yeah, you can tell me where I can find the Texas Rangers assigned here."

"Well, that may be a problem since there ain't none assigned here. They're all up at Cleburne."

"Thanks." Brody left the office, saddened to know he didn't have any help today and would have to send a telegram and see if he could get the Rangers here tomorrow.

The way to the telegraph office would take him past Dr. Wilks's office and he wanted to talk to Dash before he sent the message.

Dr. Wilks was examining a boy's arm when Brody walked into the room. "I need to talk to Dash and then I'm leaving again."

"He ain't here. He went to the saloon to play cards. Did you find out anything?"

"Yeah, I found the outlaws' hideout and there's some of the women there. I'm trying to find some lawmen to go with me to get them."

"Send a rider out to get the sheriff and his men. They are east of town, about two miles at Homer Sales's house."

"Thanks, Doctor. I'll go now and send for the sheriff."

Brody walked to get his horse and took it to the livery where he told Timmy, "Feed him some grain and leave him saddled. I also need a favor. Can you or someone you know ride east of town and have the sheriff come back here? It's really important."

"I'll take care of your horse, and I know someone that can go get the sheriff." Timmy held out his hand, and Brody put three dollars in it.

With that taken care of, he walked across the street to the saloon where Dash was playing poker. The bounty hunter looked at Brody and threw twenty on the pile. Brody stayed back, knowing that Dash had a good hand and wanted to finish it before he left the table.

Chapter Thirty-Two

BRODY SAW A TABLE OVER BY ONE OF THE windows and sat down to wait on Dash to finish the hand he was playing. The waitress came over. "Hello, Doctor, what can I get you?"

"I'll have a mug of beer."

While the woman behind the counter was getting his beer, Dash came over and sat down. He was wearing his gun and holster on his right side and a vest over his shirt that was tucked into his britches. The moccasins on his feet surprised the doctor enough that he asked. "Dash, are you feeling okay today? I noticed you didn't put on your boots."

"I feel fine, and I didn't want to strain my stitches pulling on my boots. You didn't come here to hear about me, so tell me what you found out."

Brody told the bounty hunter what he knew and that he was heading to the telegraph office to let the Rangers know so they could come and help. He also told him about sending for the sheriff. Brody drained his beer in three gulps and stood up.

"I better get that telegram sent off."

"Brody, sit back down. I'd be surprised if the Rangers come to help, so don't get your hopes up. As for the sheriff and his deputies...you would be better off taking me and some men I know with you than the local law."

"How many men can you come up with?" asked Brody.

"Maybe a half dozen or so. Give me a few hours to see what I can do. In the meantime, you can talk to the sheriff when he gets here, and I believe there's a couple of more ranchers that may want in on this. It wouldn't hurt to ask if they want to come along to get the men who have been killing their friends."

"Okay, I'll send the telegram and then start talking to some of the other ranchers."

Dash started back to the poker table and was talking to the men at the table when Brody walked past them heading to the telegraph office. He was almost to the little building next to the railroad tracks that served as the telegraph office when he saw four riders coming toward him.

"What's so important that you pulled us away from a crime?"

"Well, Sheriff, me and the hands from the Dry Creek Ranch found where the kidnapped women are being kept. There's around fifteen of the raiders there and I'm needing a lot of help to go in and get the women."

"Come to my office and you can tell me everything. I don't want everyone in town to know what we talk about."

"I'll be there in a few minutes after I send a telegram to the Rangers asking them for more help."

"Good luck with that. It may be a month before you hear back from them."

Brody went ahead and sent his message and then walked to the sheriff's office, where the same four men he had seen on the street were waiting.

It took twenty minutes to convey all that he and the cowhands had done and seen. It took another ten minutes to tell them what needed to happen to get the women back. The sheriff wasn't too happy to help out and started making excuses so he and his men couldn't go. Brody saw through his lack of care and finally stood up and said, "You and your men stay here, and I'll go get the women. I don't need the four of you getting in my way."

He put on his hat and walked out, heading to the livery stable to talk to Timmy. The boy saw him coming and was waiting out front.

"Howdy, Doctor, are you ready for your horse?"

"Yeah, and I need some information. If I wanted to get some ranch hands to help me fight those raiders, where would I go to get them?"

"I'd go to the Circle C and the Rocking M and see if they wanted to join the fight. Both of those spreads are on the road that goes east out of town and they're across the road from each other. When they come to town, it's *Katie, bar the door* with the fighting that goes on."

"Thanks, Timmy. Go ahead and get my horse, and I'll go see if they'll help me."

While waiting on his horse, Dash came out of the saloon and hobbled across the street to where Brody was. "I've been talking to some fellers and they're heading back to the spreads they work for to see how many want to join the fight."

"I'm having my horse saddled to ride to the Circle C and Rocking M to see if they will help me."

"You don't have to ride out there. I've already talked

to some of those hands as well as one from the Liberty Ranch. They're supposed to let me know today how many are willing to fight."

"Thanks, Dash. I went to the sheriff, and he started making excuses about going with me, so I left and will do it without the law. I'm thinking we hit them in the morning, right about daylight, if we have enough to come at them in three different directions."

Dash went to a bench and sat down. "Have you contacted the Rangers?"

"Yeah, but I may not hear back from them if they're in the field after outlaws."

Dash pointed a finger at Brody. "I'm going with you as soon as you have enough men, and I don't want no flak from you. Is that understood?"

Brody smiled. "Yeah, I understand, and thanks for coming with me."

"I have a Sharps .50 caliber that I'm very good with, and I'm thinking I can get where I can cover most of the place and pick off some of them men from long distance."

"That's a great idea and I know just where to put you. Now, let's hope those men you talked to come through with some fighting men."

Dash stood up. "I think you should let the men at your girlfriend's ranch know where and when to meet in the morning. Those men I talked to will come through."

"I'm going to go inside and see if Timmy can deliver a message for me, then I'm going back to the telegraph office to see if I have any messages."

"When you get finished, come to the saloon."

Brody walked into the telegraph office to be handed a message from Ranger Miller, that said: *No Ranger available. Rangers investigating crimes.*

The upset doctor wadded up the paper and threw it in the trash basket. He picked up a pencil and wrote on a piece of paper: *Me and my men will do your job for you.*

"Send this back to whoever sent me a reply," said Brody, and left the building aggravated at the Ranger's reply. He felt like they hadn't done enough when the raid on the Dry Creek Ranch happened. They were supposed to be the best lawmen in Texas and hadn't found the raiders' trail and sure hadn't found the ranch where they worked.

Brody walked back out onto the boardwalk and saw a rider coming into town from the east at a good pace. This could be the cowboy who Dash had talked to coming back with news on how many men wanted in on the fight. It was time to walk to the saloon and see for sure.

The cowboy dismounted in front of the saloon and went inside before Brody could get there. The doctor didn't change his ways in haste, but stood at the doorway until his eyes adjusted and saw Dash wave his hand for him to come to his table. The cowboy who had ridden in was seated along with two other men.

Dash motioned to the cowboy. "Dr. Brody, this is Tom Walls, and he's got a dozen men counting himself, ready to leave town at four in the morning."

Brody stuck out his hand. "Nice to meet you Tom, and thanks for helping."

Dash used his foot to push out an empty chair for Brody. "These other two are Steve Daughtery and Carl Lewis, and they're from the Cactus Bend Ranch south of here. They were hit by raiders about two years ago, but were lucky and fought them off. They'll be here in the morning with eight men."

Brody was smiling from ear to ear by the amount of fighting men he had going with him. "I want to thank you and all your men for helping out. I plan to hit them at daylight when they're least expecting it, with such force that they won't put up a fight."

"How many men are there?" asked Steve.

"I know of fifteen, and it could be more. We'll meet on the west edge of town at four in the morning and then split up when we get to their ranch. I'm hoping we're able to take most of them into custody, but if not, that's okay also, it's their call."

"We'll be here and ready to fight," said Tom.

"Thanks, I have one more thing to do before dark. I'll see you all in the morning."

Back out on the boardwalk, the doctor walked to the gun shop so he could buy another gun to take with him.

Chapter Thirty-Three

Darkness filled the early morning when Brody and Dash walked outside and headed to the livery stable to get their horses. He had paid Timmy a dollar the night before to have the two horses saddled by four, and sure enough, the boy had their mounts outside the barn, ready to ride.

Brody didn't see the hostler and figured the boy went back inside to sleep. The rest of the men would be showing up soon, and he wanted to be in place when they arrived. He had the gun and holster on his hip, the shoulder holster gun under his left arm, and the new gun he purchased in a left-handed holster. It was probably strange to some that he also brought his doctor bag. He did that in case some of the men riding with him got shot in the gun battle.

Today could be one of great joy by finding Jennifer, or it could be one of heartache. There would most likely be dead men from the ranch when the fight gets started, but that's the life those men chose when they signed on to raid and kidnap. Even though he had taken an oath to save lives, the actions of today would be up to the men they were going after.

William Longtooth taught him to have a strategy and purpose before starting a battle. The element of surprise would be his greatest maneuver with the hope of hitting them before they could put up a fight. Don't give the enemy a chance to fight back, go in with the intent to kill and only capture if they throw down their guns.

Even with a plan, purpose, and strategy, the leader had to make sure his men were mentally ready to face the enemy. This would be a three-way attack, and if the men did what he wanted, the battle should be over about as quick as it gets started.

Dash looked over at Brody. "Are you ready for this?"

"Yeah, I'm ready. I was trained for battles like this by an old Indian warrior. I'm mentally and physically ready to put an end to the raids."

"I reckon you have a place where you want me to get with this Sharps."

"Yeah, I do. I know where there's a tree located that will give you a clear view of the ranch yard."

"Look, there comes some of the men this way," said Dash, pointing to the east.

In a few minutes, twenty men joined up with Brody and Dash. The armed men headed out to the northwest to meet up with the hands from the Dry Creek Ranch.

Fifty minutes before daylight, Brody and his group came to the meeting place, and there were five men with Manuel and another four men from their neighbor's place.

Brody had the men circle around where he could talk to them.

"Men, the ranch we're going to hit is through these badlands. We know the way through, and there's a creek lined with trees to the north. That's where we'll split up and get in position to attack."

Steve moved his horse forward. "Ain't that the ranch that Colonel Musgrove owns?"

Brody didn't back off. "I don't know who owns it, nor do I care. All I know is there are two bunkhouses there. The first one is where the hands live, and the second one is where the women are. I suspect there is at least one guard on the second bunkhouse, so be aware of that."

Dash spoke up. "Look, just because Musgrove once was an Army officer doesn't keep him from being a criminal. I've taken down plenty of ex-soldiers in my way of life."

"I want Shepherd and his men to head on out and circle around to the south. Don't do anything until you see me and Dash ride out of the trees. Dash is stopping at that blackjack tree and that's going to be your clue to head to the house."

"So you want us to hit the house?"

"Yes, Manuel, take Steve and Carl's men with you and circle to the east where you were yesterday. The same thing goes for your group, except you're hitting the first bunkhouse. Hit it hard and don't give those men time to react."

Manuel moved out. "Follow me and let's get going. Shepherd also moved his men on out.

"The rest of us will ease our way through here and hold up along the trees until daylight. Dash and I will head out with you all following. Dash will stop and be set up with his Sharps and then we'll ride on in."

Brody's group of men took their time getting to the creek and let their horses drink before spreading out and waiting until their leader gave the command to advance.

It was still so dark that none of the men could see the

house or buildings yet. They sat on their horses, ready, when Brody could finally see the tree where he was going to leave Dash with his Sharps.

As soon as the dark shapes of the buildings began to show through the morning dawn, Brody thought, *it's now or never*.

"Dash, let's walk our horses toward that blackjack up ahead. That's where you'll protect us with that Sharps."

"I'm ready and so are all these men."

The two men started off and were fifty feet out in the open when the men started out. Dash dismounted, pulled his Sharps from the scabbard, and took with him his saddlebags that Brody figured were full of cartridges for the big gun.

Brody slowed his horse down enough for the men to catch up, and when they were within two hundred yards, he looked and saw the other two groups of fighters heading to their designated targets.

"Men, let's hit them hard and get this over with in a hurry."

With that said, the men out front urged their horses to run toward the house. Dogs started barking, and a light came on in the front of the house. The front door opened and out came a Black man with a rifle.

The boom of the Sharps sounded in the quiet morning, and the man on the porch was lifted up by the .50 slug and slammed against the wall. Three more men came out of the house and were met with a volley of lead from the men with Brody.

The doctor didn't pay any mind to the shooting at the bunkhouse or at the house where his men were going inside before most of the men could react. He was focused on getting to the second bunkhouse where the women were. An armed guard was hiding behind a wagon, shooting with a pistol and when he raised up to fire at the riders, one shot from the Sharps took most of his face off.

Brody jumped from the saddle and ran to the bunkhouse door, which was padlocked. He pulled his gun and fired two shots that shattered the lock.

The wood beside where he stood splintered as a bullet went past him and hit the door facing. Brody dropped down, and as he turned, he saw a man running at him, shooting with a pistol in each hand. Two quick shots, and the man went down screaming in pain.

Brody kicked the door and moved to the side in case another guard was in the large room. Nothing happened, and he eased inside and stood still.

"I'm Dr. Brody Connor, and we're here to rescue all of you and take you home."

"Doctor, are you for real? Are we really goin' home?" came an emotional voice from a woman that he couldn't see in the dark building.

"Can someone light a lantern or lamp so we can see?"

"Hold on, I can move close enough to light the lamp," said a female to his left.

In a few seconds, the shooting outside stopped, and the woman had the lamp lit where he could see ten other women who were all either tied with rope or had on leg shackles.

He wanted to throw up seeing those young women dirty, malnourished, and crying with joy for being rescued. He also felt a sense of joy and pride knowing his actions had saved these women from a life of who knows what.

"Where's the key to the shackles?" he asked.

"The guard has it."

Brody went outside and started searching the dead

men on the ground by the house where the women were. The third man he searched had the keys, and the doctor went back inside.

"Here's the key. Unlock and untie everyone, and if you want to clean up some, I'll keep everyone out until you're ready to come out."

"Thanks, Doctor. I'll let you know when we're ready."

Chapter Thirty-Four

KNEELING AND FACING THE BUNKHOUSE WERE eight men in various dress with guns pointed at them when Brody came outside. Three more men lay dead just outside the door to the bunkhouse, and he could see two more closer to the house, along with the man he shot by the wagon.

"Do we have anyone wounded?" Brody asked Manuel, who was one of the men guarding the prisoners.

"Not that I'm aware of. Did you find Miss Jennifer?"

"I didn't see her. I'm giving the women a little time to wash up and look more presentable before I ask them questions."

The Sharps barked again, and when Brody looked toward the tree where Dash stood, a corpse could be seen lying on the ground about halfway to the trees. Brody figured the man was trying to run away on foot.

"I'm going up to the house and see if Colonel Musgrove is still alive so I can get some answers."

"I don't think he was here. Shephard is up there with

his men, mopping up the place. I think everyone in the house was killed."

Brody walked to where the men were kneeling. "I'm looking for Jennifer Bernie. Where is she?"

The men looked at him and didn't say anything. Brody went to his horse, removed his doctor bag, and opened it up. His hand went inside the bag and came out with a surgeon's scalpel in his grasp.

"I'm a doctor skilled in extensive surgery applications where I can remove a man's ears, nose, or even his eyes. I'm going to start with this feller on the end, and if he doesn't answer my questions, I'm going to cut out his tongue or his eye or both."

The man at the end started getting up when the guard hit him in the back with his rifle stock. "You keep away from me with that blade. I don't know nothing."

The door to the house where the women were being kept, opened, and out came the woman that Brody had unchained. "He's a lying piece of hog crap. He's the foreman of these men, and he knows everything. They left here six days ago with Jennifer and five older women."

She walked up to the man and hit him on the mouth with a right and then went wild, hitting him with both fists until Brody finally grabbed her around the arms. She started crying, and he turned her around and let her cry on his shoulder.

"It's all right to cry and let out your anger. We'll be taking you home soon, but I have to know where Jennifer is first," said Brody, still holding the woman.

The woman settled down enough to say, "They're taking her to the gold mines in Colorado. She fought back so much that they wanted her gone."

Brody turned loose of the woman and brushed hair

from her eyes. "What's your name and where are you from?"

"I'm Regina Webb from south of Hillsboro. They were taking us to the ocean when the colonel returns."

Brody walked back to the man who was on his knees with his head down. "Two of you take hold of him." He turned back to Regina. "What's his name?"

"It's Titus, Titus March."

"Regina, what do you want me to cut off if he doesn't answer my questions?"

She looked at the man staring up at her. "Cut out both eyes and his tongue."

"Men, hold on tight, this is going to hurt him something awful." Brody grabbed the man by the hair and put the blade against the side of his left eye. "Where have they taken Jennifer Bernie?"

"I don't know."

Brody moved his hand so quick the man didn't even know he was cut until the blood started to drop off his face.

"The skin is cut, and extracting the eyeball is next. Where are they taking her?"

"To the gold mine in Summitville, Colorado. Please don't cut out my eye."

"What route are they taking and how many men and women are with them?"

"Mister, the colonel will kill me for telling you that."

"I'm going to cut you to pieces if you don't start talking." Brody made another slice with the knife, and this time the man yelled out.

"They are heading to Santa Fe and then northwest to Summitville. It's Colonel Musgrove and eight men escorting six women."

Brody wanted to cut the man's throat but refrained

from doing that. William Longtooth would have told him to kill them all but that wasn't who he was.

"Tie them up hand and foot so they can't escape and take them to the law in Waco. Have someone hook up the wagon so you can take the women back to town. I'm going to the house and see if I can find some provisions to take with me, and then I'm heading to Santa Fe."

Shephard shouted out some orders and came to Brody. "If they left six days ago, then they have a big head start on you, so I suggest you take a spare horse with you so you can swap out when yours gets worn out."

"That's probably a good idea. I'm wondering if they had a specific way they took?"

Shephard walked over to Titus. "What way does the colonel use to get to gold country?"

Titus spat at Shephard, who in turn pulled his gun and shot the man in the foot. "I asked you nicely that first time. Now, answer me or I'll shoot you in the knee next."

The sobbing man began to talk. "They go by Abilene and then by Lubbock and on to Albuquerque. They turn north at Albuquerque and follow the Rio Grande past Santa Fe and turn northwest to the mines."

Brody holstered his gun. "I'm going to the house to get some provisions, and I'd appreciate it if you would have someone saddle me a horse."

Regina came to Brody. "I need to tell you something. Jennifer is a wild one and tried to fight every chance she got. They marked up her face pretty bad this last time and broke her arm. No one is going to pay top dollar for a woman with scars and that's why he's taking her to the gold mines with the older women."

"What do you mean by marking up her face?"

"They broke her nose and busted up her lip. She had a nasty cut over her left eye when she left here. The colonel told the men if she gave them any more problems on the trip to the mine, they could have her to use anyway they wanted."

"Can you tell me about who the colonel has with him?"

"His right-hand man is Martin. You don't take him lightly. He's been known to kill some of the girls that don't mind him. Chico is a half Indian half Mexican who is the scout, and he's a killer with no compassion for anyone."

"I've played cards with Martin. Thanks, Regina and I hope you get home soon."

Brody started to the house and saw that Dash had walked up and was now talking to Titus. He didn't think nothing of it and continued to the house where he had to walk over bodies on his way to the kitchen, where he was able to pack bacon and cans of vegetables in a cloth sack. Hopefully, with two horses, he could make good time and eat his meals in towns along the way.

Dash came into the kitchen. "Doctor, your plan worked. I was told that your woman is gone and that you're heading after her. I'm here to tell you that I'm also going with you. I just found out that Porkchop is with that bunch of killers, and he's mine."

Brody smiled at his friend. "Fine by me. I'm taking a spare horse with me. I suggest you do the same."

"I also think we take a couple of blankets from here and make us bedrolls. We may have to spend some nights outside. Also, do you know how they're transporting the women?"

Brody finished putting a can of beans in the bag he found. "I didn't ask that question. All I know is that Martin is the foreman and has seven men with them."

Chapter Thirty-Five

BRODY AND DASH WALKED BACK TO WHERE THE men had finished hog-tying the raiders up. With the toe of his boot, Dash lashed out at Titus's side. "How are they transporting the women?"

"I ain't talking to you."

"My name is Dash. You may have heard of me. I'm a bounty hunter, and you don't realize it yet, but I don't have any compassion for you. Now, tell me what I want to know, or I'll take you apart a little at a time until you talk."

Brody could tell that the name of Dash got the man's attention by the way he began to sweat.

"They have them in a wagon. Chico is riding point and making sure the way is clear. The colonel ain't with them all the time. He rides into the towns to eat and sleep."

Brody stepped up. "Tell me about Martin?"

"He's the boss and meaner than a rattlesnake."

Dash had more questions. "Do they have a particular trail they use so they can bypass Abilene and Lubbock?"

"Yeah, the going is slow until they clear the Callahan Divide, then as they enter the high prairies around Lubbock, the pace is much faster. They use an old road that ain't traveled much anymore. You can't miss it if you head to the Dolan place where the wash flows into the canyon."

Dash looked at Brody. "Do you have any more questions?"

"No, let's mount up and head out. If we're lucky, we may find them before they leave Texas."

"Hold on," said Dash. "Something don't add up. Why would you have eight men escort six women who are tied up in the back of a wagon?" Dash pulled his pistol and walked back up to Titus, who was still in pain from getting shot in the foot.

"How many wagons did they take to Colorado?"

The man sitting next to Titus spoke. "They took three wagons. One for the women and two for the whiskey."

The mention of whiskey got Brody's attention. "So, you're saying they're taking two wagon loads of whiskey to the miners along with the women."

"Yeah, I've made the run twice, and it's like Titus said, they take the old road at the Dolan place, and it'll take them almost all the way to Santa Fe. They have friends along the way where they can get water and food."

"Where is this Dolan place?"

"It's six miles northwest of here, where the creek runs into the river. All you have to do is follow the river and you'll find it."

Dash holstered his gun and looked at Brody. "Let's get our horses and head on out. We may be able to overtake them in a day or so."

Shephard's men had two more horses saddled up

with lead ropes so the men could go at a fast pace. Brody knew it would be important to not work the horses too much and to swap out every few hours. With the extra horses saddled, it would only take seconds to swap.

They were covering a lot of ground when Dash slowed down. "I've been thinking about something. Why eight men? One is out front as a scout. That leaves seven men. It takes three to drive the wagons. That leaves four, and I'm thinking we should be aware of anyone we see on the trail. I wouldn't put it past them to have one or two men drop back to cover their back trail."

Brody noticed the sweat and red color covering his friend's face. "We'll worry about that when we see someone. Right now, I'm more concerned about that wound you have. We need to stop so I can take a look at it."

Dash tried to smile but finally said, "It's hurting me really bad, especially holding this lead rope. I don't know if I can make it all the way with you, Brody."

The doctor stopped his horse. "I want you to turn around and go see Dr. Wilks. If that wound gets infected out here, it could kill you, and I don't want that. I can do this on my own, and for you wanting to help, I'll kill Porkchop and bring his body back so you can collect the reward."

Dash dropped his head for a second. "Brody, I feel bad about you going up against those killers alone. I know I'm not at my best, but I'll go if you'll let me."

"Dash, I was taught how to fight by a great warrior. I've went up against men that were meaner than a cur wolf and I've faced off against gunfighters. I know how to get mean and that's what I'll do. You head on back so Dr. Wilks can take care of you, and I'll be just fine."

Dash handed the lead rope to his horse to the doctor. "You want to know something, Brody Connor. I think you'll do what you say, and I wouldn't want to be those men facing you. You take care and don't trust anyone along the road or in any of the towns you stop at. I wouldn't doubt that the colonel don't have supporters scattered along the trail, especially if he's furnishing them whiskey."

"I'll be careful." Brody stuck out his hand. "You head to Waco, and I'll see you in a week or so."

Brody picked up the pace and made the horses run until his horse was getting tired. Only stopping long enough to dismount and mount back up, he urged the horses to travel faster. After a while, he swapped for the third time.

He kept thinking about how much of a lead the wagons had on him. If they left six days ago and could travel fifteen to twenty miles a day, that meant they were little over a hundred miles ahead. He should have asked Titus how many horses were attached to each wagon. If there were only two, then fifteen to twenty miles was it, but if there were four horses to each wagon, they could get twenty-five miles a day.

At the rate he was going and using three horses, he may be able to catch them in a little over two days unless he was slowed down.

Up ahead looked like the river and the road he needed to take should be coming up soon. The banks of the river were covered with cottonwoods, elms, and willows, sucking up the moisture from the rich bottomland.

He crossed a creek that ran into the river, and as he came out of the trees, there was the old road he was going to travel. Walking his horse so he could see the tracks in the soft dirt, it was clear that wagons had used the road along with a lot of horses. Just as he was getting ready to head out faster, two men on horseback came from behind some brush and stopped in the doctor's path.

In that split second, he saw William's face and that image is what ignited him to pull his gun and start shooting. The men were bringing up their guns when the bullets began to hit them in the chest, causing them to tumble off the back of their mounts.

Brody rode on while reloading his pistol. William had always taught him to use surprise and shoot first.

By swapping out his horses when they were tired, he rode until after dark and was about to call it quits for the night when he saw lights up ahead. The lights meant hot food and maybe a soft bed and that was enough to make him continue on.

Chapter Thirty-Six

THE TOWN HAPPENED TO BE COMANCHE, AND although it wasn't much of a town, it did have a place to eat and a small hotel. Brody left all three horses at the only rundown livery in town with the instructions that he wanted his horses brushed and fed oats.

The hotel wasn't much, but he was able to rent a room and asked the clerk where he could get some food to eat.

"The best steak in town is down the street at the saloon. Ralph has a woman working for him that can really cook."

Brody put his key in his pocket. "Thanks, I'll try it out."

Not eating all day made his stomach think his throat had been cut. The so-called saloon only had five customers when the young man walked up to the counter. "Barkeep, I'll have a beer and a steak with whatever else you have."

"You won't be disappointed. I'll go tell my cook to get it started as soon as I get your beer."

Brody looked up and noticed the mirror on the wall behind the bar. It was a little odd that this little saloon had a bar mirror. The image he saw wasn't his but William's, looking back at him. He blinked, and the old Indian's face was replaced by his.

Brody turned around to look the room over and saw a man with a tied-down gun start walking toward him.

"You passing through, or do you have business here?" he asked.

Brody remembered William's face in the mirror, and he dropped down, lashed out with his leg, and swept the man's legs out from under him. As soon as the man landed on his back, Brody jumped on him and grabbed the man by his throat with his left hand while pressing his gun barrel against the man's temple.

"Mister, I'm looking for three wagons that came through here a few days ago. I reckon that you work for the colonel or you wouldn't be asking me questions. So, how long ago did the wagons come through?"

"I can't talk."

Brody squeezed a little tighter. "Sure you can. Now get to talking or you'll never talk again."

"Three days ago. They dropped off whiskey and that's all I know."

Brody knew that he should kill the man but removed his hand from his throat. "I think it's time for you to leave so I can enjoy my meal."

Brody stood up and backed up against the bar before he holstered his gun, watching the man get up, rubbing his throat. The man bent down and retrieved his hat then looked at Brody still watching.

"Me and you'll meet again, mister."

Brody nodded and knew he would have to watch his back when he left the saloon. But that didn't detour him from enjoying the steak and potatoes the cook fixed for him. When the meal was finished and the tab paid, he went to the door and stuck his head out to see if the man he assaulted was waiting on him.

The hotel was on the same side of the street as the saloon, but his training by William continued to kick in. He crossed the street and walked back toward the hotel in case the man was waiting between two buildings.

Brody walked into the hotel lobby ready for a gun battle, but the only person he saw was the clerk, who was busy. It was late, and most likely, no more guests would check in tonight, so the young doctor took his things down the hall to a different room he was assigned and opened the door.

It so happened that the same skeleton key worked on all the doors, and after going back to the room he was assigned, he fixed the bed by placing the pillows under the cover so it would look like he was in bed. He locked the door from the outside and went to the vacant room he would use for the night.

In the middle of the night, the Great Spirit showed him through haze and clouds. Twin plateaus rising up from the ground, miles in front of the rider, in the mid-morning heat of day. The road he was on could be seen skirting its way around and through trees, boulders, and brush. The dust ascending up toward the clouds was coming from three wagons being pulled by running horses.

The sound of wood breaking disturbed the sleeping doctor and made him rise up in bed with a gun in his hand. The deafening sound of gunshots caused him to rush to the door and ease it open to see the man he assaulted from the saloon back out of the room he had been assigned.

"Wrong room!" The man spun around to be hit in the chest by a bullet from the young doctor's gun. The man dropped his gun and grabbed his chest before sinking to the floor with his eyes wide open in death.

Brody slipped back into his room and pulled on his boots, reloaded his gun, and went back out into the hall as the clerk came running down the hallway in a sleeping gown.

"What happened here?"

"I had a visitor, and he busted your door and shot up your bed. I suggest you go after the law and have his corpse removed off your floor," said Brody, and went back into the room and laid back down fully dressed.

When the young warrior walked out of the room where he slept, the man's body was gone, and most of the blood had been cleaned off the floor. Down in the lobby, the clerk looked up.

"Dr. Brody, you owe me for a door and bedding."

"I don't owe you for anything. The dead man did all that damage. Get your money from him or take his horse and sell it. It ain't my concern, and you should secure your hotel better."

Brody went to the livery. "Morning, can you get my horses saddled while I find some food for breakfast?"

"I'll have them ready, and for your information, the saloon is serving breakfast."

"Good, if it's anywhere as good as my supper, I'll be pleased."

"She makes some mighty good biscuits and gravy."

"Thanks, I may give it a try."

Brody didn't think anyone was friendly in the saloon that morning. But that was fine with him. He wanted to eat and get out of the little town before he had to kill anyone else. As he ate, the vision of the dream he had last night came to mind. This wasn't the first dream where he was shown exactly where something was going to happen. All he needed to do now was pay attention to his surroundings as he hunted for the wagons.

Walking back to the livery with the safeties off both his guns, was a sense of security and not seeing his horses tied outside caused him more alarm. Was someone waiting on him inside, watching him through the cracks in the boards? Brody walked to the door, and instead of going inside, he went to one side and peered around the doorpost to see the hostler throwing the saddle on the last horse.

Brody didn't go in, but instead, he leaned his back to the barn and waited until the man walked his horses outside.

With all three horses out of the barn, Brody decided that he had gained enough on the wagons that he could leave one horse.

"Say, how much will you give me for one of my horses and saddle?"

The hostler looked at the two animals. "I reckon I could pay sixty. I ain't got much money right now."

"I'll take fifty and we'll call it even for boarding my animals last night."

"I'll go get your money," said the man, and hurried off.

He paid for the horse and took off after the wagons.

Chapter Thirty-Seven

BRODY CHANGED MOUNTS AFTER TWO HOURS OF hard riding at a small wash where the horses could get a drink. He was hoping for sixty miles today and that should be doable without wearing his horses out too much.

Shortly after noon, he crossed Turkey Creek and rode into Cross Plains, where he stopped at a café to eat dinner. No one talked to him at the café or questioned why he was there. The time he took eating gave him and his horses time to rest before they had to continue on.

After leaving the town, he once again found the old road, and the wagon tracks could easily be seen. The afternoon heat was having an effect on the horses, and he had to keep stopping for water and swapping mounts.

By dusk, both horses, along with himself, were given out and ready to stop for the day. At the first freshwater, they would make camp and get an early start tomorrow. The green leaves on the trees could be seen from a half mile away, and the smoke of burning wood was in the air.

Brody slowed his horses and made sure his pistols were ready when he could see two men camped inside the trees close to Pecan Bayou.

"Hello in the camp. Can I ride in?"

"Come on in with your hands clear."

Both men stood up, and Brody saw the Ranger badges on the front of their shirts as he came in.

"I'm Dr. Brody Connor. Myself and some men from Waco found the men that's been raiding ranches and stealing their women. I'm on the trail of some of those men who are taking six women to the gold mine in Colorado, where they will sell them to the miners. They have three wagons and a lot of rotgut whiskey with them."

"Climb on down, Brody. I'm Ranger Utah Smith, and my partner is Ranger Carl Wright. We've got plenty of venison for supper if you want to join us while you tell us everything you know about the men you're after."

The next hour was spent updating the Rangers on what they discovered when they rescued the women prisoners. The Rangers weren't surprised when Brody told them that the ranch was owned by Colonel Musgrove, in fact, they had some information on his criminal activities, including selling whiskey and rifles to the Indians.

Brody leaned back on an elbow. "I can't be more than a day's ride behind those wagons. This heat will affect their horses the same as it did mine, and I'm sure they have to rest them at night."

Ranger Utah took a drink of coffee. "I'm thinking since they have traveled this route before and know every twist and turn, that they're traveling at night while it's not so hot. They can rest during the afternoon heat and that will give them time to water and graze the horses."

Brody sat up. "That may be the way they are doing it

so those horses don't get so worn out. Are you suggesting that I do the same?"

"No. I'm saying we get some rest and the three of us leave out of here about two or three in the morning. It looks like we're going to have a full moon, so we'll ride when it's cooler, also. Tomorrow we should catch up with them someplace close to Abilene."

"So the two of you are going to help me?"

"That's right, unless you don't want our help."

Brody smiled. "I welcome your help. There is a crook by the name of Porkchop that shot a friend of mine. I promised to bring him in during the rescue."

"Is your friend a bounty man?"

"Yeah, his name is Dash, and he was a big help in rescuing the women at the ranch. I sent him back to the doctor I work for and promised to take down Porkchop."

Utah poured out his coffee. "If Porkchop gets killed by any of us, you can have the reward money for Dash. I happen to know Dash, and he's one of the good ones."

"I think a lot of him also," said Brody. "I'm about ready to call it a night and get some sleep."

The men spread out their bedrolls and went to sleep. Brody's dream had him riding down the road that went in between the two plateaus. He could see trees up ahead where three wagons were parked in the shade.

Something hit the bottom of his boot and his hand came up with the pistol in it. Ranger Utah said, "It's time to ride."

Brody saddled up his horses, and the three men took off, letting the horses set the pace they were comfortable with. The moon furnished them with an abundance of light, and their eyes adjusted where they could see as they rode across the prairie.

There were very few trees but lots of brush, a few

mesquite trees, and lots of Russian thistles that turn into tumbleweeds. By the time the sun was coming up, Utah pointed to the north. "Lubbock is that way in about five miles."

The sun was up when Carl pointed to wagon tracks leaving the road. By following the tracks, they found where wagons had parked by a freshwater spring in the shade of some big cottonwoods.

Utah went to their campfire and used a stick to disturb the coals and then put his hand on the coals. "It's still warm, so I think we're close behind them."

Brody looked west. "Is there two plateaus up ahead where the road goes in between them?"

"I don't know," said Utah.

Carl chimed in, "Yeah, there are. The plateaus ain't very tall, but there's water on the west end and a few large trees."

"That's where we'll find them holed up until it cools off."

Carl thought for a second. "It's going to be hard to go after them there. We won't have any cover and can be picked off before we ever get to the wagons."

Brody didn't like what he was hearing. "What if we circle around them and get ahead so we can hit them when they're back on the road?"

Utah took a swallow from his canteen. "I vote for Brody's idea. We can pick where we want to hit them, and the outcome will be much better."

Brody pointed to Carl. "You take the point and we circle around when you say so."

"How do you know that's where they'll stop?"

"I saw it in a dream. I spent a lot of time with an old Indian healer a few years back, and he taught me many things. He taught me about the Great Spirit and how to heal with natural plants, but the thing he taught me the most was how to fight and kill in battle. So, I had a dream where they would be."

Utah was shaking his head. "Let's hope you're right. Come on, we need to ride so we can get into position before they leave out."

Carl took off with Brody and Utah back about one hundred feet. They didn't want to eat Carl's dust on a hot morning. The plateaus were coming into view when Carl raised his hand into the air.

"We need to slow down so if anyone is watching they won't see our dust."

Brody spoke up. "There's a man that goes by Chico as their scout. He may or may not be with them."

"We know who Chico is and I'm not liking it that he's with them. He knows how to hide and blend in with the environment. We have warrants on him for murder, so don't take a chance with that one."

Carl turned south, and they started the long ride to circle around so they could get ahead of the wagons and catch the men in an ambush.

Chapter Thirty-Eight

THE DETOUR TOOK THEM MUCH LONGER THAN they thought, and it was already afternoon before they came back out onto the road. A half mile west of where the three men entered the road were some large boulders, and that's where they rode toward.

Inside the center of the boulders was an area where the horses could be hidden and safe from bullets. Carl and Utah found secure locations where they could use their rifles, but Brody hung back. He didn't feel comfortable hiding among the boulders, so he went to his horse. He wanted to be in the saddle when the fighting started. William had taught him how to fight on the back of a horse, and this was the time to use his skills.

Dusk soon approached and that's when Brody saw a lone rider coming toward them. The man was shirtless with beads hanging from his brown neck. Brody knew it was Chico without being introduced. He urged his horse out from the boulders and sat in the road waiting on the scout.

The scout reached down and touched his holster, and

the doctor knew the man had prepared it for battle. With the reins laid over his horse's neck, Brody readied himself to meet Chico.

The scout was within seventy feet when he put his heels to his horse and pulled his pistol, coming toward Brody. Brody did likewise and spurred his horse forward while pulling his gun. The difference was Brody grabbed the saddle horn with his left hand and leaned over so low that he shot Chico from under his horse's neck. Two shots were all he got off until the horses passed by each other. Brody sat back up in the saddle and wheeled his horse around and rode where Chico was still in the saddle with blood dripping out of the holes in his chest.

The outlaw scout's gun was on the ground, and he looked up at Brody and said, "You fight like Indian." Then he tumbled to the ground dead.

Carl and Utah ran out and checked to see if the scout was dead. "That was some shooting you did. You performed that little move with precision. I'm wondering what else you have to show us."

Utah pointed to Chico. "Let's get him out of the road and get ready for company. I'm sure they heard the shots and may send a couple of men to investigate."

Brody helped drag the corpse of Chico behind the rocks and then went to his horse. "I fight better on the back of my horse, so I'm going to those boulders we passed by and find me a place to rest. When the wagons come by, I'll hit them from the rear while you two hit them from the front."

"That sounds good to us." Utah started walking back to his hiding location while Carl pointed east. "If they send anyone to see what the shots were, they may not ride the road."

"I'll watch my back trail. Let's hope they get here

before dark," said Brody, and rode east fifty yards and found where a boulder cast a shade he could sit in. His horse found a small patch of grass to graze on, and now it was time to wait.

THE SUN HADN'T COMPLETELY GONE DOWN when Brody heard the wagons coming down the road. He stayed hidden until the third wagon went by and then he mounted up and rode around the boulder and onto the road. No one looked back, and he was able to get in closer before Utah and Carl opened fire on the two riders in front of the wagon.

Brody spurred his horse and was coming in on the two rear riders when he began to shoot and saw both men fall from their horses. He leaned over the neck of his horse and was coming up beside the last wagon when he shot the driver, and he slumped to the side and fell off the wagon.

He could hear more shooting, and as he came up to the second wagon, he saw that the driver was dead and the horses wanted to run. By getting beside one of the lead horses, he grabbed hold of the bit and made the animal stop. Turning back to the wagon, he rushed to set the brake before making his horse run after the lead wagon, which was heading down the road by the scared team.

As he got even with the wagon bed, he saw Jennifer sitting there with the biggest smile he had ever seen. He blew her a kiss and took off to the lead horses so he could get the team settled down.

It took a few hundred yards before he got the team settled down enough for the wagon to come to a dead stop. After setting the brake, he walked to the back of the wagon. "Hello, ladies."

"Brody Connor, what took you so long? Get these ropes off me."

He hopped into the back of the wagon and untied her hands and feet. He then went to the other women, freeing them. When he finished, he went back to Jennifer and extended his hand so she could stand up.

As soon as she was on her feet, he put his arms around her and kissed the woman of his life on the lips. He felt her wince in pain as his lips touched hers and knew it was from the cut on her lip.

"I'm sorry, I forgot about your lip."

"Brody Connor, you're my hero and can kiss me anytime you want. I'm so darn glad to see you." And then she kissed him.

The rest of the women were up and coming to thank him and some even kissed his cheek. He hopped off the wagon and helped the women down, and it wasn't long until Utah and Carl rode up.

When they dismounted and came with their canteen, Brody put his arm around Jennifer. "Gentlemen, this is the reason I came out here, ain't she the most beautiful woman you ever seen?"

Jennifer hit him on the shoulder. "You stop that. You know that I'm cut, bruised, and filthy."

Brody looked at her and put his hand on her cheek. "I don't see the bruises or the dirt. I see the beautiful woman that I'm in love with."

She started to cry and put her arms around his neck. "I love you too."

Utah came over. "I hate to break up the reunion but it seems that we're short a couple men. I don't see Martin, or the colonel anywhere."

Jennifer took hold of Brody's hand. "Martin went to Abilene, and I have no idea where Colonel Musgrove went. We've only seen the colonel once since we left the ranch."

Brody pointed back to the dead men. "Which one is Porkchop?"

"He ain't here either," said Jennifer. "The colonel rode off with Porkchop and Twisted Nose back at Comanche a few days ago."

Brody took a deep breath. "Utah, I would appreciate it if you and Carl would get the women back to Waco. I can't go back until I find Martin, the colonel, and Porkchop. If they leave Texas, you and Carl can't go after them, but I can."

"Brody, are you sure you're up to going against those men?"

It was Jennifer to answer this time. "He's more than adequate to go up against those men. I've seen my man in action, and he's hell on wheels when he gets riled up."

Utah started laughing. "I totally agree with you. In fact, I'd like to deputize you, Doctor."

"No thanks, I may have to do things my way, and the badge could get in the way."

He again brought Jennifer up against him. "Do you want to go with me?"

She kissed him on the lips. "You know I do. Get me a gun and holster off one of those dead men."

"Brody, this is not a good idea," said Utah.

"Utah, she can handle a gun as good as any man. I don't want to lose her again, so she's going with me."

Chapter Thirty-Nine

NONE OF THE DEAD MEN'S HOLSTERS WOULD FIT Jennifer since she had lost so much weight. She hung it off her saddle horn with the pistol handy. As they were riding away, she asked, "Brody, did you graduate from doctor school?"

"Yes, I graduated at the top of my class and had some very good job offers. I knew I had to find out why you stopped writing me, so I loaded up and headed to Central Texas. Everywhere I inquired, no one could tell me anything that would lead me to you. I went to work for Dr. Wilks and met a bounty hunter that helped me out. Your ranch hands and I found the place where the other women were being held. I had a lot of help, and we stormed the ranch and rescued all the other ladies. That's how I knew where to find you."

"You don't know how many times I prayed for you to come get me."

"I knew where you were before we found you. I seem to have a gift from the Great Spirit, and he showed me in a dream where the wagons were camped on the road between the two plateaus."

"Are you serious? Have you ever had dreams like that before?"

"Yes, I have. When I left to come here, I stopped by William Longtooth's house and he hadn't been there in a long time. I went looking for him, and I saw in a dream where he was. I didn't realize it at the time but now I know when I see visions."

"Maybe you'll have a dream telling us where we can find Martin and the colonel."

"It could happen. I have a question. On the morning of the raid, who came to the house on the chestnut with a star on its forehead?"

"I don't know his name other than they call him Blade. The morning he came to the house was the first time I had ever seen him. He claimed to have a ranch east of us. I saw him a lot on the colonel's ranch, and he always stayed in the big house with the colonel."

"That makes me think that he's a relative or a partner. Do you know where he's at now?"

"No, I ain't seen him for a few days before we left. I think he has something to do with money."

"What do you mean by that?"

"I overheard him and the colonel talking one day, and he was saying something about investing in railroads."

"Look, Abilene is up ahead. How about I rent us rooms and then we can go to the gun store and buy you a holster."

"Let's get rooms and then you buy me a holster and new clothes. I feel so dirty and ugly, and I need a bath in the worst way."

"That sounds like a plan."

They chose the second hotel since it was newer and

most likely had modern plumbing. When Brody checked in, he found out that the bathtub was inside the room. He smiled at his plan as he walked back out and they walked their horses to the gun shop.

Jennifer walked in. "Mister, I need a holster and belt that will fit me. I have my own gun, but I'll need enough bullets to fill in the loops plus an extra box."

"Yes, ma'am, follow me." The man handed her three holsters until she chose the third one. After filling all the bullet loops and taking the extra box outside, she said, "Let's take the horses to the livery and then I'll go buy some new clothes."

Brody didn't see anyone when he stuck his head inside the livery barn. "Hello, anyone in here?" With no answer, he began to walk to the back of the barn and suddenly stopped in front of a stall. Inside the stall was a beautiful chestnut with a star on his forehead. Moving closer, he looked at thc horse's legs and sure enough, it had two white stockings.

The hostler came in through the back door. "Howdy, sorry I had to do my business out back. What can I do for you, mister?"

"I need my horses taken care of for the night. Who rides this chestnut?"

"That's Blade Musgrove's horse. Ain't he a beauty?"

"Yes, he is. Do you know where I might find Mr. Musgrove?"

"He's probably at his saloon down the street. It's the Cattleman's Saloon."

"Thanks, I may go by and meet him later tonight."

Jennifer had a stern look on her face as they started across the street to the clothing storc. "I'm going with you to the saloon."

"Of course, dear, but we have things to do first that's more important."

She was able to buy two changes of clothing, along with new boots and a hat, before they headed back toward the hotel with the packages. As they were passing the Baptist Church, Brody saw a man and woman walking into the building. The man was dressed nice and had a Bible in his hand.

"Excuse me," he called out. "Are you the preacher?"

The man turned. "Why, yes I am. How may I help you?"

"Would you marry us right now?"

Poor Jennifer almost choked on her tongue, and he had to hold her up. "Brody, are you sure about this?"

"I've loved you from the first time I saw you, and you're the only one I want to spend the rest of my life with. Jennifer Bernie, will you marry me?" He went down on one knee and looked up at the woman of his dreams.

"Get up. You know that I will. I've also loved you after that first meeting. Let's go get married."

THE PREACHER PERFORMED the simple ceremony where Brody and Jennifer spoke of their love for each other. After they completed their wedding vows, the two newlyweds headed to the hotel. She looked back at the Cattleman's Saloon. "I think visiting the saloon will have to wait until tomorrow."

"Maybe, pick up the pace. We need to get to the hotel."

That was short-lived when Jennifer squeezed Brody's

hand. "That man up the street is the one they call Porkchop."

Brody took a deep breath, and he felt his blood turn cold as he looked at the heavy-set man with a full beard wearing farmer overalls.

"Darling, what're you going to do?"

"I'm going to confront the killer and put a stop to his criminal life once and for all. When we get closer, move over a few feet and be ready to join the fight if he has a partner."

"I'm joining the fight whether he has a partner or not. I plan on killing every one of those murdering scum that killed my daddy and friends."

"Go ahead and draw your gun and hold it on your hip. I don't want you practicing your fast draw just yet."

While biting his bottom lip, he kept his eyes on the man walking toward them, and when the vile outlaw was within twenty feet, Brody stopped. "Porkchop, go for your gun."

The big outlaw was shaken for a second and then he was pulling his gun as two shots filled the evening quietness. Brody and Jennifer had both fired, and the large man was looking at them with blood seeping out of two holes in his chest. He tried to raise the gun, but Brody walked up to the man and pulled the gun out of his hand.

Jennifer walked up to Porkchop and kicked him in the crotch so hard that he bent over and tried to puke, but all it did was finish him off, and he fell forward on his face dead.

The couple heard boots pounding on the boardwalk and turned to see two lawmen coming their way.

"I'm Dr. Brody Connor, and that's a wanted outlaw by the name of Porkchop. You should have a paper on him in your office. I'll come by tomorrow to pick up the reward. If you need us for anything, we'll be at the hotel."

Jennifer took hold of her husband's hand and said, "We need to get off the street and go to our room for a hot bath."

Brody wanted to tease her. "What about our supper?"

She smiled at the man she loved. "Pay the hotel clerk to have us supper delivered."

Chapter Forty

BRODY WOKE UP, AND THE SUN WAS ALREADY showing around the edges of the curtains covering the windows. He hadn't slept this late in a long time, and as he threw the covers back, he saw his wife in all her beauty. He was a lucky man to have such a beautiful, hardworking, intelligent, funny woman as his wife.

The grateful husband sat on the side of the bed and was putting on his britches when he felt a warm hand rubbing his back.

He turned to Jennifer and they kissed. "Are you going to stay in bed all day?"

She threw back the cover. "No, I'm hungry as a caged bear since you didn't have our supper delivered to the room last night. Let's get dressed and have steak and eggs for breakfast."

Brody finished dressing and was combing his hair while standing in front of the mirror, looking at his reflection. "I may go by the barbershop to get a haircut and a shave."

Jennifer was buttoning up her shirt. "That's a grand

idea. I haven't had my hair cut in over six months. Maybe there's a woman's hair place I can go to."

Brody looked at his wife. "Darling, you're the prettiest woman I've ever laid eyes on, and with those new clothes you're wearing, I'm keeping the safety off my gun so I can shoot the men away."

She smiled at her silly husband. "Of course you will. You're a jealous warrior."

Brody reached out and took her by the hand. "Come on, let's get going so we can get finished before dark." The bath and clean clothing had done wonders for Jennifer from what she looked like riding in the back of the wagon.

They had breakfast at one of the cafés and Jennifer asked the waitress, "Is there someplace in town where I can get my hair cut?"

"Yes, ma'am, right down the street at a place called Linda's. Ms. Linda has fancy dresses, makeup, and a lady that cuts women's hair."

Brody reached into his pocket, pulled out a roll of greenbacks, and handed his wife a few of the bills. "Here, buy whatever you want. While you're at the lady's shop, I'll get a haircut and a shave. I may even get some information about Blade."

They parted ways outside the café, but Brody watched her until she entered the dress shop. He, in turn, went to the barbershop where he was able to get in one of the two chairs. Not many places had two barbers in the same shop.

"I'd like a shave and a haircut."

"Would you like some of our tonic? It's only a dime."

"Does it smell good?"

"Oh, yes, sir. It's got lilac in it."

"Well then, put some on when you're finished."

The barber went to work on the hair first. "Are you new in town or passing through?"

"I haven't decided just yet. I'm interested in playing cards at the Cattlemen's Saloon, but I've been told that the owner may have a stacked game."

"I wouldn't know about that. Mr. Musgrove seems to be a straight shooter, and he is hardly there anyway. Some say he stays out at his place most of the time, taking care of his ranch, but I can't confirm that."

"That's fine. That name brings back a memory of me meeting a man with the same last name. If I remember correctly, his name was Colonel Musgrove. I wonder if they're kin or know each other?"

"The older Musgrove is his pa. He was in here for a trim a few days ago. I reckon that he's at the Two Creek Ranch, also."

Brody didn't want to press for answers, so he changed the subject to herds coming through heading north. Some more customers came, and he stopped talking and let the barber finish shaving off his facial whiskers.

Walking across the street and looking inside Linda's store revealed Jennifer in a barber chair with wet hair. He figured she would be there long enough for a visit to the livery stable.

"Good morning," said Brody when he walked into the barn.

The hostler looked up from raking the floor. "Morning, do you need your horses?"

"No, not yet. I may a little later. Do you know Blade Musgrove?"

"No, and I don't want to. He's left his horse here a few times, but he usually keeps it tied up at the saloon."

"What kind of man is he?"

The hostler looked around before he spoke, "Mister, I

would rather not answer any questions about that man. It could get me hurt or killed."

"I understand," said Brody. "I do have one more question if you would be so kind as to answer. Where's the Two Creek Ranch located?"

It's north of town between Elm and Clear Creek."

Brody handed the man a couple of greenbacks. "Thanks, I'll keep this between us."

Jennifer should be getting close to being finished, so he walked back across the street and sat down on the porch, watching people. There wasn't much to the town, and the cattle drives supported most of the businesses.

Colonel Musgrove was at the barbershop a few days ago. But was he at his son's ranch or had he gone someplace else? Thinking back to his training, he knew that the colonel had to die for the evil he had done. The only problem was locating the former Confederate officer.

Why would anyone who owned a large ranch with cattle want to raid and plunder? Let alone kidnap women so he could sale them into slavery and prostitution. Greed, power, and pride have been the downfall of many men over the years. They never have enough with an attitude that they can take what they desire.

That was also the kind of man Mama's dead husband was. He thought he could beat his wife and her son the way he ran roughshod over the men who came to his tavern. It's been over three years since he killed the man for beating his mama, and he still didn't have any ill feelings about the death of Ludwig Muller.

The door opened behind him, and when he turned around, there stood his wife looking so beautiful. Not only had she got her hair cut, but the woman in the shop had applied makeup, which consisted of powder and rouge, on her face to cover up most of the bruises and scars.

"What do you think of my new look?"

"Jennifer, you look so beautiful. I love the hair and makeup."

"Thank you, darling. You look really handsome yourself."

"Let's walk to the marshal's office and see if I can collect the reward for killing Porkchop. I promised my friend Dash that I would collect it and give the money to him for helping me."

"Sure, did you find out any more about the men we're after?"

"Yeah, Blade owns a ranch north of town, and the colonel may be there also."

The city marshal was in the office when they came in.

"Hello Marshal, do you have the reward money on Porkchop?"

"I do, I got it from the judge this morning." He went to the desk drawer and pulled out the money. "Here it is. It's sixty dollars. You can count it if you want."

Brody counted the money and put it in his pocket. "Thanks, Marshal, we'll be on our way now."

"Good, I'm not fond of bounty hunters in town."

Jennifer pointed her finger at the marshal, but Brody took her by the arm and pulled her along with him through the door. "I don't trust these small-time lawmen, and he doesn't need to know any more about us or what we plan to do."

Chapter Forty-One

Jennifer stopped walking when they were in the street. "I'm thinking we ride out to Blade's ranch and see if the colonel is there with him."

"I'm not sure that's a good idea. I don't know how many men he has or if we can even get close enough to see anything."

"I bet the hardware store has one of those telescopes we can buy so we can see a long ways," said Jennifer, and started off to the store.

Brody caught up with her. "You realize that it may be dangerous to go out there, don't you?"

"No, darling, it's not dangerous. I have you going with me to kill whoever tries to harm us."

Brody laughed and shook his head. "Although they had just gotten married, he knew better than to argue with her. A spyglass would come in handy so they could watch the ranch from afar."

The clerk in the store was more than helpful and showed them three different telescopes. While Jennifer was looking through them and talking to the clerk, Brody saw a Sharps .50 caliber behind the counter. He remembered how Dash had killed at least three of the men at the ranch when they rescued the women.

Brody had never shot one of the large, heavy rifles but knew that he could.

"Sir, could I see that Sharps you have behind the counter?" asked Brody.

"Yes, sir. Let me go get it. We purchased it used from a man that was going to use it to kill buffalos, but his wife changed his mind. As you will see, it's been shot a few times, and I'll have to have forty-one dollars for it."

The man handed the rifle to Brody, who opened the breach and then looked down the barrel. It was the heaviest rifle he had ever handled, but it felt good when he put it to his shoulder. He raised the back sight and adjusted it while looking at the notches along the metal on each side of the sight opening.

"I'll give you forty-one dollars for the rifle and three boxes of bullets."

"Forty-two and it's yours," said the clerk.

Jennifer laid the looking glass she wanted on the counter. "Darling, what do you plan on shooting with that cannon?"

He smiled and handed it to his wife. "I'm going to shoot some varmints."

She picked out an apple from a barrel and laid it on the counter beside the spy glass and went outside. Brody paid the man and carried his rifle with him outside where Jennifer was standing. He handed her the apple and she took a bite.

"Let's go get the horses and go somewhere so I can practice shooting this gun at different distances."

"Brody, are you thinking about shooting Blade from way off?"

"No. I'm taking it with us in case his men see us and ride out to kill us. I can pick a few of them off before they get into range and return fire. You know that I would never shoot a man in cold blood."

"I know you wouldn't, but I might if I had to. Especially if it's the colonel or Martin."

They walked to the livery stable. "Howdy, can you get our horses saddled, and I'd like to know how to get to the Two Creek Ranch."

"I don't know nothing about that ranch."

"Okay, thanks anyway."

Brody took Jennifer by the arm. "Come on, dear, let's go across the street for something."

The newlyweds walked to the gun shop, where Brody bought a used scabbard to carry the rifle in, and the man in the shop gave them directions to the Two Creek Ranch.

By the time they returned to the livery, the hostler was finishing up. He stopped what he was doing and looked out the door to make sure no one was watching. "Brody, if you go to the Two Creek Ranch, be watching for his men. It's been said that some of them watch who comes there. Blade has a Mexican woman who lives on the north edge of town in a little white house. You may want to ride by there to see if his horse is tied out front, and don't tell anyone what I told you."

"Thanks, we'll do that, and my lips are sealed."

EVENTUALLY, they did find the house where the Mexican woman lived, but the chestnut wasn't tied out front. Two miles from Abilene, Brody set up targets at different ranges and started sighting in the big rifle. He went through an entire box of bullets before he was satisfied with his marksmanship.

"I feel good shooting this buffalo gun and I think I can hit what I aim at. I've seen what one of these guns can do when the big slug hits a man's body."

"Are you ready to go on to the Two Creek Ranch now?" asked Jennifer.

"Of course, dear."

The two rode for four more miles when Brody pulled up. "Let's ride to the creek and follow it so we can stay hidden in the trees."

They were able to ride the creek bank until they could see the tops of the buildings. Brody was ready to get closer when Jennifer reached out and touched his arm. She pointed across the prairie where she could see a horse tied in a clump of trees with green leaves.

Brody pulled out the looking glass and was surveying the area when he saw the man sitting on the ground with his back to a tree, sound asleep.

Jennifer took a look. "What do you want to do with him?"

"I don't know. We can't go any farther with him out here, so I'm thinking I'll ride back the way we came and try to get in as close as I can. You ride up on him, and when you have his attention, that's when I take him down."

Jennifer shook her head. "Honey, I know you mean well, but that's the lamest plan I've ever heard. We ride over to him and take him down."

"You can't be serious."

"Yes, I am. We have to be the aggressor and take the fight to him."

Brody made a face. He knew she was right, and that's the same thing William had always said—*be* the aggressor.

"Okay, let's go."

They rode within twenty feet of the man before he woke up with two guns pointed at him.

"Well, crap," said the man, looking back toward the ranch headquarters. "What do you want?"

"Unbuckle that gun belt and let it drop off, then lie on your stomach."

"Mister, if you shoot me, five or six men will be here in a jiffy to kill you."

Brody dismounted. "That's what I'm hoping for. The truth is, you'll already be dead by the time they get here."

The man did as he was told and laid on his stomach while Jennifer dismounted.

"Here, use this rope to tie him up." Jennifer threw him a length of rope that she removed from the man's saddle.

Brody tied the man's hands and legs so he couldn't move. Not wanting him to holler out, Brody stuffed the man's handkerchief in his mouth.

The couple mounted back up. "He's already told us that there are five or six men at the house, so let's see if we can find a good location to watch the house, barn, and bunkhouse."

"Fine by me. Let's ride."

Jennifer was the first one to see the top of the barn and slowed them down. "Let's walk the horses so they don't stir up dust."

"We should go over to the creek and use the trees so we can get closer," said Brody, pointing to his left.

They were weaving around trees and following the stream until they had a good view of the house and all the buildings. Leaving the horses tied along the creek bank, Jennifer led the way, carrying the looking glass, and Brody came behind her carrying the Sharps.

Chapter Forty-Two

STANDING BEHIND A LARGE TREE UNOBSERVED, Jennifer took her time watching the ranch yard and buildings through the looking glass while whispering what she was seeing to Brody. Suddenly, she gasped. "Brody, are you seeing this?"

A half-naked girl ran from the house and was headed toward the road when a man came running after her. Then another man came out of the house with a rifle and just stood watching.

Jennifer whispered, "That man on the porch is Blade, and I bet that poor girl is one they kidnapped from one of the ranches. Brody, we have to do something to save that girl."

"I agree. What do you want to do?"

"Shoot Blade with the Sharps. You kill him, and the rest will run away."

"Dear, you know that I'm not one to shoot a man in cold blood."

The man was catching up to the girl when she stopped, and the man running after her caught up and threw the poor girl over his shoulder. Then a man on a horse came running his mount down the road toward the house and stopped in front of the porch. He stayed in the saddle while talking to Blade as the man carrying the girl stepped onto the porch. Blade grabbed the girl by the hair and tilted her head up. He lashed out with an open hand and slapped her across the face twice while saying something to her.

The man carried her on into the house, and Blade continued to talk to the man on the horse. The man carrying the girl came outside, and Blade said something to him, and the man ran toward the bunkhouse.

A few seconds after he rushed into the bunkhouse, five armed men came outside and went to the corral, catching horses and getting them ready to ride.

Blade had gone inside his house while Brody and Jennifer stayed put watching the activity at the barn. In a few minutes, Blade came outside and seemed in a hurry as he walked to the corral and mounted up on the chestnut.

"What do you think this is about?" asked Jennifer.

"I think Blade just got news about the wagons getting hit. Let's stay here, and as soon as they're far enough away, we'll ride in and rescue that girl."

"I like that idea."

Blade led the way as all the men rode out of the ranch yard, raising up a dust cloud as they galloped toward the road. Brody had to keep Jennifer behind the tree until he couldn't see any of the riders.

Brody started to his horse. "Let's ride in and see if we can free that young woman."

With the Sharps laid across the saddle, they rode into the yard and up to the front porch.

"Jennifer, put your gun in your hand and go inside.

I'm going to stay here in case there's still someone in the bunkhouse. Don't mess around, free the girl, and let's get going."

Jennifer dismounted and was on the porch when an older man came out of the bunkhouse with a repeating rifle and commenced to fire. Brody raised the Sharps, took a deep breath, took aim, removed the slack from the trigger, and squeezed. The big gun bucked in his hand, and smoke came from the end of the barrel, and the big slug hit the man he was shooting with such force that he was slammed against the wall.

Brody ejected the spent hull and put another bullet in the chamber. Nothing else happened, but he knew that Blade and his men heard the roar of the Sharps and would be coming back to see what was happening.

The wait was short and out came Jennifer with a girl who couldn't be a day over fourteen. Her face was bruised and bloodied from the beating Brody and Jennifer had witnessed. Even her arms were bruised from trying to protect herself from her attackers.

"We have to leave now! Blade and his men will be back any second now."

Jennifer mounted, and the girl got on behind her. Brody led the way, and they took off to the trees along the creek. They wanted to go in a different direction than Blade and his men, so Brody rode north from the creek, and that's when they urged their horses to go faster. Jennifer's horse was carrying two, and she had to slow down after a few miles.

"We need to change directions again and get to Abilene, where we can find a safe place for our new friend," said Brody, and looked at the girl. "By the way, what's your name?"

"It's Melinda Roberts, and I'm from east of Abilene.

They killed my folks and stole me and my sister. I haven't seen her in weeks."

Jennifer turned in the saddle. "I know your sister Susan and she is safe in Waco. We're going to take you to the law in Abilene, where you'll be safe."

"No, don't do that. A deputy from Abilene comes to the ranch all the time to talk with Blade. His name is Randall, and I'm sure he's on Blade's payroll."

Brody kept looking in the direction that Blade and his men took. Although he knew he was a gallant fighter, he was not going to be effective going up against six armed men.

When he turned back to the women, he said, "We need to get going, and we'll take Melinda to the hotel by the back stairs. She can get cleaned up and in some better clothes, and I'll find a way to keep her safe."

The three of them rode into Abilene by way of going down alleys and on streets in the residential part of town. When they were behind the hotel, Brody went inside by the front door and made his way to unlock the back door.

Jennifer stayed with Melinda while Brody walked to the sheriff's office. He opened the door and walked inside to find the lawman cleaning his gun.

"Sheriff, I'm Dr. Brody Connor and me, along with two Texas Rangers and some other men, rescued some of the kidnapped women that the raiders stole. I have another young girl in my custody that we rescued from Blade Musgrove's ranch. The Musgrove's are the ones behind all the raids, and I have reliable information that a local lawman may be on Blade's payroll. His name is Randall."

The sheriff abruptly threw the towel he had been using onto his desk. "I don't like it when some stranger comes into my office accusing one of my deputies of wrongdoing. I have a good mind to run you and whoever you have with you out of town."

Brody took a step toward the sheriff when the door swung open and in walked Ranger Utah, Carl, and another Ranger Brody didn't know.

"Hello, Brody and you also, sheriff," said Utah.

The sheriff's face had turned white as cotton at the sight of the Rangers. "What brings you fellers to my county?" asked the sheriff.

Utah didn't answer the lawman but instead turned to Brody. "Did you find the man you came here for?"

"Not really. We found the colonel's son, Blade, on his ranch with one of the young girls they stole. While we were watching the place, a man came riding up and talked to Blade and then all six of the men at the ranch rode off. Jennifer and I went in and rescued the girl and brought her here. Jennifer is with her, and I came to tell the sheriff that a deputy by the name of Randall is taking money from Blade. He seemed upset and even threatened to have me run out of town."

Utah sat down on the corner of the sheriff's desk. "Lonnie, we did away with the raiders that have been terrorizing Central Texas and while doing that, we were able to question one of the injured men before he died. By his testimony, you and your men have been taking money from the Musgrove's while they transport women and whiskey through here."

The sheriff's eyes grew large, and sweat had popped out on his forehead. He looked down at his gun that was still in pieces on the desk. Ranger Carl walked around and stood behind the sheriff.

Utah stood up. "Lonnie, you're a disgrace to that badge you're wearing. Take it off and stand up so Carl can make sure you don't have another weapon before we lock you up."

"Utah, let me explain what I know."

"Go ahead and tell me."

"Randall is Blade's cousin, and he's the one that started taking money from the saloon so we wouldn't interfere with the card games, whiskey, and women upstairs. I never knew they were the ones doing the raids, killing all those folks and taking those women through here."

"Get up and raise your hands, Lonnie. I never said anything about them taking women through here. Lock him up."

The third Ranger that Brody didn't know went to the window and looked south. "Utah, five riders on lathered-up horses just pulled up in front of the saloon."

Brody walked to the window to see. He turned to Utah. "Blade ain't with them. I wonder where he went? Is the wagons still out there where we hid them?"

"Kinda, we used one to haul all the corpses back to town and soaked the other two in whiskey before we set them on fire. The ladies rode the dead men's horses back to Cross Plains, where we met up with two more Rangers. Ranger Dooling is taking the women back to Waco, and Ranger Cartwright came with us."

A man on a fine-looking chestnut rode by and went to the saloon where the others were.

"Blade just rode by," said Ranger Cartwright.

Chapter Forty-Three

RANGER UTAH GOT UP, CAME TO THE WINDOW, and watched as Blade went inside the saloon. He turned to Brody. "How do you want to do this?"

"There's six of them and four of us. No, wait. Jennifer will want in on this, so it's six against five. I like those odds pretty good, so I'm thinking me and Jennifer go inside the saloon and then the three of you come inside after a minute. We'll go to one side of where the men are sitting and you men can go to the other side. Don't give them a chance to fire the first shot. As soon as the three of you are in position, we'll start shooting."

"That sounds good to us. We'll make sure Lonnie can't escape and warn his boss. We'll wait here until I see you and Jennifer head to the saloon. Then we'll be coming in behind you."

Brody nodded and went to the door, where he looked both ways before walking to the hotel.

He knocked and waited until she opened the door. "Jennifer, three Texas Rangers are waiting on us. We saw

Blade and those men go into the saloon and we're going in there after them."

"Thank you for coming for me. I have a bone to pick with that scum." She pulled her pistol and checked to make sure the cylinder was fully loaded. "Melinda, you stay here and don't open the door for anyone. We'll be back soon so the Rangers can take you to your relatives."

The girl nodded her head, and Jennifer grabbed her hat. "Let's go."

Brody glanced over to the sheriff's office as they walked down the boardwalk and saw the door open. As they were walking up to the saloon doors, Brody said, "Close your eyes for a few seconds so you can see when we get inside."

He squinted his eye and could barely see as they came to the batwing doors and entered. He stood still for only a couple of seconds and started to the bar counter where he could face Blade when the time was right.

"What are you drinking?" asked the barkeep.

Brody was looking at Blade and his men from the mirror behind the counter. Without taking his eyes off the table where they sit, he replied, "Beers."

The man was filling two mugs when the three Texas Rangers came in and started toward the table where Blade and his men sat drinking whiskey. Brody saw Blade stop his hand midway to his mouth and say something, and this was his clue to get the party started.

Brody nudged Jennifer and then he turned and pulled his gun as Blade was standing up. The doctor fired at Blade and then turned to hit another of the men before he holstered his gun and pulled the shoulder gun. That move saved his life since the barkeep had reached under the counter and was coming up with a shotgun when Brody shot him between the eyes.

The shooting had stopped, but the air inside the saloon was filled with gunpowder smoke and the smell of death as the six men sitting at the table were all on the floor, bleeding out. The bartender was laying behind the counter with the back of his skull missing.

The Rangers were checking to see if any of the men were still alive. Utah came to Brody. "That's the second time your plan has worked. Those men didn't have a chance in a crossfire."

Brody was reloading his pistols when he said, "I'm wondering why Blade came in later. Is there a telegraph or post office here?"

Carl spoke, "Yeah, it's over about two or three blocks. The railroad is coming through here soon and it's close to the new track location. Why do you ask?"

"I'm thinking Blade may have gotten word to the colonel about the wagon train getting hit and that his whiskey and women are gone."

Utah smiled. "You have a good idea. Come on, I'll go with you in case the operator doesn't want to talk."

Jennifer came to Brody. "I'm going back to the hotel. Let me know what you find out. Utah, can one of your men take over caring for the girl we saved from Blade?"

"Yes, ma'am, I'll have someone take her to her relatives."

"Thanks."

Brody and Utah took off to the telegraph office, and as they were walking that way, they saw a man riding toward town with a badge on his shirt.

"Do you reckon that's Deputy Randall?" asked Brody.

"Could be. Let's have a little fun."

The deputy was coming up on the two men when Utah pulled his gun. "Deputy, keep those hands where I can see them. What's your name?"

"Now, look here. I'm a sworn-in deputy, and you can't be pulling iron on me."

Brody pulled his gun too. "The Ranger asked you what your name is."

"It's Randall. Why do you want to know?"

Utah walked up to the horse and took hold of the bridle while pointing his gun at Randall. "You're under arrest for taking bribes from Blade and the colonel. Blade and all his men are dead in case you're thinking about trying your luck with that gun."

Randall looked at Utah and Brody for a second before he raised his hand shoulder high. "I ain't goin to try anything. I'll go with you in peace."

"Unbuckle your holster and hand it over. Then I want you to dismount."

Brody watched as the deputy did as he was told and handed over his holster. When he was on the ground, Brody tied his horse to the hitch rail, and he and Utah escorted Randall to the jail. After locking Randall in the same cell with Lonnie, the two men once again headed to the telegraph office.

The operator was writing down a message coming over the key when Utah walked up to the counter. He let the operator finish what he was doing before he said, "I need some information. Did Blade Musgrove send a message a few minutes ago? Before you try to waste my time, I'm a Texas Ranger and I'll arrest you if you don't tell me the truth."

"You are really putting me in a rough situation. I'm not supposed to give out information on who sends messages."

"Is there a law that prevents you from giving the law information?" asked Utah.

"No, not that I'm aware. It's just a company thing, I reckon."

Utah tapped his fingers on the counter. "There's a law about someone withholding information about a crime. We believe that Blade and Colonel Musgrove are criminals who have murdered and kidnapped women. This law says that I can arrest you for withholding valuable information that we need. So start talking or come with me to Austin."

"Yes, Blade was here and this message that I just wrote down is his reply. He sent a message to the colonel that said, *Wagon train destroyed. Men dead and cargo gone.* Here's the reply: *Leave now and come to the Brazos River.*"

Utah looked at the message and then asked, "What does this mean?"

"I don't know. Unless he has another ranch on the river."

Utah read the message again. "This could be anywhere on the river. How do you want to handle it?"

Brody thought for a few seconds. "Let me talk to Jennifer. She may know what it means. How about we meet you at the sheriff's office in a few minutes so you can take possession of the girl we have?"

"Okay, I'll see you in a few minutes."

Chapter Forty-Four

BRODY, JENNIFER, AND MELINDA WALKED OUT of the hotel to be met by the three Rangers and their saddled horses from where they had left them earlier.

Utah pointed to Ranger Cartwright, who was holding the reins of a spare horse. "Young lady, if you'll mount up and go with the Ranger, he'll take you to your kin. Mrs. Jennifer, do you have any thoughts on what the message meant?"

"No, I'm sorry, but it doesn't ring a bell with me. The Brazos is a long river, and he could be anywhere. I'm more concerned on where Martin is. Other than Blade, he was in charge when the men went off to raid and steal."

"I appreciate the two of you solving who was behind these terrible raids and rescuing the women. I'm sure the colonel has sold way more than we got back, but we'll continue to look for him and Martin. Good luck, and I hope we meet again. Me and Carl have more work to do."

Utah turned his horse, and the two Rangers headed

out. Jennifer went to Melinda and hugged her. "You know where we live and you're welcome to come live with us if things don't work out with your aunt and uncle."

Melinda wiped a tear from her eye. "I know. I really love you for rescuing me from that awful man."

Brody helped the girl get mounted, and they watched Melinda ride off with the Ranger before they mounted up to head home.

They weren't out of town when Jennifer asked, "What do we do when we get back to Waco?"

Brody didn't reply for a few seconds, but then said, "I think we get a room at the hotel and I go back to work. You can find a carpenter to build us a new house on your land while I work. I'm thinking if you can find one that has a large crew, they can build it fairly quick."

"What about finding Colonel Musgrove and Martin?"

"I happen to know a bounty hunter that owes me a favor. What if he helps us out and goes after the colonel? I have a feeling that Martin will come back to Waco someday, and we will face off. In the meantime, you and I have to get on with our lives."

She smiled at her husband. "Dr. Connor, one of the things I love about you is your ability to plan. What kind of house are you thinking of us building?"

"Well, since we kind of need it fairly soon, I'm thinking one story with three bedrooms, a kitchen, living room, and one of those fancy indoor toilets that flush and has the tub inside."

"So, you don't mind us splurging and having some fancy things in the house?"

"Jennifer, I love you and plan on spending the rest of our lives together. This will be where we raise our children and entertain guests, so yes, make it as fancy as you want."

She was smiling at her husband. "I love you and we'll work together to make sure the house is our home. But I've been thinking about something also. You know that you can quit your job at Dr. Wilks's office and run the ranch with me."

"I appreciate you suggesting that, but I'm a doctor and want to help people. This has been my dream for years, and I want to pursue it. I'm going to talk to Dr. Wilks about him and I going in together and building a hospital. I worked in one while going to school and there is a real need in Waco. Right now, the only hospital is the one owned by the town and it's not much. I'm sure that if we build one, it would be full of patients most of the time."

"I have another suggestion if you want to hear," said Jennifer.

"I'm open to all suggestions, my dear."

"What if we built you an office at the ranch so the country folks could come there to be treated. That way, you could also work at the ranch when you weren't doing doctor work."

"That's a possibility. I'm open to all suggestions, but first we need to get our house built."

They rode their mounts hard until they came to Comanche, Texas, and spent the night. Word had already gotten out about them solving who were behind the raids and murders. The clerk at the hotel treated them like royalty when he read the name on the ledger.

THE FOLLOWING MORNING, they were once again on the road home by daylight and had already decided to ride until after dark that night until they were back at Waco.

BRODY LET Jennifer off at the hotel in Waco to check them in while he took the horses to the livery stable. He was dead tired and was ready to eat and get some sleep.

The hostler woke up when he heard the door open to the barn. "Who's out there and what do you want?"

"It's Dr. Brody, and I need my horses taken care of."

"I'll be right there, Doctor."

"I hear that you've been a busy man."

"I'm hungry and tired. Is there someplace we can get something to eat?"

"Yeah, The Spur Saloon has a feller that will cook for you. He cooks a good steak if he has any."

"Thanks," Brody said, handing the man a few dollars.

He then walked toward the hotel where Jennifer stood on the porch. "Do you know where we can get some food?" she asked.

"I was told that the Spur Saloon has a man that's a good cook. Let's go there and see what he can fix for us."

The saloon was still going strong when Brody and his wife walked in and looked around the room. He saw a few familiar faces and headed to the bar to see if they could get some food.

"Evening, Doctor, what can I get for you?"

"As you can see, I have Jennifer with me, and we got married in Abilene a couple of days ago. I was told by the man at the livery that we can get some food to eat."

"You bet, I'll go tell Willie to fix you and the misses

whatever he has. By the way, congratulations on your wedding."

It was Jennifer who replied, "Thanks, we'll also have some beer to drink while we wait."

The bartender went to see the cook and then came back to pour their beers. While they waited on the food, Brody asked, "Has Martin been in lately?"

"He ain't been in here in a couple of weeks, but I heard that he was in at the Reservation last week. You watch your back with that one. Not only is he a dangerous man, but he has friends that watch his back."

"You're the second person to tell me that. I'll keep your advice in mind."

They heard a loud whistle come from the back room, and the barkeep took off. He returned with two heaping plates of eggs, ham, and potatoes.

Brody and Jennifer ate their food and finished off another round of beers before walking back to their room for the night.

Chapter Forty-Five

THE FOLLOWING MORNING, BRODY AND Jennifer didn't leave their hotel room until nine to eat breakfast. Brody noticed that the bruising was almost gone from her face and arms. He smiled at his wife and took her hand.

"I'm the luckiest man alive to be married to not only a beautiful woman but one who is good with a gun and can hold her own with anyone. You make me a better man just by being close to you."

"Hush your mouth, Brody Connor. I know you're up to something, so you might as well tell me."

He started laughing. "I'm going to the office and start back to work. I also need to talk to Dash and see if he can find Colonel Musgrove and Martin. I'm sure Dr. Wilks is covered up with patients since I'm not there to help out."

"Dear, I wouldn't think nothing less of you. I'm going to see the family lawyer and then go to the bank. After that, I'm finding a carpenter that can get started on our house."

"Okay then, I'll see you at the hotel when I'm finished at the doctor's office."

Jennifer leaned over and gave him a kiss. "You save some energy for me later."

Brody walked outside and started to the office where he could see patients sitting outside under the porch. He really needed to find Martin and stop him from hurting anyone else. As for Colonel Musgrove, he was the leader of the bunch, and although he had never seen the man, he figured that he was a small man with a big ego and only dangerous when he had the drop on someone.

As he walked up onto the porch, he stopped. "Hello everyone, I'll be with you in a jiffy."

"We sure are glad to see you back, Dr. Brody."

"Thanks," he said, and as he grabbed the doorknob, a lady reached out and took him by the arm. "Is it true that you rescued all them young women and even found Jennifer Bernie?"

"Yes ma'am, we found the women, and I have my Jennifer. Just so you all know, she and I got married in Abilene a few days ago."

"We all heard that you and her got hitched but I didn't want to pry into your personal affairs."

"Thanks, I better get to work before Dr. Wilks fires me." He opened the door and went to let Dr. Wilks know that he was here. "I'm back and ready to see patients."

The older doctor motioned to the waiting room. "Let's see if we can clear out the ones waiting in the reception room first."

By two that afternoon, Dr. Brody had treated an assortment of ailments and one broken leg. The boy only needed a cast and given some laudanum to ease his pain. When the nurse escorted the boy and his mama out of the doctor's office, she came in and sat down.

"Dr. Brody, it's time you tell me what's been going on."

"As you probably heard, me and some men found the kidnapped women and rescued them. I also found out some more of the men had my Jennifer and was taking her to Colorado to sell in the gold mine town. A couple of Texas Rangers and I rescued her and five more women."

"The rumor is that you and Jennifer got married. Is that true?"

"Yep, we were married in Abilene."

"Congratulations on finding her and for getting married. Are you going to continue to work here or will you become a rancher?"

"I'm a doctor and that's what I plan on doing. I went to school to help people and that's my passion."

"You may not know this, but the talk of the town is about the young gunfighter doctor. They say you're one heck of a fighter, and some say you're as fast as any gunhand that's ever been through here."

"Let them have their rumors. You know that fantasy is always more fun than real life." Brody wanted to stop this conversation. "Is Dash still in the back room?"

"Yes, he pulled his stitches, but he's doing fine now. I'm sure he's in his room since it's too early to go to the saloon."

"I'll be in his room if you need me."

Brody walked to the back rooms and found Dash sitting in a chair, reading a newspaper. "It looks like you're doing much better."

"Yeah, and I have to thank you for sending me back here. I tore some of the stitches, and Doc Wilks had to fix me back up. Tell me what happened."

"I ran into a couple of Texas Rangers and we maneuvered around in front of the wagons, and when they came near, the Rangers took the front, and I came in from the rear, and we killed all the men. Jennifer was in the wagon and then she and I went on to Abilene and found Blade Musgrove at his ranch. One of his men came, and let him know that the men with the wagons were all dead. Blade and his men took off, and we were fortunate enough to rescue a young girl and take her back to Abilene. The Rangers rode in, and then Jennifer, the Rangers, and I went to the saloon and killed Blade and his men."

"What about Colonel Musgrove and Martin?"

"They weren't there, but Blade sent his pa a telegram telling him that the wagons were gone and also the cargo. The reply said to leave and go to the Brazos. We don't know what that means."

Dash started to laugh. "The Brazos is a saloon where Aquilla Creek runs into the Brazos River. It's a real dive and a man could catch death there if he ain't careful."

"Well, I'll be. The old feller is closer than I thought. I may have to find this Brazos place and meet Colonel Musgrove," said Brody.

"Not by yourself. I'm coming with you if you go to that hellhole. By the way, did you kill Porkchop?"

"Yeah, I killed him and brought you back the reward money. I have it at the hotel. If you go to the saloon tonight, I want you to meet Jennifer, and I'll give you the money."

"Brody, you earned that money, so you keep it. I've been getting lucky playing cards, and I'm fine on money right now."

"No. I told you I would collect the money for you, and I'm a man of my word. When do you think you can ride again? I want to get this settled so me and my wife can get on with our lives."

"Wife. You didn't tell me you got married."

"Yeah, we did it in Abilene with a preacher."

"Give me until tomorrow, and I'll ride to the Brazos with you. We may need some extra guns when we get there."

"I have one other gun. Jennifer wouldn't miss this for the world."

"Are you serious? Your wife wants to go?"

"Oh yes, and don't take her lightly. She can use a gun with the best of them. You rest some more, and we'll pay Colonel Musgrove a visit."

Chapter Forty-Six

JENNIFER WAS WAITING IN THE HOTEL LOBBY when Dr. Brody left the office for the day. He wanted to eat a good supper and then talk to his wife about what Dash told him about where the Brazos were. She met him when he entered the lobby and gave her husband a kiss. "Are you ready to go eat, or do you need to go up to the room?"

She brushed hair from her face. "I'm starved. Let's go."

"I have a lot to tell you, but I'm going to wait until we're seated for supper," she said.

"Fine, I have a lot to tell you also."

She reached out and took hold of his arm. "Tell me while we walk."

He started laughing. "Let's wait until we're seated."

"I guess I deserve that."

They were able to find a table where they could have a conversation without everyone in the café hearing. The waitress came over. "Hi folks, we have a really good roast with potatoes and carrots, or steak and potatoes."

Brody was hungry, so he went first. "I'll have the steak and potatoes with water to drink."

Jennifer said, "I'll have the same, but I want coffee to drink."

"Yes, ma'am, coming right up."

Brody looked at his wife. "Okay, we're seated so tell me what you know."

"I hired a carpenter and he's already started. He and some of his men went to the burned-down house and started cleaning the place up so they can get to building. He's hiring more workers so they can get the house built as quickly as possible. He will put us in a modern toilet and running water in the kitchen."

"How much is it going to cost?"

"I went by the bank before I started talking to the carpenters and found out that we have enough money in the bank to pay for the house, and I did something that you may not like. I asked the carpenter to build another smaller house close to ours."

"Why do you want another house?" asked Brody.

"Wouldn't it be nice for your mama to live close to us?"

Brody bit his bottom lip, and his eyes got a little wet. "Yes, it would. Thank you, Jennifer."

"So, what news do you have?" she asked.

"I talked to Dash, and he knows where Brazos is. It's a saloon where Aquilla Creek flows into the Brazos. It's a really rowdy place and he's wanting to go with me to see if the colonel is there."

"I'm going with you. If it's that bad, we'll need all the firepower we can get. Do we leave tomorrow?"

"I'm leaving that up to Dash. He may want to scout the place out since it's not that far away. He said we can be there in an hour."

The waitress brought their food, and the conversation stopped since both had missed dinner that day. Brody was thinking about tomorrow when he said, "Let's walk to the saloon and see if Dash is there. I think it would be wise to speak to him about tomorrow."

The saloon wasn't busy, and Dash was sitting at one of the poker tables by himself, shuffling cards when Brody pulled out a chair for Jennifer to sit in. He also sat down and asked, "What's your plan for tomorrow?"

Dash placed the cards in front of Jennifer.

She reached out and cut the card.

He picked them up and started dealing them out. "I'm thinking we ride that way about three tomorrow afternoon. If Colonel Musgrove is there, he won't be at the saloon during the day. I'm betting that he has a house nearby where he can keep up with who comes and goes."

"You're probably right about that and it may be better for us so we don't have to shoot it out with a bunch of hard men," said Brody.

Jennifer looked at her cards and flipped them onto the table. "I win, I have four aces."

Brody and Dash started laughing. "Dear, don't play cards for money with Dash."

"Oh, you hush," said Jennifer.

"Jennifer and I will be ready to leave at three. We must excuse ourselves and head back to the hotel."

Jennifer was quiet on the way to the hotel. When they were in the room, she asked, "Do you think that Martin will be at the Brazos?"

"No, I think he's too smart to be there. In fact, I think he knows the entire operation has been taken down, and as soon as his boss is dead, Martin will head someplace where no one knows about the raids."

BRODY WAS DEAD TIRED, and after a hot bath, he drifted off to sleep. Sometime after midnight, he began to dream and saw a man in the street coming toward him with his hand close to his gun. The next thing he saw was the man lying in the dirt street, dead. He sat up in bed with sweat covering his face.

Brody got out of bed and went to the window to let the breeze cool off his sweaty body. Why did he have these dreams? Even though he didn't know the reason, the truth was, the dreams came true, and he was thankful for the heads-up.

Jennifer got out of bed and came to her husband. "Did you have a bad dream?"

"I don't know if it was bad or good. I told you about seeing the wagons camped where we found you. I also saw where my friend William Longtooth was lying dead. Tonight, I saw a man coming toward me on the street. The next thing I saw was the man lying in the dirt. Was the dream telling me that I would kill someone in a gunfight on the street?"

"Dear, it wasn't you in the street dead, so it must be a good vision. Come on, let's go back to bed."

Brody lay awake for a long time listening to Jennifer breathe. He knew it was a blessing that she was here with him, and he also knew that the Great Spirit was taking care and watching over him.

The dreams weren't just dreams, they were divine visions, and he was grateful that he was chosen to live the life he had. Tomorrow, men would die, and that's a shame, but they chose this life. As for Colonel Musgrove, he was a military officer and had went against everything he was taught in the Army. Why did a man of his stature stoop so low to raid, murder, and kidnap women? Worse than that, he was selling the women into a life of abuse and slavery.

With his eyes closed and trying to will himself to sleep, the face of William Longtooth appeared. Brody knew that the old Indian had something to say, so he just lay in his bed and kept his eyes and mouth shut.

"Brody Connor, you are a warrior. Attack and fire the first shot. Look at the beads. Don't leave any alive. You go and I go with you."

The vision of William disappeared, and Brody smiled. William had given him advice, and he needed to listen to his mentor. But what did he mean by the beads? William never said anything unless it was important, and he would make sure he looked at the beads wherever they were.

The talk had done something else, it had given the young healer a calm about tomorrow, and he fell back to sleep.

Chapter Forty-Seven

THE FOLLOWING MORNING, JENNIFER HAD TO shake Brody to wake him up. "Sleepyhead, we need to get dressed and have breakfast. I have lots to do today and so do you."

"I know, I laid awake a long time before I went back to sleep but it was worth it. I had my eyes closed, trying to sleep, when William appeared to me."

"Did he tell you anything?"

"He told me to be the aggressor, to attack and shoot first, and look at the beads."

"What about the beads?"

"I don't know. I just have to watch for the beads. The rest will come when I see them. I believe it's a gift that I see things in my dreams. I just hope that I'm disciplined enough to pay attention and do what the dreams reveal to me."

"You keep having dreams of visions. They haven't lied to you yet, so cherish them and do what you're told, because I agree with William. We go in there today shooting and figure it out after everyone involved with Musgrove is dead."

Brody finished dressing and escorted his wife to the café where everyone greeted them as they found a table. Brody was the only man in the building drinking milk with his breakfast. When he finished his food, he reached out and took hold of Jennifer's hand. "I'll leave early enough to go get the horses from the livery stable. Where do you want to meet?"

"How about I get the horses and come to the clinic and get you? I'm going to be out and about most of the day ordering materials for the house."

"That sounds even better. I need to go, I'm sure I have patients waiting on me already."

They parted company outside the café, and the doctor continued to the office where a family was waiting outside on the bench. "Morning folks, let me get the door unlocked, and you can come on in."

Only the woman and a young girl who was holding her belly came into the examining room. "What seems to be the problem?" he asked.

"She had a stomachache all afternoon and night. I swear, none of us got any sleep."

"Let's get you up on the table so I can examine you."

He helped the girl up and began to feel her stomach when he stopped and asked, "What have you been eating?"

"I ain't ate nothing since yesterday morning."

"Did you eat any green apples or pears?"

"Yeah, I ate pears."

The doctor looked at the child's mama. "She has a common stomachache from eating green pears. I'm going to mix up some medicine for her to drink, and it will take care of the problem. The next time this happens, mix some baking soda with water and have her drink it."

Brody gave the child the medicine, and as soon as he got it down, she let out a big burp and smiled. "I feel better now."

The woman grabbed the child by her arm and pulled her to her feet. "You caused us to come all this way so you could burp. I'm going to wear you out if you eat another one of those green pears."

"I'm sorry, Mama. I was hungry."

"Remember, baking soda mixed with water, and you owe me a quarter."

The woman paid him the money and was still scolding the child as they left the office.

Dash walked into the room. "Morning, Brody. I'm going to scout out the place on the river and will be back in a couple of hours. Are you and Jennifer still on for three this afternoon?"

"Oh yes. I have another matter to discuss with you. I need to find Martin, and I'm willing to pay you if you're up to finding him."

"With everything that's happened, it may be difficult to hunt him down. Martin is smarter than the colonel and I figure he's already on his way out of Texas. Word gets around fast, and I'm thinking as soon as he heard about the wagons and Blade getting killed, he took off to greener pastures."

"I'm thinking the same thing, but if you run across him or hear anything about where he is, I'm willing to pay for the information."

"Doc, I owe you my life, and you won't owe me anything if I find that man."

"Thanks, and you don't owe me anything. You paid me back by helping me rescue those women. When you find him, I'd appreciate it if you would let me settle the score with him."

Dash nodded his head. "I need to get going so I can be back by three. If something happens and I don't make it back, ride the river and we'll meet up."

"Okay, you be careful."

Dash left, and Brody had to get his mind off of what was going to happen this afternoon. He started seeing patients so he could stay focused and provide them with the best care possible. By noon, he had forgotten all about what was about to happen until an elderly man came in with beads hanging from his neck. Brody couldn't let it go, so he asked, "Why do you wear the beads around your neck?

"I'm part Indian and wear beads as part of my spiritual connection with the Great Spirit."

"I also believe in the Great Spirit. Maybe I should wear beads."

"You don't need beads. You the healer, and the Great Spirit gives you visions to help people."

Brody was at a loss for words after being told that. "How can I help you today?"

"I have pain on my back that I can't get rid of."

"Get on the table and lie on your stomach." Brody began to rub and push on the man's back. "Tell me where the pain is."

When Brody hit the area, the man said, "There."

The doctor massaged the area and then put the heel of his hand beside the backbone and pushed. The bones began to move, and he could hear them as they crunched. "Go on home and try not to overwork your back today. It should feel better tomorrow."

After the man left, Dr. Brody stood looking out the window. William had told him to look at the beads. Was that a spiritual connection that his old friend was using to connect to him?

Brody was disturbed by Dr. Wilks. "Doctor, we're caught up if you want to go on and meet up with Jennifer."

"Thanks, Dr. Wilks. By the way, I did check on that girl the day I went to the Dry Creek Ranch. When I examine her, I found that her heart skipped a beat on a regular basis."

"I'm glad you found that also. I thought I heard it but wasn't for sure. I sent a telegram to some doctors and they only said that it should get in regular rhythm as she get older."

"That's good to know. But we should keep monitoring her as she gets older.

"I agree. Go on and take care of your business."

"Thanks, Doctor. I'll see you in the morning."

Brody walked out and headed to the livery stable to see if he could get there before Jennifer. The hostler was in fact finishing up on his horse when Brody walked into the barn.

"Afternoon, Doctor, your wife said you would need the horses by three, so I went ahead and got them saddled."

"Thanks, I'll take them now."

Chapter Forty-Eight

JENNIFER WAS COMING OUT OF THE HOTEL when Brody rode up. "Hello, dear. Are you ready for a ride?"

"Yes, I am. Where's Dash?"

"He left earlier to scout out the saloon and will meet up with us on the trail."

Jennifer had her gun on her right hip and was dressed in britches, boots, long-sleeve shirt, and a hat. Brody had on both of his guns and was mentally ready to get this over with.

They rode along the riverbank like Dash had instructed, and thirty minutes away from Waco, they saw their friend coming to meet them. Brody pointed to a shade, and that's where he and his wife waited for the bounty hunter.

"What do you think?" asked Brody.

"He was in the saloon with his men when I left. But don't fret none if he ain't there when we arrive. The colonel's staying in a house about a hundred yards up from the dive. I saw him walk to the saloon, and when I eased up where I could see inside, there were five more men in there besides him. I recognize two of the men from when I was on a hunt in Indian territory a year or so ago. They're brothers who will kill for the fun of it and have ridden with Porkchop in the past. The other three I don't know but I'm thinking they are part Indian since they have on beads."

"Did you say beads?"

"Yeah, beads around their necks, but for some reason they don't look right on them."

"That's because the beads don't belong to them. Those are the beads that Porkchop and Twisted Nose stole off of my friend when they killed him. Is Twisted Nose in there?"

"He could be, I couldn't see some of the men very well."

"So that's what the vision was about," said Jennifer. "You're supposed to get William's beads back and keep them as your own."

Brody nodded his head at his wife. "Dash, I only know one way to do this and that's going in there shooting and don't give them a chance to respond."

"For some reason, I knew that you would say that. I'm fine with that if you are."

Jennifer pulled her gun from the holster. "Dash, is there another door to the place?"

"Yeah, there's a back door."

"If you take the back door, then Brody and I will come in through the front, shooting."

Dash wiped the sweat off his forehead with a handkerchief. "We can leave our horses over by the oak trees where the well is and stay hidden until we're ready to go in. I'll give you a thumbs up when I'm in position and we can all go in at the same time."

"Fine, lead the way," said Brody.

The three rode until they could see the saloon that looked more like a rundown shack. There were five horses tied out front that looked like they had been there for a while by the way they were standing on three legs and their heads down.

Dash motioned for them to dismount. He removed his spurs and gave a nod before he started toward the back of the building. Brody and Jennifer made their way to the front and stayed where they could see Dash.

Brody had a gun in each hand. Jennifer had her gun in her hand with the hammer cocked ready to fire. Brody saw the thumbs up from Dash, and that's when he stepped through the door, and his first shot hit one of the men wearing the beads. The second shot hit the other man, who also had on beads. He turned his gun and was firing at the men still sitting at the table, and all he could hear was gunfire beside him and to his left.

The shooting stopped, and Brody was already reloading his guns. He looked over at Jennifer, and she was reloading her gun. The man wearing the Confederate uniform dress jacket was looking up at the young woman as she reloaded her gun. The man raised his empty hand and pointed his index finger at her. "Bang, bang," he said in a weak voice.

"Colonel, you're responsible for killing my pa and many others because you wanted more money. As your judge and jury, I condemn you to hell." She pointed the gun and pulled the trigger. The bullet hit the man between his eyes and his head bounced off the floor as the lead exploded out the back of his skull.

Brody walked over to the two men he shot who were wearing the beads. He grabbed the men one by one and carefully removed the beads from around their necks. He held them up at arm's length. "William, this is for you, my friend."

Dash was checking out each man and removing what money they had when Jennifer went to the door and then turned back. "Dash, is that house up there on the hill where you saw the colonel come from?"

"Yeah, the house on the hill." He got up and came where she was and pointed to the house.

"Brody, I have a feeling in my stomach that we need to check out the house."

Brody and Jennifer walked up the hill to the house, and when he tried the door, it had a padlock on it. With one powerful kick, the door frame shattered, and as they walked into the front room, Jennifer grabbed him by the arm.

"Listen, I heard a moan. Let's check the bedrooms."

The first room was empty and hadn't been used. The second room was also empty, and that's when Jennifer took a few quick steps and flung open the third bedroom door. She almost sank to her knees when she saw the girl with her hands and feet tied to the bedpost and a rag stuffed in her mouth.

"Come on, Brody. Let's get her untied and make sure she is not injured. There's no telling what that evil man has done to her."

"Sweetie, I'm Jennifer, and I was also taken prisoner by the colonel, and this fine man rescued me. We're going to get you untied and take you home."

As soon as Jennifer removed the gag, the girl started to cry so hard that she shook. Brody untied both feet and was working on the hands while Jennifer continued to talk to the frightened child.

"What's your name and where are you from?"

"It's Susan North, and I live close to Comanche. They

killed my mama, pa, and brothers. I don't have anywhere to go," said the child in between sobs.

After Brody finished untying the child, he started looking around the room and saw a leather bag practically under the bed. Out of curiosity, he opened the bag to find it stuffed full of money.

"Do you have any shoes or other clothes here?"

"No, ma'am. This is all I have."

Jennifer went rummaging around and found a shirt that she put over the girl's nightgown, and they started outside and saw Dash standing outside with the horses.

"I see you found another one." He pointed to the saloon. "What do you want to do with the dead inside the building?"

With a somber look on her face, Jennifer said, "Burn the place down like they did my home."

Dash looked at Brody, who also said, "I'm fine with that."

"You all go ahead and get mounted, and I'll get the fire started so if anyone sees us here, they can say you didn't do it," said Dash.

"Come on, dear, we need to go. I'll help Susan up behind you."

The three started off, and when Brody looked back, fingers of fire were coming out the windows, and he saw Dash mount up and come up behind them.

"I know one thing for sure. I don't ever want either of you two mad at me. I've seen a lot in my years, but that attack just now was a fine piece of work," said Dash.

"What are your plans now?" asked Brody.

"I'm going to start looking for a couple of men that I have wanted posters on. Hopefully, I'll find out something for you about where Martin is." Dash looked over at Jennifer and the girl. "Jennifer, what are your plans now?"

Jennifer turned toward Dash. "I'm going to find Susan a good home and do everything I can to get her in possession of her folks' land. Then Brody and I will continue to rebuild our home. He's going to be the best doctor in Waco while I'm going to be the first woman rancher in the area."

Dash smiled at the strong-minded woman. "I do believe the two of you will accomplish every bit of what you just said, and more."

Chapter Forty-Nine

DASH LEFT THREE DAYS AFTER THE INCIDENT AT the Brazos Saloon, and neither Brody nor Jennifer ever heard one word about the dead bodies inside the burned-out saloon. Jennifer kept Susan with them for a week until a cousin with her husband came and took the girl back to her family's farm. They were going to stay there and work the land so she could keep it in the family.

For the next two months, Jennifer spent most of her days shopping for items to go in the house and was keeping up with the progress. The sooner they could get out of the hotel, the better.

Dr. Brody stayed busy taking care of patients and seeing to their needs. Many times, he or Dr. Wilks would have to make house calls. He wore the beads that belonged to William around his neck as a spiritual connection and as a conversation piece with the townsfolk.

One thing he hadn't told anyone except Jennifer was the leather bag of money he found at the house where Colonel Musgrove lived. It turned out to be a little over six thousand dollars. Do they try and give some of the money to the victims, or do they keep it for themselves? They both confirmed that the money had to be divided to the victims and Jennifer was in charge of distributing it.

He hadn't had a dream or vision since William directed him to look for the beads. He didn't know if his life was so good that he didn't need the dreams or if they had stopped for good.

As he reflected back on the dreams, there was still one that hadn't happened and he had figured that one out. He would eventually meet Martin in the street, and the two men would shoot it out, and Martin would die. It was sad that men had to kill other men, but that was life, and there were evil men out there who would do just about anything for money or fame.

The two doctors were caught up on patients and were in the kitchen, where Dr. Wilks was drinking coffee and Brody was having a glass of water.

"Dr. Wilks, I've been thinking about something and I'd like to talk to you about it."

The older doctor moved his cup closer to the edge of the table. "Tell me what you've been thinking about."

"We have a lot of patients, and many times either you or I have to make house calls that take away from other patients. What if we had a hospital where we could have those patients stay, and we could see them daily? I actually worked in a hospital in Kansas City, and I treated many of the residents that were there."

"I've been to the hospital in Houston at the medical school where the students treat the patients, and I'm not keen on the care at that hospital."

"I understand, but I'm talking about a private hospital that will be managed by us. We set the standard of care and hire all the nurses, orderlies, and maybe even some more doctors. Think about this. We have our office as part of the hospital where we see patients. We have one or two rooms dedicated to surgery. Another thing we had in Kansas City was a pharmacy that had all the medication and specialized instruments that we could use. Also the patients could buy all their medications from the pharmacy."

"Do you have any idea how much that would cost us to get started?"

"Yes, sir, I do. We could take on partners who would invest in the business, and we would pay them back with a portion of the profits. One thing we would have to implement is that our patients would have to pay for our services, and I don't know how many will be able to do that."

Dr. Wilks started to laugh. "So I could stop taking chickens and pigs as payments?"

"That's right, or we would have to make sure they were actually worth what we charge. There are benefits and there are downfalls, but I think the benefits are positive."

"Tell you what, I'll consider it if you'll come up with a cost and a plan on getting the money. You may want to talk to Winston Thomas at the Bank of Waco. He's a fair man and may want in on the project. The other thing you need to do is talk to the city mayor and get his blessing. You know that he's on the board at Waco University, and he can be very influential?"

"I didn't know he was associated with the university and that's a very good idea. If he's against it, then the city could fight it, and we lose a lot of money."

"Brody, how many hospital rooms are you thinking about starting out?"

"I was thinking we build a new office that will house

four doctors. The hospital will have two operating rooms and ten patient rooms, along with three rooms for new mothers. Those rooms need to be separated from what I call the sick rooms. Babies cry and can be disruptive, plus as you know, patients can holler and cry also."

Dr. Wilks got up and went after the coffee pot. He poured himself another cup and set the pot down. "Brody, I don't have that many years left to treat patients. I'm thinking about going in on this crazy notion you've come up with. I suggest you go see Larry Boatright over at the surveyor's office and have him draw you up a set of plans so you can take it to the bank. If I was you, I would set up a meeting at the bank with Winston and Charles, the mayor. You can show them the building plan and maybe a chart of charges for all the things we charge for."

"I think that's a great plan and I'll talk to Jennifer about helping me when she is bored here in town. The house is coming along really good, and she thinks we can start moving in a couple of weeks."

The older doctor took another drink of his coffee. "I just thought of something else. I live south of town, and Jennifer's ranch is southwest of town. We could relocate to the south or even the southwest area of town, then we wouldn't have as long a commute as I do now."

"I thought about that, and I'm also curious if we could buy and remodel the old tanning factory. The building doesn't look very old, and it seems to be in great shape. If we could purchase it for a good price, that would save us a lot of money."

"The bank holds the note on the building, and I'm sure that Winston would love to have some of his money back that he loaned to the business."

Brody thought about it for a few seconds. "The

factory sets back far enough from the street that we could build the new examination office in front and then build out the inside for the hospital."

"Remember when drawing up the plans to add a kitchen in it. We'll have to feed the patients three meals a day."

"I'll do that. I'm going to see Larry in a little while and see if he will go look at the abandoned factory. He may be able to put us something together quicker by remodeling that building."

"Go ahead. I'll probably close up and go home myself."

Chapter Fifty

Dr. Brody started the process of building a hospital by going to see the surveyor and talk to him about purchasing the old hide factory and turning it into a hospital.

"Dr. Brody, I know that old factory building pretty well and I think it would cost more to remodel it than it would to build a new modern hospital. I've also done some drawings for the Waco University, and off the top of my head, I'm thinking it could cost as much as $20,000."

Brody took a second to take that in. "That's a lot of money, and it will take years to pay it back. What if I build a place with four patient rooms, a toilet room, a reception room and two examining rooms?"

Larry thought about that for a few seconds. "I'm thinking $4,000 could build that and buy the property here in town. Property prices have gone up along Main Street."

Brody thought about that. He got up and stuck out

his hand. "Thanks, Larry, I'll think about all this and see you around town."

It was still early in the afternoon, so Brody walked to the livery and collected his horse. The ride to the ranch went by fast since he was deep in his dream of building a hospital.

He was surprised at the progress of his and Jennifer's house. In fact, it looked like it was finished, but he knew the men were still working on the inside, and that's where he found Jennifer and the carpenter planning out cabinets.

"Hello, dear, doesn't the house look so nice?"

"Yes, it does. It won't be long until we can move in."

The carpenter whose name was Woody Oak said, "I can probably be finished in two weeks with this house and a week later with the small one."

"How much would it cost me to have an office and hospital built here on the property?"

"Well, that's according to how big you want and how fancy you want it."

"Excuse me, I need to go outside," said Jennifer, and took off out back.

"I'm thinking about having a reception room where patients can sit. Then there would be two examining rooms and a storage room. Then I want four small bedrooms for patients and a modern toilet room."

"I'm thinking the reception room and storage room will be small, like ten by ten. The two examining rooms will be bigger and need some cabinets and drawers. Those could be a little bigger. The patients' rooms will be small, and then the toilet. I'm thinking around $3,000."

Brody turned his head and saw his wife in the backyard, throwing up. "Excuse me, Woody. I need to check on Jennifer."

Brody walked outside. "Dear, are you all right?"

"Yeah, I must have picked up a stomach bug."

He felt her forehead and touched her stomach. "How long has this been going on?"

"The last four days, and it's mostly when I eat."

Brody put his arms around his wife. "Honey, you don't have a stomach bug. You have a baby growing in that little belly."

She looked at him with a blank face for a couple of seconds. Then her face lit up and she started laughing. "We're pregnant," she said, blushing.

"Yes, dear, we're pregnant and I'm thinking that you could be around two months."

"Brody, I want you to send your mama a telegram and ask her to come live with us. She needs to be around you and our children. We can catch the train and get her if she'll come."

"Jennifer, I have a lot going on with work, and I don't know if the time is right to be going to Wichita after her."

"You show the carpenter what you want and have him go ahead and start your office and hospital out here. We have the money in the bank, and I want you close to me and our baby. Dr. Wilks will be retiring soon and you need to start putting your plans in place."

"I'll think about it on my way back to town. In the meantime, I don't want you doing a lot of heavy lifting or exerting yourself."

She smiled. "Yes, Doctor, now give me a kiss."

Brody had an entire new set of thoughts to plan out. His wife was with child, and he had the means to have his office and small hospital built at their house. Of course, he wouldn't have the amount of patients that he would have in Waco but the country folks could come to him and not have to go all the way into Waco. The hospital would also be a lifesaver for a lot of folks and he could use the ranch cook to fix all the meals. One important thing he would need is a nurse to work there. That may be a problem to hire someone this far out.

Dr. Wilks would hate to lose him, but he had to do what was best for him and his family. If the hospital works out, then he can show the bank how profitable it would be, and he could build a bigger one.

What about Mama? He told her when he left that he would send for her when he got settled. What better time to have her move here, where she can help raise his kids. She deserves a new home where she's safe and around her son and daughter-in-law.

The ride back to Waco was a time of decision, and he rode to the telegraph office where he sent a long message to his mother. He didn't figure he would hear back until tomorrow and then they could start planning the trip to Wichita.

The train depot ticket office was his next stop.

"Hello, sir, I would like some information on how long it will take me to get to Wichita, Kansas?"

"Well, sir, give me a few minutes to see where you will have to change lines." The man pulled out a map and started following the lines. "You will have to change lines four times, and it will take you about three days to get there. Should I go ahead and put the tickets together?"

"No, not yet. Thanks for the information."

Brody took his horse back to the livery stable where the hostler came and took his pony inside.

Brody was tired of thinking about the future and walked to the saloon for a beer. One of the poker tables only had three players, so he took his beer and went over. "Howdy, can I take a seat?"

"Sure, Doctor, your money is as good as anyone's."

After five hands and two beers, he called it a day, left the saloon, and decided to go by the telegraph office. Sure enough, he had a reply that was simple: *Come on, I'm waiting.*

He knew she was ready, and now he had to talk to Jennifer so he could tell Dr. Wilks about his plans.

It was getting late, and he knew that Jennifer would be back in town soon, so he went to the hotel, took a bath, and changed into clean clothes before supper.

Jennifer arrived, and as they went out for supper, he updated her on the message he received from his mama. "I need to know when we can leave to get her. We will probably be gone at least a week."

She thought about it for a few seconds. "What if we leave the day after tomorrow?"

"Fine, I'll talk to Dr. Wilks tomorrow and buy the tickets."

They finished their supper and returned to the room.

Chapter Fifty-One

THE FOLLOWING MORNING, WHEN BRODY walked by the telegraph office on his way to work, the operator came out. "Doctor, I have another message for you."

Brody, don't come. I'm getting on the next train. See you in three days.

He started laughing. His mama wasn't waiting on him, she was doing it on her own. There was so much to do, so he turned around and went back to the hotel where Jennifer was still in the room. He knocked on the door. "Jennifer, it's me, open up."

She opened the door. "What's wrong?"

He handed her the message from his mother. "We have to change our plans. Can you ask the carpenters to work later and get the houses finished in a few days? Also, tell him that I want to get started on my office and hospital when they finish with the houses."

She put her arms around his neck. "I'm so glad you've decided to do that, and I'm sure you'll have more patients than you can treat."

"Speaking of that, with Mama here, she can help me in the hospital and office. That will give her a way to make money and meet people."

"Dear, you need to talk to Dr. Wilks today and let him know what your plans are. I assume that you'll continue to work for him until your own office is finished."

"Yes, I'll talk to him today. I really hate to do this to him, but I have to pursue my own dreams. I'm sure he'll support my decisions and still be my friend."

"You go on to work, and I'll go out to the ranch and talk to Woody about getting the houses ready to move into."

After a kiss, Brody left for the office, where no one was waiting outside when he opened the front door. He hadn't been there but a few minutes until both nurses arrived and started working in the kitchen area, washing towels and getting water boiling for sterilizing more bandages.

Brody was in his examining room when Dr. Wilks came in. "Good morning, Dr. Brody."

"Good morning, Doctor."

"About what we discussed yesterday. I spoke to my wife and we came to the decision that I'm too old to tackle such a big project, so I'm out. The truth is, I would like to sell out and retire. Would you be interested in buying me out?"

Brody started to laugh. "Doctor, I was going to tell you that I was also out on that idea. It's way too expensive here in town. Jennifer is pregnant, and we've talked to my mama about coming here to live with us. Jennifer came up with another idea that I really like. I'm going to build me an office and a four-room hospital out on the ranch."

The older doctor smiled. "That may be the best idea

that you've had in a long time. The folks living in that direction won't have to come all the way into town and you won't have to make house calls."

"As for buying you out...I'd be interested in purchasing your equipment, instruments, and all the medical supplies. I wouldn't have a use for the building."

Dr. Wilks thought about that for a few seconds. "I'll sell you everything inside the office since you'll need most of this stuff anyway. I'll sell the building to someone else."

Dr. Wilks stuck out his hand, and they shook to seal the deal. "Brody, I'm glad you decided to go out on your own. I've been wanting to quit for some time, and when you came to work here, you revived me for a while, but I've been doctoring a long time, and it's time for me to enjoy the years my wife and I have left."

"Help, I need help!"

Brody took off to the reception area, where a woman was trying to hold up a man with his shirt covered in blood. Brody went to the man and helped the woman. "What happened to him?"

"He's been shot in the chest."

Dr. Wilks took the woman's place, and the two physicians got the man into the examining room and on the table. Brody tore the man's shirt open to see the small hole where the bullet went in. He turned the man enough so that he could see if the bullet went all the way through and if there was no exit wound.

"Dr. Wilks, I have to remove the lead, and from the look of the blood, I would say it's in the liver or close to it. Have the nurses bring lots of towels and let's get the area clean and disinfected so I can start. I'm going to wash my hands."

Dr. Wilks and both nurses assisted while Dr. Brody

went to work on removing the lead from the man's chest. It was too deep and the hole too small for the long-nosed forceps, so he took a scalpel and went to work opening up the man's chest so he could get to the bullet. It was a bloody mess until he finally found the bullet and then looked at the older doctor.

"He's losing a lot of blood, and I think we need to cauterize some of the area to stop the bleeding."

Dr. Wilks then said, "Nurse, take my place, and I'll go get a red-hot instrument to stop the bleeding." Brody was getting what he needed to close up the chest when the older doctor came in carrying a red-hot knife. Brody took it from him and started touching it to the flesh where most of the bleeding was coming from.

When he was satisfied, he began the process of closing up the cut he had made. By the time he was finished and the nurses had the man cleaned up, Brody was exhausted.

"Let's move him into the room where Dash was and see if he lives. I'm going out to talk to his wife."

Brody went out where the woman was sitting. "Ma'am, I have the bullet out, and he's still alive, but it's going to be a wait-and-see if he makes it. We have him in a room if you want to go sit with your husband."

The woman frowned. "He ain't my husband. He's just some man that's been coming around courting me. He got out of line, and I shot him with this little .32 that I carry."

Brody was somewhat shocked and didn't know what to say for a few seconds.

"Well, ma'am, do you know his name?"

"Yep, it's Bill Oliver. I'm sorry he ain't doing good, but he needs to know that he can't go around putting his hands where he ought not. I'm going home now, if that's all right."

"Yes, ma'am, that will be fine, but I'd like to know your name also."

"It's Shelly Moose, and if you think I'm paying for all this, you have another thing coming. It's all his fault, and he can pay."

"Yes, ma'am. I'll give him the bill."

The woman got up and left with Brody shaking his head in disbelief.

Chapter Fifty-Two

BRODY CHECKED ON BILL FREQUENTLY FOR THE rest of the day, and by the time he left, the man was awake and had taken a few sips of soup. Brody didn't want to go off and leave him, but he also had things to do and would come back before bedtime to check on him.

He told Jennifer about the deal that Dr. Wilks had made with him and that he would continue to work in Waco until Woody had his office finished.

"I talked to Woody, and he'll be finished enough so we can start moving furniture into both houses in three days. He's hired a few more hands and they're working late each day until they're finished."

"I look for Mama to be here in three or four days. She can stay at the hotel for a few days if need be. How much furniture have you purchased for our house?" asked Brody.

"Not much. I've been waiting on the carpenters, but I better get busy tomorrow. Do you think that you can come with me tomorrow?"

Brody thought about that. "If I can get away, I can. I have a gunshot patient that I have to go check on later. If he's doing all right tomorrow and we're as slow as it was today, I'll have plenty of time to shop with you."

"When are you going to check on your patient?"

"I can go now. It's getting late, and if he's still doing okay, he'll be fine, I think."

"Do you mind if I go with you, and then afterward, maybe we can window shop on the way back?"

"Sure, let's go."

When he went into the room where Bill was recuperating, he found the man asleep, snoring up a storm. That's all he needed to see and then eased his way out and went to Jennifer.

They walked hand in hand along one side of the street, looking in windows at furniture, drapes, lamps, and at one store, they put their hands against the glass so they could see beds.

Jennifer looked at her husband. "I think that we should start with the kitchen and work our way to the bedroom."

"I agree with the kitchen, but then the bedroom next and the other rooms last."

"Brody, have you thought about baby names yet?"

"No, I haven't. I must admit that I'm new to all this and I don't know anything about baby names."

"Do you have a preference on what you want it to be?"

He looked at his wife. "I don't care. I'll love it regardless of what it is."

They continued on, and as they were passing by the newspaper office, something caught his eye, and he stopped to look at the newspaper in the window. The headlines weren't what got his attention, it was a sub-article: *Bounty Hunter killed.*

Brody had a hard time seeing what was written, and Jennifer was the one to see it and put her hand on his arm. "Dear, it says that Dash was killed in a gunfight in Abilene. He had an argument with some gambler, and the man shot Dash in the back as he left the saloon."

Brody looked at his wife. "The gambler was Martin. He hasn't left the area after all. From now on, I want you to carry your gun with you."

"Brody, it didn't say anything about it being Martin. It could have been any gambler that shot him."

"I don't think so. I know it was Martin, and I wouldn't be surprised if he doesn't come back here."

They had started walking again when he said, "I'm going to kill Martin when he gets here. The man's destiny is already planned out, and I'm the one to send him to hell."

"Brody, you're scaring me with that kind of talk."

"Jennifer, I saw it in my vision, and I'm confident that we will meet right out there in the street. I'll kill him and then I don't know what my next dream or vision will be."

They arrived at the hotel, and Brody stood on the boardwalk for a few seconds, looking up and down the street. Jennifer knew what he was doing and stayed by his side.

They went inside, and she went on to bed while he took a hot bath and thought about the time when he operated on Dash, and by all accounts, probably saved his life. After his bath, he lay in bed and went off to sleep.

SOMETIME BEFORE MORNING, he saw inside a smoke-filled saloon and the smell of cigars, sawdust soaked with spit and beer filled his nostrils. He was in the room, but he was above everyone where he could see every movement. Dash got up from the poker table and walked to the bar where he placed four bits on the countertop. He turned and had almost made it to the door when another of the men at the table got up and rushed after him. The man pulled his gun and began to fire into the back of the bounty hunter. He turned back to the crowd, and Brody looked into the eyes of Martin.

Someone cracking a whip out on the street woke Dr. Brody Connor up. He lay with his eyes closed, thinking back to what he had seen and knew that this was coming to a showdown soon.

He got up and picked up the beads of William and placed them over his head, and then he went to his bag and retrieved the medicine pouches that William had also given him. Without a shirt on, and only the Indian beads and pouches hanging from his neck, Brody went down onto both knees and closed his eyes. He raised both hands above his head like he was presenting himself to the heavens.

He kept his eyes closed and focused his entire being to the Great Spirit. He prayed for understanding, wisdom, and for the courage of a warrior going into battle. When he finished, he raised up and there was Jennifer watching him from the bed. He nodded to her, and she wiped tears from her eyes.

With sweat covering his face and upper body, he removed the beads and bags before taking another bath. While he was washing off, Jennifer climbed in with him.

"You had another vision during the night, didn't you?"

"Yes. It was Martin who murdered Dash. As Dash was leaving the saloon, Martin got up and rushed after him and shot him in the back. Then he turned and looked at me."

"You saw all that in a dream?"

"You may not understand this, but I was there in the spirit. I was hovering above them, looking down and saw it all."

Jennifer reached out and took his hand. "Brody, what're you going to do now? Are you going to Abilene after Martin?"

"No, he'll come here when the time is right."

"When will that be?"

"When God decides."

"Let's get dressed and get busy."

Chapter Fifty-Three

THE FOLLOWING TWO DAYS FOUND DR. BRODY and Jennifer busy buying furniture, kitchen tables, and bedding. They made arrangements to have most of it delivered, and some of the ranch hands also came to town with wagons to haul some of it to the house.

Brody kept checking at the railroad for his mama and knew it could be today or tomorrow before she came in on the train. The excitement of seeing his mama grew each day since he knew that she was coming to live there. The last three years have been hard on her, being alone in Wichita with him on the run and then off to medical school.

Dr. Wilks wasn't coming into work most days now, and Brody had to see the patients by himself and also watch after Bill, who was improving each day. The good thing about running the office, he could come and go as he pleased and didn't have to answer to anyone.

He heard the train whistle, and when he finished with the patient he was seeing, he walked down to the depot and waited. As the passengers began to disembark from the cars, he saw his mama and went to her. She had put on a few pounds and looked so much happier than the last time he saw her.

"Hi, Mama. Give me a hug."

She grabbed him and squeezed. "I've missed you so much. Where's Jennifer?"

"She's at the house getting it ready for you. Let's get your bags, and I'll hire us a buggy to take us to the ranch. You're going to like your new house."

"As long as I'm close to you and Jennifer, I'll be happy. Is she showing yet?"

"No, but she will be soon. She's having some morning sickness, but it's not really bad."

They talked all the way to the ranch since Brody wanted to know how Dr. Milrose was doing and what she did with her house and furniture. It turned out that she sold the house and furniture to the same man who purchased the tavern from her. He paid her a fair price, and she was happy.

A person would have thought that Ellen and Jennifer had known each other for years, the way they were getting along. Ellen loved her new modern house with the inside toilet and running water. After an hour of reminiscing and talking about the future, Brody had one of the ranch hands saddle him a horse so he could ride back to the office and make sure there weren't any emergencies.

On the ride back to town, he was so happy that his mama was here, where she could be part of his and Jennifer's life. She would be such a blessing when the baby gets here.

Suddenly, the day clouded up to the point that it was almost dark and then he heard a voice: *Brody Connor, healer, warrior. It's time.*

The dark clouds drifted away, and he smiled as he rode with a piece that calmed his mind. He knew what was about to happen and that it would end in the middle of the street today.

He rode to the livery stable and dismounted.

"Did you get another horse, Doctor?"

"Yeah, but just for today. Feed and water him, I have something to do."

Brody started walking down the street and stopped in the middle of the road with wagons and horses going around him. He was watching the saloon door and then there he was. Martin stood in the doorway of the saloon for a moment before he removed his jacket and laid it across one of the hitchrails.

He started across the street and had to walk toward the sun as he started where Brody stood.

"Martin, you're a murderer, a kidnapper, and a terrible cheat at cards."

"So, the so-called fast gun doctor thinks he can take me down. I'm going to kill you and then kill your wife and child."

The words of William came to him: *"Draw first and show no mercy. You're the warrior."*

Brody smiled. "The devil is waiting on you." The doctor drew his gun and fired the first shot before Martin cleared the holster. The bullet hit the thug in the chest, making him take a step back.

Brody started walking toward Martin. "I'm so much faster and better than you ever were." He fired another shot that hit the man in the face and exited through the back of his head, taking brain, skull, and blood with it.

Martin lay dead in the street just like in his dream. The townsfolk watched as the new doctor ejected the spent shells and reloaded. He turned around and walked toward the office to see if he had any patients.

It just so happened that he was alone in the office where he again went to his knees and prayed a prayer of thanksgiving, and forgiveness. The killing of Martin happened the way he saw it in his vision, and he didn't have any ill feelings about shooting the man. The Great Spirit had shown him the way, and now it was time to go see his wife.

BRODY RODE into the yard at the ranch and took the horse to the barn where one of the hands cared for him. As he walked toward the house, Jennifer came outside and ran out to meet him. She threw her arms around his neck, crying with joy. "You killed him, didn't you?"

"Yeah, it's over. He was in town when I got back."

"Thank you, my darling, for putting your life on the line for not only me, but for all the good men they murdered and for the women that suffered at the hands of those men. All the murderers that did those horrible crimes are dead, and me and the other victims can begin to heal and get on with our lives. Brody, you're my hero, and I love you."

"I love you too. Now let's get this place in shape."

A Look at: Card Jordan Volume One

by Monty R. Garner

VENGEANCE FORGED HIM. DUTY DEFINED HIM. LEGEND MADE HIM.

From the blood-stained plains of Texas to the lawless edges of Indian Territory, Card Jordan's rise from heartbroken boy to hardened lawman unfolds in five gripping Western adventures.

When sixteen-year-old Card returns home to find his family murdered and a taunting message carved into the dirt—*CARD, KILL THEM ALL*—his quest for vengeance sets him on a path he can never turn back from. Across these first five novels, Card hunts killers, rescues the innocent, uncovers conspiracy at the highest levels, battles rustlers threatening his land, and confronts outlaws who push the limits of justice and honor.

But every fight carries a cost. Every choice carves deeper into the man he's becoming.

Perfect for fans of Louis L'Amour and classic frontier justice, Card Jordan Volume One *includes the first five novels in the Card Jordan saga. Stories of grit, high-stakes action, and a gunslinger who refuses to back down, no matter the odds.*

AVAILABLE NOW

About the Author

Monty was born and raised in Southeastern Oklahoma in the small town of Sawyer, which is nested along the banks of the Kiamichi River. He's owned horses and cattle, riding the former and working the latter. Over the years, he formed a deep connection and respect for the Old West and the courageous folks who braved the wild frontier.

Monty is an avid reader and is particularly enthusiastic when it comes to Western authors and novels. His love of reading sparked his desire to write his first short story. He loves writing about real places and landmarks from the 1800s. In college, he wrote a ten-page paper about his grandmother, born in 1886, who married at fourteen and took in five orphaned nieces and nephews shortly thereafter. Monty's love for history and penchant for storytelling earned him an A+, and he hasn't looked back since.

Now retired, he loves to travel, fish, spend time with his four grandkids, and tell stories. He looks for inspiration for future books wherever he goes, and he is a member of the Western Writers of America Inc.

www.montygarnerauthor.com

www.ingramcontent.com/pod-product-compliance
Lightning Source LLC
LaVergne TN
LVHW040216110826
845146LV00005B/1302

* 9 7 9 8 8 9 5 6 7 2 6 3 1 *